ALL'S FAIR IN BLOOD AND WAR

ALL'S FAIR IN BLOOD AND WAR

THE KURTHERIAN ENDGAME™ BOOK FOUR

MICHAEL ANDERLE

DISRUPTIVE IMAGINATION

ALL'S FAIR IN BLOOD AND WAR TEAM

Thanks to the JIT Readers

Diane L. Smith
Kelly O'Donnell
Jackey Hankard-Brodie
Jeff Eaton
Mary Morris
Jo Owen
Nicole Emens
James Caplan
Angel LaVey
Misty Roa
Keith Verret
Daniel Weigert
John Ashmore
Peter Manis
Larry Omans

If I've missed anyone, please let me know!

Editor
Lynne Stiegler

To Family, Friends and
Those Who Love
to Read.
May We All Enjoy Grace
to Live the Life We Are
Called.

Immersive Training and Recreation Scenario: High Tortuga, Southern Continent, Plains (Eight Months of Real Time/Nine Years of Game Time Later)

Tabitha woke up at the crack of dawn with a dull ache at the base of her spine. She pushed away the obvious reason for the pain and crawled out of her tent on her hands and knees, grumbling at the thought of trying to do such a simple thing in the real world with what her real body looked like right now.

She didn't even want to *think* about stretchmarks.

Any longer in here and she would be giving Gabrielle a run for the longest pregnancy in human history. Which seemed like an awesome idea when she expected it to last for five years.

However, things had gone a tiny bit differently than planned. When the neurological issues that came with adjusting time for long periods inside the game had come to light, it had been too late to just pull the three of them out.

The only solution had been to extend their time inside the Vid-docs from twelve weeks real time and five years game time to the eight months real time and nine years that Tabitha, Alexis, and Gabriel had experienced so far.

Tabitha hummed as she placed a few pieces of fire log on the dying embers of the fire and waited for it to catch.

You're chipper this morning, Achronyx remarked.

Yeah, well, my confinement is almost over.

I still do not understand why you were so happy there was an issue in the first place.

Because, Tabitha told him, *I got to spend my whole pregnancy without any of the restrictions women have to suffer through.* Fuck! She doubled over as the cramp that had been building bloomed in her lower abdomen. *Shit. I can't avoid this one, though.*

Braxton-hicks again? Achronyx asked.

I don't think so. My boy is impatient to see the world. He's not going to wait much longer. She reached for normality as the universe fell out from under her feet, grabbing a pan, which she put over the fire to heat. *I'm pretty sure he'll hang on until after breakfast.*

Achronyx was silent for a moment while he checked her over. *You're right. All the indicators are pointing toward an impending shift in your hormonal balance. This looks like early labor. We should return to the base and exit the game as soon as possible.*

Tabitha had come to *that* conclusion when the cramp hit, but she wasn't in such a hurry that she had to upset the twins. Besides, she'd added maple smoked bacon to their inventory for that morning. *You should inform Eve, but I'm not leaving Alexis and Gabriel without telling them where I'm going.*

I already have, and Eve is putting your birth plan into action, Achronyx told her calmly.

She doesn't hang around. Tabitha tapped on Alexis' and Gabriel's tent, chuckling at the sleepy protests from within. "Rise and shine, kiddos. It's a brand new day, and you've still got some fun planned with Addix before you go back to the base."

Alexis poked her head out, her dark hair obscuring her face. "That sounds like you're leaving."

Tabitha winked. "It's almost time."

Alexis squealed at that ear-shattering pitch almost exclusive to teenage girls. "Really?"

Tabitha nodded. "Yup. Pretty sure I just had a contraction."

Gabriel's head appeared next to his sister's. "Does that mean Mom and Dad might let us out of here at last? I miss them."

Tabitha did her best not to be amused by the way his voice slid around. "I don't know," she admitted. "You'll have to ask them."

"I'm calling Mom right now." Alexis pulled her head back inside the tent, causing Gabriel to stumble forward.

Gabriel rolled his eyes at his sister and crawled all the way out of the tent, enticed by the smell of bacon. "Oh, good. Breakfast." He wandered over to check the pan.

Addix emerged from her tent, rubbing her eyes in bewilderment. "It's not like you to be first up." She read the tension in Tabitha's shoulders despite the rude awakening. "Is everything all right with the children?"

"Sure, but I'm in labor, so Eve will be getting me out of here soon." Tabitha put a brave face on, a hand straying to her flat stomach as another cramp began to wind itself up inside her.

Addix's mandibles twitched in concern. "I still do not understand why you would choose to endure this or why Eve would allow it."

"Trust me," Tabitha ground out with something between a chuckle and a gasp, "it's not fun. But this is part of the bonding experience." She nodded toward the tents. "Do you mind coming up with something to do with Alexis and Gabriel? I could use the time to think while I get their breakfast ready."

Eve's avatar appeared beside them. "Breakfast will have to wait. It's time to go. Everything is waiting for you, just like we planned."

Tabitha hesitated. "What about Alexis and Gabriel?"

"We're fine with Aunt Addix," Gabriel called.

"Yeah," Alexis chipped in from inside the tent. "Call us when he's born so we can meet him at last."

Tabitha reached for Eve's outstretched hand for a quick exit.

High Tortuga, Space Fleet Base, Michael's Offices, Vid-doc Suites

The first thing Peter heard when he entered the room was Bethany Anne talking in hushed tones to Alexis on the side monitor. "What do you mean, she's in *labor*?"

"Tabitha's in labor?" His hands dropped to his sides, releasing the bag holding his quick and dirty dinner without a second thought.

Eve sighed at the puddle of spilled Coke coming from the dropped bag at his feet. "Yes, Peter. We can't delay the birth any longer; the baby is on his way. Don't worry, they're both in good hands." She wiggled her fingers at him, then went back to typing instructions into Tabitha's Vid-doc console.

A moment later a cleaner bot appeared and nudged Peter's foot gently. He stared blankly at the bot when it bumped him a second time, which Peter thought was a little insistent.

Bethany Anne left the console and walked over to steer

Peter over to the couch. "I know we'd hoped to give them all another month or two, but Baby's not giving us an option. We're going to take care of Tabitha, then Alexis and Gabriel."

Peter appeared to be paying more attention to the cleaner bot than what Bethany Anne was saying. She looked at him with concern and waved a hand in front of his face, startling him.

"Peter, you okay?"

Peter ran a hand over his head. "It's just sudden, is all. I'm good."

"You sure? You zoned out for a moment." Bethany Anne noted Peter's trembling hands. "Just take a minute. Eve is pulling Tabitha out of the game, and that takes some time." She reached out to pat Peter's shoulder. "It's all going to be better than fine. Just wait and see."

Eve pushed a gurney over to the side of Tabitha's Vid-doc. "She's in the rejuvenation cycle now. Three minutes."

Peter straightened his shoulders. "There's no time for that. We're about to become parents."

High Tortuga, Space Fleet Base, Medical Unit, Corridor

"My nanocytes had better fix," she indicated her distended stomach with a hand, "this!" She gritted her teeth against another contraction. "*Fuuuuck!*"

Bethany Anne winced when Tabitha grabbed her hand and squeezed hard.

Tabitha growled at Bethany Anne as the contraction peaked. "Serves you right for not telling me how much this fucking *hurtssss!*"

Bethany Anne took the pain of her crushed fingers without complaint. "Um, about that. I had TOM and ADAM dial down most of my labor pain."

Tabitha glared and squeezed a little bit harder.

"Twins, Tabitha," Bethany Anne stated. "Wait until you've had *one* baby and tell me if you want to go through the experience a second time right after."

Tabitha turned away, pouting when she realized through the fog that the person on the other side of her moving gurney was Peter—the cause of all her pain.

She pulled her hand free of Bethany Anne's and pointed a wobbly finger at him. "This is all your fault, you... You..."

She would finish telling him later. She felt really sleepy, which was weird since she'd technically been asleep for the last eight months.

Peter waited for the slip into Spanish that told him Tabitha wasn't really too mad at him. Of course, when she *did* do it because she was mad, it meant he'd better clear out of the way before Mount Tabbie exploded in his face.

He didn't get the chance to find out. Before she got to the cursing him out part, Tabitha's eyes rolled in her head and she sank back against the pillows. "Tabbie?" She didn't respond.

Peter almost lost his shit there and then. *"Tabbie!"* Somehow, he held on. This was not a situation that could be improved in any way by dropping a terrified Pricolici into the middle of it. He turned to Eve. "Do something!"

Eve started pushing the gurney a lot faster. "Hold on!"

Peter grabbed his side of the gurney, and he and Bethany Anne kept it stable while Eve powered her way to Tabitha's birthing suite.

They had two rooms on standby. The first was candlelit and had a warm pool and whale music for Tabitha to mock, where Peter would feed her bonbons and fan her while she brought their son into the world.

Eve directed them toward the second, where the freshly-scrubbed surgical team waited for Tabitha under too-bright lights. The door was opened by a pair of nurses, and another stepped forward to guide Eve into the theater.

Eve sailed through with the gurney, but Peter found his way barred.

Peter tried to push past the nurse who blocked his way, frowning at the man whose nametag went unnoticed in Peter's worry. "What are you doing? Let me in."

The nurse, clearly used to dealing with distraught fathers-to-be, raised a hand to ward Peter off. "I'm sorry, Commander. Medical personnel only beyond this point until we know the cause of her collapse." He pointed to a sign on the wall by an alcove a short way along the corridor. "There's a waiting area there if you'd like to take a seat and gather yourself. Otherwise, I'll have to ask security to come down here, and none of us want that."

Peter didn't care if he had to fight his way to Tabitha. She and their baby were vulnerable, and they needed him right now. He growled deep in his chest. "Let me pass. I'm staying with Tabitha."

The nurse looked at Bethany Anne as the voice of reason.

It was only when Bethany Anne moved Peter firmly but forcefully away from the doors to the operating theater that he realized he'd been too close to insisting the nurse let him in or face the painful consequences, and *that* wouldn't do at all.

Peter held up his hands at the nurse who'd blocked his way. "Sorry. You're right. It's been a hell of a day, but that's no excuse. Didn't mean to make your job harder." He turned to head for the waiting area to prove he was done being difficult.

The nurse looked at Peter with understanding. The man was clearly concerned but resolute. "It's not an easy time, but your wife is in the best hands." He slipped back behind the door and closed it firmly.

Peter looked down at his feet while he and Bethany Anne walked over to the waiting area and murmured, "If you find my wife, you'll have to introduce us." He smirked for a moment, but it faded just as quickly. That was one of Tabitha's less cutting lines whenever anyone assumed they were married.

The thought of how it would feel to never hear Tabitha verbally flay another asshole in response to their ignorance was unthinkable, and yet it kept trying to *be* a thought.

He couldn't bear it if anything happened to Tabitha or their child.

However, he had to trust Eve and the surgeons to do their best work. He wondered if whatever was wrong was another adverse reaction to spending so long living life on fast-forward.

He hadn't been affected by the issue, since over the last few months Bethany Anne had wanted him focused on working with the Admiral's wife on integrating the masses of new recruits into the Guardian Marines.

Coordinating their training and deployment around

the various locations Bethany Anne had collected in the years since the acquisition of Devon was a full-time job, so he'd only spent short stints in the game construct during Tabitha's pregnancy.

However, for Tabitha and the twins, it was more serious. Once game time began to pick up speed to compensate for the twin's rapid growth, their visitors started to get severe headaches if they stayed for more than a few hours real-time.

The side-effect was spotted by TOM after Bethany Anne had stayed with the twins for two months in game time. Her nanos cleared up the headache just fine, but further investigation had revealed potentially life-threatening consequences for anyone living at a different speed for a protracted period of time if the issue wasn't addressed.

Everybody was quite ready to get out, even though Tabitha had initially been a little too happy with the news that she and the twins would have to remain in the Vid-docs while their time perception was slowly adjusted back to the normal rate.

Peter was well aware that her snark was just a cover for her fear of being a terrible mom. Their conversation kept coming back to Nickie, and what she saw as her failure to steer her niece straight.

Peter's personal opinion was that everyone had done plenty for the girl, *especially* Tabitha, and she'd still turned out the way she had. It was up to her to sink or swim now.

That was just how it went sometimes when a kid got everything handed to them. If *anyone* understood that kind of rebellion, it was him.

Tabitha didn't want to hear it, but Peter knew that Nickie would return a changed woman when her time was up. In the meantime, being exiled to experience life as the majority lived it could only do her good.

Bethany Anne's shadow passed over Peter, tearing him from his brooding. "I'm going to find you a hot drink and something to eat. Do not move from that spot." She raised a finger to be sure he knew she wasn't kidding. "I'll be back soon. Understand?"

Peter nodded and she walked off, leaving him to work out how to live through the agony of the minutes crawling by while he waited for any scrap of news.

It didn't take long for his thoughts to wander again. Tabitha had nothing to worry about. They were going to be great parents, whether she believed it or not. He decided to focus on that, and what he could do to make Tabitha's life easier once their son was born.

They had talked endlessly over the last few months—or years if he looked at it from Tabitha's perspective—and he had listened to her fears and acknowledged them. That she wasn't any kind of disciplinarian. That she was going to fuck their child up because she had to have a certain amount of chaos going on to be happy.

Tabitha couldn't see what Peter could: being responsible for Alexis and Gabriel had changed her. She'd become comfortable with the idea that having authority didn't necessarily mean being the authoritarian during her time in the game world.

Bethany Anne returned what felt like an eternity later with a familiar-looking paper bag in each hand. "You didn't get to eat your dinner earlier. It's amazing what you can get in the middle of the night if you're not too fussy."

"You are the literal best," Peter told Bethany Anne sincerely. He took the bag she held with a grateful grin. "And you'll take that back when you eat one of those fries. They're wonderful."

Bethany Anne tipped a finger at him and sat down to open her own bag. "We'll see. Eat up, you need your strength." She waved a fry at him before biting down on it and chewing thoughtfully for a second.

"It didn't take you long to run out for this," Peter mused idly, more interested in his second chance at dinner than how it had been procured.

Bethany Anne grinned guiltily. "Okay," she admitted. "They're good. I called ahead and had our order ready to pick up. I didn't know which one you prefer so I got you one each of the specials."

Peter unwrapped the first burger. "You pretty much nailed it."

She rummaged in her own bag and came up with a carton of hash brown fries for him and a Coke for each of them.

Peter bowed to Bethany Anne before taking them from her. "*Totally* nailed it," he amended. "Kerry's fries are the best. I can't believe nobody thought of making hash browns this way before."

They chatted while they ate. Bethany Anne kept the conversation superficial. She talked about the potatoes they were growing that were very close to Earth-equivalent, including the taste, when fried, seeing that was what he needed.

Peter made short work of the burgers stacked inside his bag.

After they'd eaten, he went to find a trash can for their empty wrappers, needing to stretch his legs after sitting still for the last couple of hours.

When he returned, Bethany Anne was talking to the nurse from earlier.

The nurse spotted Peter. "He's here. Commander Silvers, if you'd like to come this way." He broke into a smile. "It's time to meet your son."

Peter's knees went wobbly for what seemed like the millionth time that long day when he heard a faint snuffly cry and Tabitha's soft murmur.

"They're okay?" he asked.

The nurse nodded. "They are. Mother and baby are in perfect health. We were just waiting for you to get back to complete baby's registration paperwork."

Peter frowned for a second until he realized what the problem was. "She wouldn't tell you his name? I wouldn't worry about it. She wouldn't tell any of us."

Bethany Anne groaned. "For crying out loud! This has been bugging me for *months*, Peter!" She pushed him. "Go in there and find out."

Peter winked and headed for the door. "That's the plan. Tabbie has to tell us his name now he's been born."

"The surprise was that Alexis knew the whole time and didn't give it up."

They turned at the sound of Michael's voice.

Bethany Anne's smile lit the corridor when she saw her husband walking toward them. "You made it!"

"Glad you did," Peter agreed. "Tabitha wanted you here."

"I wouldn't have missed it for the world," Michael told them both. "Eve has been keeping me updated. As well as a few others, who will be here shortly."

Bethany Anne waved Peter toward the nurse. "Go, see Tabitha and meet your son. We'll hold everyone off when they get here and give you three a minute to get acquainted before we welcome him to the world."

"And find out his name," Michael added, the tiniest of smirks gracing one corner of his lips.

Bethany Anne pointed at Michael. "Yes, that too."

High Tortuga, Space Fleet Base, Medical Unit

Peter hesitated outside the door to Tabitha's recovery room to listen to her singing to their baby.

A second later, the lullaby stopped and she snorted. "Are you going to come in and say hi or are you planning on hovering there until you take root?"

He pushed the door open, careful not to flood the softly-lit room with the harsh light from the corridor. "Hey, beautiful. What's a fine chick like you doing in a place like this?"

Tabitha was mostly upright on the bed, leaning on the mass of pillows behind her with the baby in her arms. She narrowed her eyes playfully, her fire undiminished by the ordeal of giving birth. "Some charmer talked me into bed. It's sad, really. Taken out of the game at the peak of my hotness."

Peter grinned as he closed the door with a barely audible click and walked over to the bed. "Your peak started when the year still began with a two, and it's not showing any signs of ending any time soon."

Tabitha grew slightly pink in the cheeks. "You're too smooth for your own good, Pete. I look really messy, but I don't care. Come see the tiny human we made!"

She looked just perfect to Peter, from her hospital gown and her hair sticking up all over the place to the dark circles under her eyes. He leaned over and kissed her. "I wouldn't change a thing about you. How are you feeling after the cesarean?"

She patted her bed with her free arm. "I'm feeling good, a bit achy where the nanos are working on deep tissue still. Sit with us."

He sat down on the edge of Tabitha's bed and held out his hands for the blanket-wrapped bundle. "You ready to share a moment?"

Tabitha smiled as she gently placed the baby in Peter's arms and he got his first glimpse of his son. He was mesmerized by his miniature fingers and toes and the dark, downy hair on his head. The way his face was arranged in a perfect copy of his mother's most petulant pout. "He's so beautiful."

The baby began to squirm, reddening as he drew breath to protest being parted from his mother. Peter ran a finger over his son's forehead to soothe him. "Hey, little man. No need to cause a ruckus. You and I are going to be best buddies, just wait and see."

Tabitha's eyes shone. She leaned over carefully and whispered to the baby, "Say hello to your Daddy, Todd."

Peter felt his heart contract. He met Tabitha's eyes. "Todd? Really?"

Tabitha nodded and smiled beatifically at their son. "Yup. Todd Michael Nacht-Silvers. Any objections?"

Peter looked into Todd's eyes, which seemed to be tracking him already. "It's perfect. *He's* perfect." He scooted along the bed so he could wrap his free arm around Tabitha. "And so are you. Well done, Mama. I'm so proud of you."

There was a quiet tap, and Bethany Anne slipped through the door. "You've got visitors." She caught sight of Todd and crossed the room in an instant. "But me first. Aunt's privilege."

Peter looked questioningly at Tabitha.

She waved him off, stifling a yawn. "I'll be fine as long as it's a quick visit. But then Todd and I have to get some sleep."

"If you say so." He stood and prepared to transfer his son to his Aunt Bethany Anne for a snuggle.

Bethany Anne brought baby Todd in close and cooed to him. She grinned at them both. "He's beautiful." She whispered to Todd before looking up again. "Congratulations to all three of you. We'll talk about Todd's birth gift tomorrow. For now, just tell me when you've had enough of visitors, and I'll clear everyone out."

The door opened again, and there was a moment's chaos when everyone tried to get through at once. They heard the nurse scolding someone. Possibly John, from the rumbling reply.

Bethany Anne rolled her eyes for Tabitha's benefit. "Here, you take him back while I teach these grown-ass men and women how to use a door."

Tabitha snickered, accepting Todd into her arms. She

stared at him as she'd been doing from the second the surgical team had placed him in her arms. She couldn't get over him. He was a perfect blend of Pete and her.

Bethany Anne had arranged her visitors into manageable groups of two and three. Tabitha nodded and smiled and replied to their praise, her eyelids growing heavier during the gaps between well-wishers.

Todd fell asleep, so Peter took him from Tabitha and gently laid him in the bassinet attached to the far side of her bed.

Without the baby to keep her alert, Tabitha's eyelids fluttered closed in a matter of minutes despite her best efforts to stay awake. Peter tucked her in while Bethany Anne cleared the room like she'd promised she would.

Peter sighed a huge sigh of relief when the door closed behind John and Jean, who were the last to leave.

Bethany Anne kept her voice low, not wishing to disturb Tabitha or Todd's sleep. "Interesting day, huh?"

Peter nodded solemnly as he took the chair beside Tabitha's bed. Sitting down, he breathed in twice before answering. "I've never experienced anything like it."

Bethany Anne chuckled softly. "This is only the beginning, Peter. Sleep now. I'm not going anywhere until morning."

Peter squirmed to get comfortable enough to fall asleep. He opened one eye as he drifted off. "Thank you, BA," he mumbled.

Bethany Anne, who was arranging all the welcome gifts, paused. "It's what family does," she replied softly as he began to snore.

2

High Tortuga, Space Fleet Base, Barnabas' Office

It wasn't *technically* his office, but Barnabas had claimed it long ago and stenciled his name on the door regardless. Tabitha had taken the one down the corridor just to annoy him, but she never used it.

Finders keepers.

Barnabas enjoyed the solitude in this re-creation of his office on the *Meredith Reynolds*. He never felt alone on the ship, given Shinigami's efforts. But here he had this office, and the empty underground part of the base it was situated in was the closest thing to a quiet place he had found.

He was somewhat out of touch with goings on around the base, having had his hands full with the taming of Shinigami for the last few years.

However, maybe it was time to reconnect. Barnabas had an idea that Bethany Anne had some plan in mind. He could see no reason she would use resources doubling up on defenses otherwise.

As if karmic intervention had drawn the object of

Barnabas' thoughts to him, Bethany Anne walked into his office and took a seat in the dark leather wingback chair opposite the desk from him.

"How's it going, Uncle Barnabas?" She crossed one leg over the other and leaned into the chair's comfortable padding. "Tabitha told me you stopped by to see her and baby Todd today."

Barnabas flushed with delight. "I did indeed. It's always a pleasure to welcome a new member of the family." His smile morphed into a knowing look. "But that's not why you're here, is it?"

Bethany Anne gave him a wry smile. "Straight to the point as always. Your efforts on the vigilante front have not gone unnoticed." She inclined her head a touch. "You're doing a great job cleaning the place up so far, and you know how much I appreciate what you're doing."

Barnabas arched an eyebrow, knowing full well what was coming. Bethany Anne hit him with that disarming smile, the million-watt one nobody could say no to because you just *knew* that smile was based on her faith in you to do whatever task she had in mind. "Whatever service I can give my Queen, I would be glad to provide," he replied.

Bethany Anne's smile impossibly grew brighter. "Great! You'll love this, I know it. How would you like to reduce your coverage area for a while? Like, to this planet?"

Barnabas steepled his hands in front of him on the desk. That sounded like something he would not mind happening at all. "Because you're preparing to leave and fight the Ooken."

Bethany Anne nodded, drumming her nails on the arm

of the chair. "You've got it. Almost. The Ooken are preparing to move."

Barnabas inclined his head a touch. "But you *are* ready for them." It was a statement, not a question.

Bethany Anne grinned. "Of course I'm ready. The time for licking wounds is over. I have all my pieces lined up on the board, and they're playing kiddie checkers."

Barnabas chuckled. "When do you leave?"

"Not long now," she confirmed. "I'm expecting to hear that the fleet is fully operational when I speak to the Admiral late tomorrow. Alexis and Gabriel get out of the Vid-docs today, and not a day too soon. Even though I spent a lot of the time in there with them, the nine years was a long time for us to be apart as a family. As soon as they've recovered, we're good to go."

Barnabas flexed his fingers while he considered the information. "So you want me to watch over this planet while you're gone? What about Devon?"

Bethany Anne waved unconcernedly. "Phase Three is complete. Devon has begun to settle of its own accord, the defenses there are all in place, and the *Guardian* is completed and is fully operational. That end of the Interdiction is complete, and all records of High Tortuga's location are being scrubbed from existence and replaced with Devon's coordinates instead."

Barnabas dropped his hands and leaned back in his chair. "An impressive feat."

"Yeah, of ADAM's," Bethany Anne clarified. "I'm not going to pretend to understand how or what he did. As long as it works, I'm happy." The corner of her mouth curled in satisfaction. "By the time he's done, not even the most insignificant independent captains will escape with their maps intact." She got to her feet, impatient to leave. "I have to get to the Vid-doc suite, but I can give you until tomorrow to think on this. If you don't want the duty, I can make other arrangements."

Barnabas shrugged. "You can have my answer now. I'm happy to remain behind. I'm enjoying my work here. It's therapeutic."

Bethany Anne raised an eyebrow. "There *are* ways of relaxing that don't involve killing, you know. You could play a bit more chess. I've heard it's good for the mind."

Bethany Anne winked and stepped into the Etheric, leaving an annoyed Barnabas gasping at his desk.

High Tortuga, Space Fleet Base, Michael's Offices, Vid-doc suite

Michael paced the room to work off his excess energy. The children would exit the Vid-docs soon, but it couldn't be soon enough for him.

Eve turned from the console where she was monitoring the Vid-docs to give him a stern look. "Such repetitive motion only causes the perception of time to be altered, so you experience *more* of it."

Michael paused and raised an eyebrow. "You mean that a watched pot never boils?"

Eve bowed her head. "A rose by any other name." She snorted softly and turned back to the console.

Bethany Anne appeared in the transfer area. She strode out of the recess and over to the wallscreen, which showed Addix waiting patiently in the game version of the Vid-doc room. Bethany Anne had to look around, but she spotted Alexis and Gabriel sitting with their backs against the wall, talking quietly. "Am I late?"

"You're right on time," Eve assured her. She instructed Addix, Alexis, and Gabriel to get into their Vid-docs. "It's not technically necessary, but it will help to prevent you from feeling disjointed when you wake."

The Vid-docs on both sides lit up and the screen went dark as all three went into the rejuvenation cycle.

Bethany Anne and Michael moved as one to stand by the twins' Vid-docs.

"One minute," Eve told them.

The lights on the Vid-docs went out and the opaque tint drained from the window in the lid, revealing the occupants.

Michael's brain tried to trick him. For a fraction of a second, he half expected to see Alexis and Gabriel as the five-year-olds they had been when they entered the Vid-doc.

Of course, his children now had the bodies to match their minds—and the experience of the years lived in-game to go with their upgraded bodies. Of course, he had spent as much time with them while they were growing these last months as possible, and it had still been slightly jarring to witness the change each time. If not for his regular visits then it would have been difficult to recognize them.

Bethany Anne drew a breath when the Vid-docs began their unlocking sequences. "*My babies.*"

"You realize our son is taller than you now?" Michael pointed out. "While I'm well aware that you could still quite easily carry either of our children on your hip, I can't see Gabriel wanting to be cosseted. Alexis even less so."

Bethany Anne dismissed Michael's good sense with a wave. "I don't care how big they get. They are my *babies*. That's all there is to it."

Michael chuckled at his wife's soft heart when it came to their children as the Vid-docs' lids clicked open.

Alexis was first to wake, followed by Gabriel, and lastly, Addix. Bethany Anne, Michael, and Eve helped them down.

While Addix had the advantage of being quadrupedal to balance her, Alexis and Gabriel held onto their parents for the moment. Although their muscle tone was fine, their legs were wobbly, which was no wonder after aging nine years and growing several feet in height.

Bethany Anne examined them closely while Eve took care of Addix. "How are you both feeling? Any pain or dizziness?"

"No, I'm good," Gabriel replied. "But I don't think those are actually my legs." He poked his thigh and gazed at Eve. "Why do they feel so weird?"

"The Vid-doc was not intended for this. Consequently, the development of new neural pathways in your brains and the growth in your bodies were two separate process-es," Eve explained.

"So why are we able to stand?" Alexis asked. "Without the movement to develop our muscular structure, we should be flopping around on the floor like fish." She looked down at herself. "I feel fine. Weak, perhaps, but fine."

Eve waved her hands as she answered. "We used mild

electrical impulses to sync your movement within the game with your bodies. The connections are somewhat weak at present, but you two are strong and your bodies semi-active. Plus, your nanocytes are now fully functional. I suspect you will return to peak health in no time."

Alexis turned to her parents. "When can we see Aunt Tabbie and the baby?" She paused for a beat. "Whose name I don't know," she finished in a dull monotone, her eyes shifting as she spoke.

Gabriel laughed. "You're the worst liar ever." He sucked in a breath when her elbow met his ribs.

Shhh!

Bethany Anne and Michael exchanged an amused look.

"I'm pretty sure you can lie better than that," Michael teased.

Bethany Anne rolled her eyes. "We're having dinner with Tabitha and Peter later," she told the twins. "You can see Todd then if he's awake. First we go home, where I have a surprise for you both."

The twins quickly regained full use of their legs.

Bethany Anne called Alexis and Gabriel back from the door with her hands outstretched toward them. "It's a lot louder than you're used to out there. You get to ride in Mom's taxi today."

The twins giggled at her lame joke. Bethany Anne took their hands and pulled them into the Etheric, Michael appearing beside them in the mists a moment later.

I take it this will be a surprise to me also? Michael inquired as Bethany Anne led the way to their quarters.

Of course, Bethany Anne replied in a tone of voice that

implied she was a little offended he even had to ask. *I had their room remodeled.*

Michael's mouth was a straight line. *I thought we were done with remodeling?*

Bethany Anne looked at her husband in disbelief. *You haven't been in their room since they went into the Vid-doc, have you?*

Um, no? Michael replied. *The children weren't using it, so there was no reason to go in.*

Alexis read the silent conversation passing between her parents and pointed it out to Gabriel.

Gabriel snickered. "Uh-oh, Dad's wearing the look he gets when Mom's been shopping."

"Yeah, but Mom has the one she gets when she's won." Alexis giggled. "Hey, Mom. Now that I'm all grown up, does that mean you'll share your shoes with me?"

Bethany Anne narrowed her eyes at her daughter and held up a finger. "First of all, you will *not* be 'all grown up' for a long time." She held up a second finger. "Secondly, I would give you my empire if I still had it, but if you touch my shoes without permission, we're going to have some very serious words." She raised an eyebrow, smiling at her daughter. "Besides, don't you want to start building your *own* collection now you're out of your atmosuit phase?"

Alexis' eyes lit up, and she clapped her hands. "Oh, Mom, you have no idea!"

Michael groaned at the same time Gabriel did.

"Oh, God, *no*." Michael started.

"It's bad enough that Mom is obsessed. Not you, too!" Gabriel finished.

Bethany Anne and Alexis flashed identical grins and

walked off arm-in-arm to discuss the difficulties of finding a shoe designer who understood that "killer heels" should mean *just* that.

Michael and Gabriel shared a look common to despairing males everywhere, of whatever species, in whatever system one found oneself.

Except the Sardis system, but it was universally agreed the laws of relationships totally bypassed *that* group.

"Where are they planning to put all these shoes?" Gabriel wondered aloud.

Michael shrugged and patted Gabriel's back as they walked. "I've no idea, son. But don't be surprised if your mother decides she wants some extra storage and a part of the base vanishes behind a wall."

Gabriel nodded somberly. "I wouldn't even blink. I know my mother."

Michael chuckled as Bethany Anne and Alexis stopped ahead of them. "Looks like our stop."

Gabriel sighed. "Lame, Dad."

Michael lifted his hands. "What? It was funny when your mother made a similar joke."

"Yes," Gabriel replied slowly. "Because it's Mom and she's funny even when we don't get what she's talking about."

Michael raised an eyebrow as Gabriel walked off. "And it's not funny when I make a joke?"

Gabriel turned back, copying Michael's shrug. "Well, if you're comfortable admitting it…"

Michael saw the flash of panic in Gabriel's eyes when he realized what he'd just said. He laughed. "You have been spending entirely too much time with Tabitha."

Gabriel's nervous grin dropped. His confusion at his father's reaction was more than enough to satisfy Michael.

I love watching you bond with the children, Bethany Anne told him, a hint of a chuckle lacing her mental voice.

Of course, my love, Michael agreed. *And what better way to open up to the children than to let them see my legendary sense of humor?*

You do mean legendary like Bigfoot is legendary, right? Bethany Anne teased.

TOM says that there were aliens that looked like Bigfoot who would occasionally get stranded on planets. Their technology wasn't great. It's feasible that Bigfoot was merely a stranded alien, and not legendary as in "not seen."

I've been nothing but nice to you, Michael. Why would you shaft me like that? Have I ever suggested I wanted my words to be used in an argument between you and Bethany Anne?

What are you doing, interrupting?

The Etheric is causing you guys to flex your mental muscles differently. It's like the walls between us are too thin when you are talking.

Huh, was all Bethany Anne offered in reply.

She took Alexis' and Gabriel's hands and the four exited the Etheric into the transfer room of their home.

Bethany Anne was first to the door. "Okay, cover your eyes and follow my voice."

The twins did as they were asked. Bethany Anne backed down the corridor toward the twins' room. "This way, keep going. Gabriel, step left before you hit the table."

Alexis opened her fingers to look at Bethany Anne. "Is the surprise in our room?"

"Mmhmm," Bethany Anne answered vaguely. She waved for Alexis to cover her eyes again. "I'm opening the door, no peeking!"

She guided Alexis and Gabriel into their room. Which was now somewhat larger, suited for teenagers rather than small children, with their sleeping Pods separated from the main room by a Japanese-style partition wall boxing each one into its corner of the room. "Stop right there. You can open your eyes."

Alexis dropped her hands and ran over to her Pod, squealing. "It's exactly the same as our room in the base scenario!"

Gabriel wandered around checking things. "Mom, how did you get all the details right?" He closed the drawer he'd just opened and went to look in the closet.

Bethany Anne tapped the side of her nose with a finger. "Secret Mom magic."

Michael suppressed his chuckle, knowing full well that Eve held the blueprint for every scenario. "We'll leave you two to get ready for dinner."

QT2, QBBS *Helena*, Thomas Family Quarters

"Did you just say your mother is coming to stay?" Admiral Thomas put his stylus down on the breakfast table next to his tablet. His schedule could wait a moment. "Is now really the best time, sweetheart? You have enough on your plate with the station filling up, and there will be a war on our doorstep at any moment. Isn't that enough to deal with without getting worked up about Helena being here for an extended period of time?"

Giselle looked up from her own preparation for the upcoming week, exasperation clear in her tone. "Was that the only thing you heard in everything I just said? That's exactly why I'm *not* getting worked up. Mother is coming to help me with the home side of things. It's the perfect solution to our childcare issues."

The Admiral raised an eyebrow over the cup he'd just picked up. "We wouldn't *have* childcare issues if you were willing to settle for anything less than Mary Poppins' more competent colleague." He waved off her argument. "I'm not saying that for any reason other than concern for your wellbeing. Helena has a way of getting under your skin, whether she means to or not."

Giselle's smile tightened slightly. "Yes, well, that was before she had grandchildren to focus her attention on. This is the perfect time for us to work past all that." She flourished a hand. "Look what can be accomplished in just a few months' time."

Admiral Thomas wasn't sure whether his wife was referring to the completed defenses or their newborn son in his bassinet on the other side of the room. "You're right. I'll anticipate her arrival." He returned his wife's smile—without adding that his anticipation was the kind people had the night before their execution—and finished the last few bites of his breakfast.

There was a soft *ping* from the speaker, and CEREBRO spoke. "Admiral, your transport has arrived."

He sighed inwardly in relief and changed the subject quickly, standing to take his plate to the kitchen. "I was hoping the children would wake before I left."

Giselle got to her feet and began helping clear up the

breakfast things. "They're perfect monsters in the morning. Consider it a lucky escape."

"Never," he vowed.

Giselle laughed. "See if you still say that when the baby is crying, the twins are arguing over who gets to eat the blue crayon, and *you* haven't even had coffee yet. You'd better get going, Your Admiralness," she teased, tiptoeing to drop a kiss on his cheek as she took the plate from his hand. "Good luck today."

"You could use my middle name."

She gave him a pointed look. "Or I *could* use your first name since it wasn't the name of one of my monumental boyfriend screw-ups."

Admiral Thomas shrugged. "'Your Admiralness' it is."

Giselle snickered. "Whatever you say, Barty."

He turned his head at the last second to catch the kiss on his lips and surrendered his plate to Giselle in favor of quickly packing his tablet into his briefcase, which was waiting on the sideboard by the elevator door.

Admiral Thomas made his way down to the public concourse in the elevator, one of the perks of his wife's position as station manager, and climbed aboard the transport waiting for him. It was one of the automated roamers that had been built for getting around the station when it was still a shell.

The roamer set off, its destination preprogrammed. The early morning bustle was encouraging.

Admiral Thomas had never thought he'd be glad to be part of rush-hour traffic again, but here he was, in a line behind three other roamers waiting to use the diversion around Central Plaza.

People were settling in.

He allowed his gaze to linger on the barriers blocking off the very center of the plaza, where final preparations for the upcoming ceremony were going on.

The ceremony was going to be a double-edged thing. He was grateful that Bethany Anne would be speaking.

Since it was partly a celebration of construction being completed and partly a memorial to the souls lost in the first clashes of the war, he fully expected emotions would be running high.

What they needed was an outlet for the tension, *not* the continued ratcheting up of pressure aboard the station to the point where morale was affected.

That was the last thing he wanted.

He resolved to speak to Giselle about arranging some entertainment as the roamer entered the transfer station.

The roamer passed the turns for the public transport links and took the route to the lines reserved for military personnel. There were roamers waiting here too, but his rank came with clearance to pass them and use the express line.

This was the Admiral's favorite part. He sat back and waited for the roamer to seat itself on the mag-rail.

It moved toward the circular door, picking up speed once the wheels had retracted.

The circular door spiraled open and Admiral Thomas drew a deep breath, as he always did when the roamer shot down the rail into open space.

Or at least it appeared that way. In reality, the chameleon tech they'd gained in the battle with the grub-like aliens had been used to create tunnels for the rail lines that reflected empty space where the rails ran while appearing completely transparent from within.

Defensive weapons, the smallest of which were the size of two or three large humans, were mounted at both ends of the transfer rails, set to incapacitate anything that threatened the integrity of the rails.

That wasn't *all* the technology had been used for. The Admiral frowned, momentarily reminded of the new *Shinigami*-type ship Bethany Anne had sprung on him.

The majesty of the shipyard came into view a moment later, and the annoyance passed when he saw all the ships he now had in return for not kicking up too much of a stink about the *Izanami*. Qui'nan was a genius, and he didn't care who he bored with the knowledge.

After Michael's visit, the Yollin architect tweaked the design of the shipyard to allow for continuous production —just in case Bethany Anne ever did turn up and drop an impossible order on them.

Since that visit, they'd produced sixteen new ships of varying class, all valuable additions to the fleet and not a disappearing ship among them.

They were not truly superdreadnoughts except in size, and while they were all equipped with a version of the Ooken plasma weapons that used the Etheric instead of plasma, they varied in specification.

Admiral Thomas spotted the *Ulysses* and the *Atlas*, the *Ballista*-class world-killers at berth. The rear of the *Grieving Widow* was just visible around the curvature of the shipyard.

That wasn't all of them. The ancillary fleet had also been beefed up—upgraded weapons and shielding on the smaller battleships, and more EI-controlled guard ships to back them up.

He had a team who was close to working out how to miniaturize the gigantic plasma weapons they'd stolen from the Ooken—and improved on—by enough to mount them on *every* ship.

It was a good start.

The roamer reached the shipyard transfer station. Admiral Thomas waited for the roamer to pull to a stop and headed in the direction of Qui'nan's library, where she could usually be found at this time of day.

He had a slight spring to his step as he walked. The Ooken might have the numbers, but he had the beginnings of the fleet of his dreams coming together.

When he was done, they wouldn't have a tentacle to stand on.

3

Devon, First City, The Hexagon

"Jacqueline! Jacqueline! Jacqueline!"

Ricole soaked in the chant of the crowd. She stood up with her hands on the console, leaning into her microphone as she looked down from the commentary box to the Hexagon below.

Sabine stood in the center of the ring with her whistle at the ready.

Ricole began her introductions. "A warm First City welcome to the challenger, Shast*aaaa* the Im*mov*able!"

At Ricole's announcement, the crowd went wild.

With boos.

Ricole chuckled. "Play nice, now," she told the crowd, who ignored her and continued to chant for Jacqueline.

They do not like the rock alien, Demon observed from her perch on the seat beside Ricole's. *Is it because he is inedible?*

The aforementioned rock-based alien mounted the steps to the ring, clutching his boulder-sized hands above his head in a premature victory pose.

"And in the other corner," Ricole continued, "We have everybody's *favorite* furry fury, the woman you've *all* bet on to win tonight, *Jacqueline!*"

The crowd went completely wild for Jacqueline. Her fans were out in force tonight, eager to earn a few credits on the outcome of the fight.

The Immovable challenger took one look at the young human female approaching the ring and folded his arms. "Oh, no. Nuh-uh. I'm not fighting her. I'm all for having the advantage, but *this*? This is going too far for the sake of entertainment."

Jacqueline nodded to Sira as the young Noel-ni let her in through the cage door. "I know, right? " she called out loudly. "It's totally unfair. But I keep breaking fighters, so the public vote went toward finding me a more durable opponent." She laced her knuckles and stretched her arms. "You seem pretty honorable, so I'll go easy on you."

I love this script, Ricole told Demon over the team link.

Demon purred. *Only Mark could have gotten her to agree to the next part, which is too funny.*

Shasta is kind of hamming it up, Mark grumbled, *but I think it's adding to the drama. Maybe we should plan to include this kind of performance for the next show.*

Maybe, Ricole ventured. *If the audience approves. I'm still not sold on this "acting" instead of having a straight-up fight. Isn't the whole "a stranger comes to town and gets his ass kicked by a waif" routine a bit much to swallow?*

"But you're so *tiny* and fragile!" Shasta's booming voice proclaimed from inside the six-sided cage, one hand on his chest as he swept the other behind himself dramatically.

You're wrong, Sabine interjected. *Look, they love it!*

The massive screens around the events arena showed a close-up of Shasta, who was milking every second of the crowd's attention.

The hand on his chest moved to his head, palm out. "I could *never* do such a thing."

The crowd, for their part, had changed their opinion of Shasta.

He said in his interview that he'd done some work as an actor, Mark told them. *I think he was a good hire.*

Ricole sent an update out to the others. *We're getting a flood of bets on him. Wow. I'd complain about how fickle they are, but Shasta really likes the attention, and I really like the profit that's generating.*

I bet he'd love a t-shirt line or something, Sabine remarked dryly. *Actually, that's not a bad idea. Let's start looking into whether it's worth getting into merchandise.* She raised her hands and blew her whistle, signaling for the fight to begin.

Jacqueline suddenly gained three feet, serrated teeth, and a set of claws just *perfect* for digging through whatever was in her way. "Arrre you *suuure* about that?" she asked in a low growl.

"What is this I see before me?" Shasta threw up his hands in mock-horror, and the crowd broke into laughter.

Jacqueline began to circle Shasta slowly. "My, myyyy. What biiiig eyes yoooou have." *Seriously, Mark. I hate you right now.*

Mark's deep chuckle rang out across the link. *Sorry, babe. The opportunity was there, and just...too tempting. I couldn't pass it up.*

Yeah, well I don't think Yollywood will be calling anytime soon. Jacqueline took her cue to launch into the first action sequence. *And the thought of what* you're *going to do in return for me playing along will get me through this just fine.*

Mark was quiet after that.

Bad dialog aside, Jacqueline still found joy of a sort in the choreographed techniques.

There were much worse things to do than this. Like half-contact sparring, which she hated. She would get to let loose for the final round, and that was worth all this ridiculous acting.

Sabine blew the whistle to call the first round, which ended with both of them scoring pretty evenly, but with Shasta slightly ahead.

The crowd didn't know how to react.

So they bayed incomprehensibly for the next round to begin.

The second round went mostly the same, but this time Jacqueline took the lead by a small margin.

Again, the crowd were on their feet by the time Sabine blew the whistle.

Ricole whooped into her microphone, whipping them up further. *You did great with the choreography, Sabine.*

I had some help, she replied modestly.

Send Lover-Were my regards, Jacqueline half-teased. *Seriously, these techniques are decent.*

Sabine scoffed, feeling her cheeks warm. *You would know them already if you trained with the Guardians a bit more.*

Round three began, and Jacqueline had the smallest of smiles hidden at the corner of her mouth as she faced Shasta for real.

"You fight well," Shasta praised Jacqueline at the top of his...lungs? "But you can't beat me. I am—" he stretched up to his full height and pushed out his chest, "The Immovable!"

"Ass warrrrts," Jacqueline blurted. "They'rrre immooovable, too."

Laughter rippled through the crowd, growing in volume as the spectators' translation software dealt with the way Jacqueline's Pricolici mouth stretched the words.

Shasta frowned. "No ad-libbing!" he hissed out of the corner of his mouth.

Jacqueline shrugged and moved in to attack. "That's exactly what we do in this rrround." She struck him in the side on which he'd landed a little awkwardly in an earlier maneuver. "It's tiiime to get *rrreal.*"

Shasta got his guard up a touch too late. He bent to absorb the impact, then stepped back and rolled his head from side-to-side.

Jacqueline made a face at the grinding coming from what she assumed was Shasta's neck. "Ewww." She shuddered as the noise ran through her, amplified by her enhanced hearing.

Shasta saw his chance. He feinted and caught Jacqueline in the jaw with a wide swipe when she dodged the first strike.

She stumbled back a few steps, wiping the blood from her nose while her loose teeth were rooted back into her gums by her nanocytes. "Good trrry. Now it's myyy turrrn."

Shasta took an involuntary step back as three hundred and ten pounds of snarling Pricolici bounded toward him.

Jacqueline howled her laughter and swerved around him at the last minute, deciding to wing it on a whim and make this the best show since they'd opened the Hexagon for business.

She launched herself at the cage, using it as a landing pad to reach the lighting rig above. She grabbed it and swung once to gain momentum before letting go with her feet pointed directly at Shasta's chest.

It was a risky move, and Jacqueline gave it almost no odds of success.

However, Shasta's species must be somewhat lacking in the fight-or-flight department. Either that or the sight of her descending was enough to circumvent the instinct completely, because he stood rooted to the spot with his stony mouth making a rough "o."

Jacqueline's feet found their target and Shasta went down like the ton of rock he was.

"Ohhh shiiiit!"

Jacqueline's knees bent to absorb some of the massive shock, and she just managed to jump off his chest before he crashed into the side of the cage, unconscious.

The crowd went insane. Their screams and cheers shook the rafters as Sabine came forward and raised Jacqueline's now-human hand. The medics came in to tend to Shasta, who had regained consciousness and was sitting in a daze with his back against the wire.

Ricole jumped around the commentary box with the mic in her hand. "We have our winner! By knockout, *Jacqueliiiineeee!*"

Sabine took one look at the crumpled cage wall. *Can we get through one night, just* one, *without breaking anything?*

. . .

High Tortuga Space Fleet Base, Meeting Room

John was last to arrive at the meeting room, just behind Gabrielle.

Bethany Anne raised an eyebrow at Gabrielle but allowed her to take her seat. "John. Nice of you to join us."

Ah, shit. He leaned against the doorframe. "I have a perfectly good explanation for being late."

"I'd love to hear it," Bethany Anne told him, a hint of her amusement showing. Her fingers tapped slowly on the table. "But we have a meeting. Sit down already."

Eric, Scott, and Darryl snickered quietly. John glared at them and counted his blessings as he made his way to his seat. He passed Bethany Anne, Michael, and Scott, taking the empty seat beside Tabitha's at the far end of the table.

Tabitha stuck her tongue out at him while Bethany Anne was occupied with talking to Michael. "You would never have gotten away with that if she wasn't so focused. Do you remember when she would have had you do push-ups on the table for the entire meeting?"

John grunted his agreement. "I kind of miss those days. You know, like you miss a giant pain in the ass when it's not there anymore?" He chuckled softly. "How's Todd doing? He started climbing the furniture yet?"

Tabitha shrugged. "Give him a minute."

Bethany Anne cleared her throat to end the conversations around the table. "Okay, we're all here. We have just one item on the agenda today, which is the fucking Ooken —and what we're going to do to get a lead on the Kurtherians."

A murmur of agreement went around the table.

Bethany Anne quieted them with a hand. "Largely

thanks to the efforts of ADAM and the scout ship fleet, since our energy has been concentrated on upgrading the main fleet, we have more information than we did about those thieving murderers."

John caught Bethany Anne's attention. "Is this everything we've found out since Loralei got us the coordinates for the second splinter colony?"

"Yes." Bethany Anne waved a finger, and a holo-map appeared in the center of the table. She indicated the multiple markers that were widely spread out over a large portion of the map. "The green markers belong to me. The red markers are Ooken splinter worlds."

Gabrielle sucked in a breath. "There are *how* many?"

"That we know about *so far*," Bethany Anne modified. "However, we cannot assume these are all of the colonies, and we don't have the location of the homeworld yet."

John examined the map, tapping a finger on the table as his eyes roamed over it. "We're placed well for defense."

"That's not an accident." Bethany Anne got to her feet to pace while she worked through the explanation of her plans. "Phase Three is complete. That includes work on the Devon side of the Interdiction, as well as the garrison at QT2. I am headed over to the *Helena* in a few days to speak at the completion ceremony." She paused and turned to face the table. "We are now in Phase Four."

There was a slight scuffle as Gabrielle kicked her husband under the table. She shrugged when Bethany Anne paused and looked at her. "Eric would like to be reminded of what exactly is going to happen in this phase."

Bethany Anne turned her glare on Eric. "Eric didn't ask because he knows how I feel about repeating myself." She sighed. "Fine. Phase Four. It's time to allow trade to resume. Under my watchful eye, of course."

Michael pursed his lips. "Isn't that a risk?"

"It is," she concurred, "But it's a risk I have prepared for. It was always in the plan to open up High Tortuga again to a degree. We have the Interdiction as protection from outsiders looking to take the planet's wealth for themselves, and Barnabas will remain here to keep a rein on things while we're gone."

Gabrielle tilted her head. "How well is Devon protected? I haven't been there for a while."

"They have the *Guardian*—which coincidentally is just *full* of Guardians. I figure that was a well-named ship—and all the ships and weapons they need to defend against assault from any direction. The station is linked to EI-run outposts, and they have the standard BYPS system, as well as a few other fun surprises for uninvited guests."

"Devon is doing well," Tabitha cut in. "Or at least, Sabine and the others are doing well on Devon, which is pretty much..." She paused for a moment, then smirked, "Actually, that's not the same thing." She yawned. "Shit, sorry. Long night. Peter's been coordinating with both stations on Guardian Marines stuff, and he talks about how things are going. It's all well, right?"

"Not exactly," Bethany Anne countered. "Devon has expanded a lot faster than I anticipated, even with the measures I put in place. I'm meeting with Peter later in the week to talk about what he and Giselle are doing to cope with the high number of Wechselbalg drawn to the relatively relaxed rules there."

"They want in on the fights," Michael interjected. "Let's

not kid ourselves. Tabitha is right; the older children are making a name for themselves by creating a system that favors the fighters."

"I like what they've done with the place," Bethany Anne agreed. "The fights needed some sort of regulation. There were too many unscrupulous bastards making money on the fights and not paying it out to those doing the fighting."

"Things are a bit less wild there these days," Michael supplied. "It seems unlikely, but the small amount of order we've instituted is drawing people in."

Tabitha snorted. "Maybe because none of those rules interfere with the right of the people to live their lives without being told how to do it."

Bethany Anne waved her hands. "We're getting distracted. I don't want to leave until I'm completely sure I'm not leaving *anyone's* ass hanging in the wind. High Tortuga will be protected, as will Devon, as will my outposts."

Tabitha interrupted, her face wearing a carefully neutral expression. "Are we leaving for good?"

Bethany Anne shook her head. "We will come back here when we're done with the Ooken. *But*—when we return, it will only be to rest and recuperate for a short time before we take care of our unfinished business with the Kurtherians."

Gabrielle's brow furrowed. "What then?"

Bethany Anne spread her hands wide, a smile playing on the edges of her lips. "Who the fuck knows? Let's concentrate on getting through what's coming next." She chuckled as a thought occurred to her. "Maybe after that, Hell will freeze over, and the never-ending supply of assholes in need of correction that the universe seems intent on sending my way will finally dry up."

John scratched his chin. "Can't see it, Boss."

"I'd *better* fucking see it," Bethany Anne retorted. "Otherwise, what have I spent the last two hundred years working for?"

She banged her hand on the table. "There *will* be peace."

High Tortuga, Space Fleet Base

Tabitha watched Peter playing with Todd on the rug. He lay on his stomach beside their son's bouncer seat and dangled the shiny stuffed toy above his head. "You two are the cutest."

Peter flashed a grin at her. "I'm not the star of this show. Watch this." He jiggled the toy and moved it slowly for Todd to follow with his eyes. Todd's tiny hands waved and reached out in an uncoordinated attempt to grab the toy.

Peter placed the toy on the bouncer seat's tray, and they both laughed when Todd's efforts to get his hands on it resulted in the toy being knocked to the rug.

Todd's tiny face screwed up and went a very specific shade of red.

"I'll get the diaper bag," Tabitha trilled. "It's my turn to change him."

Peter held a hand over his nose. "Sure thing, babe. But you're sort of too happy about changing a smelly butt."

Tabitha shook her head as she took the mat out of the bag and laid it on the rug, along with everything else she needed.

Todd was beginning to make grunts about the load in

his diaper, but Tabitha was already there, lifting him onto the mat. "Who's my big stinky boy?"

Peter made an exit as she opened the diaper. "It used to be me," he complained good-naturedly, stifling a gag as he went by. "But as long as you take care of the poop, I'm good with the transition. I feel bad, but a deal's a deal."

Tabitha waved him off. "Don't worry about it, I'll get him cleaned up. You can take over on dinner. Bethany Anne, Michael, and the twins will be here soon."

"I love that a weekly dinner is becoming a tradition," Peter called from the hallway, pausing a beat before continuing, "if three consecutive weeks counts as a tradition?"

Tabitha smiled at her son as Peter headed to the kitchen. "I think I got the better end of the deal," she confided to Todd while she cleaned him up. "Poop's not the worst thing a child can get everywhere, and you're going to grow out of needing help with *that* in no time."

The baby kicked his legs and gurgled contentedly.

Tabitha smiled as she fastened Todd's romper suit. "I know, right? You're such a clever little guy. Yes, you are. Mommy loves you. Yes, I do..."

By the time Todd was clean and sweet-smelling again, Tabitha heard a commotion at the front door. She carried Todd to the hallway, but Peter had beaten her to the door.

He had barely opened it when Alexis swept past Peter and headed straight for Tabitha and Todd with her arms held out. "*Todd*! Hi, little one. It's your cousin Alexis."

Tabitha made a show of checking whether she was still there. "Nope, I'm definitely present. It must be the baby. Does he make me invisible?"

"Sorry, Aunt Tabbie." Alexis looked anything but. She still wasn't looking at Tabitha because she was making faces at Todd, much to the baby's delight. "Can I sit with him until we eat? *Pleeease?* I'll be *very* careful."

Tabitha glanced at Peter, who came over and took Todd from her and nodded toward the living area. "We can sit in there. Wait until you see what he can do already."

Bethany Anne raised an eyebrow at Tabitha. "Anything we should know about?"

Tabitha's eyes misted over a moment. "He's advanced; we can tell that much already. He's been tracking things with his eyes since day one, and he has more control than he should at this age."

"He's growing rather quickly, too." Bethany Anne's eyes flicked through the door to the twins. "If he continues to grow at that rate, you should get his nanos checked out."

"Already on it," Tabitha assured her. "His first checkup with Eve is tomorrow."

Dinner passed pleasantly, if too quickly, and Tabitha soon found herself at the door saying goodnight while Peter fed Todd before bedtime.

It was only when she shut the door that the tears came.

Peter returned from tucking Todd in for the night as she was scrubbing her cheeks dry. "What's wrong?"

Tabitha shrugged. "I dunno. Nothing?"

He gathered her into his arms. "Come on, Tabbie. If you're sad, I'm sad, too. What am I sad about?" He kissed the top of her head. "I don't know, because you won't tell me."

"I'm not sad," she insisted. "I'm just...not happy about us being split up. You heard Bethany Anne at the meeting and at dinner tonight. She's planning on an extensive campaign against the Ooken, possibly immediately followed by the war we came out here for. We just had a baby. Tonight was perfect. I don't want a thing to change right now."

Peter held Tabitha close as she began to cry all over again. "Me either, babe. But you know we'll deal, same as we always do."

"I know." Tabitha sniffed, her supply of tears finally exhausted. "Damn hormones. What are we going to do? I don't want to take our son into a war, but the war will come to us if we don't take it to the Ooken first."

She looked up at Peter. "And we *have* to win." She held Peter tightly for a moment, looking around their home. "We'll lose all of this forever if we don't."

4

High Tortuga, Space Fleet Base, The Dome

Bethany Anne led Alexis and Gabriel along the corridor into the main chamber.

"This is our classroom!" Alexis exclaimed. "But...the door in the garden..."

"Doesn't exist," Bethany Anne reminded her daughter gently. This was why she had insisted on reality as much as possible within the game's base scenario. "The entrance has been hidden. You can only get here through the Etheric now."

Gabriel scanned the dome suspiciously. "Why's that, Mom? Is it not safe to be down here?"

Bethany Anne shook her head. "It's safe, but the old entrance had to be guarded. Besides, I don't want anyone who can't defend themselves against what happens in here to stumble in and get killed."

"Killed?" Alexis asked, wide-eyed. "What are *we* doing in here?"

Bethany Anne smiled at her children. "You want to come with your father and me when we leave? You need to learn magic."

It's not magic, TOM huffed.

Shhh! I'm creating a **narrative** *here!*

TOM sniffed. **My apologies. Please continue.**

Don't make me come in there.

Alexis frowned. "But we're not in the game, Mom. We have technology to use, not magic."

Bethany Anne waved a hand, and three seats and a table rose out of the floor.

Both children were amazed.

Bethany Anne indicated that they should sit. "A very long time ago, someone wrote something that made me think. He said, "Any sufficiently advanced technology is indistinguishable from magic."

Alexis nodded. "That was Arthur C. Clarke, Mom. I read him a year ago. But that's *fiction*. It can't apply here."

Bethany Anne tilted her head. "Can't it?"

Gabriel roused himself from thought. "It's not too far a stretch. I remember thinking the Etheric was made of magic when I was younger."

"So what you're saying," Alexis dragged out her thought to ensure she got the wording right, "is that to someone who had no knowledge of the Etheric and no access to advanced technology, *we* would appear to be using magic?"

"Sweetie," Bethany Anne shook her head, her lips pressed together and a brief sadness crossed her face, "to somebody like that, we would appear to be *gods*."

Alexis sighed. "That sounds tedious. But you don't want to be a god, Mom. You're really clear about that."

Gabriel snorted. "Mom didn't want to be an empress, and she's clear on *that*, too."

Bethany Anne's mouth twitched. "True, but duty and responsibility are two things that come above the personal feelings of any leader worth their salt." She leaned into the chair's soft back and waved a hand dismissively. "Thankfully, I'm done with all that now."

Alexis tilted her head toward her mother in confusion. "But you're building again. Do you even want this war we're getting into?"

Bethany Anne tapped her fingers on the table while she considered how much of the truth to share with her children.

On the one hand, the truth was something Alexis and Gabriel would learn by themselves as time went on. On the other, she didn't believe sugar-coating it would do them any good whatsoever in the long run.

"Mom?" Gabriel pressed.

Bethany Anne ceased her tapping and looked her children in the eyes. "Leadership sucks," she told them. "It's giving every bit of yourself endlessly with no break, no rest, and no choice but to bear it—or crumble under the weight of responsibility."

"But." She raised a finger before Alexis could interrupt, "there is no more honorable calling than protecting others. There is nothing more rewarding than knowing people lived because you acted." She placed her hands flat on the table.

"Is that why you were a cop before you met Dad?" Gabriel leaned forward with his elbows on the table, completely entranced by his mother's words. "Because it was honorable?"

Bethany Anne laughed, waving a hand at her son. "Oh, honey. I didn't care one bit about honor. I wasn't a cop, either, but I cared about the same thing I've always cared about—Justice for those who can't get it for themselves. Each time it meant taking on a greater role and more responsibility, I did it gladly, knowing I served a greater purpose."

"Like the time Aunt Addix killed those idiots who kidnapped us," Alexis offered. "She wasn't happy about it, but she was glad they wouldn't kidnap anyone else."

Bethany Anne got to her feet, gesturing for the twins do the same. "I don't think we will be executing anybody anytime soon." She rolled her eyes at the disappointment she saw in the twins' eyes, along with their massive relief. "This isn't a game. I know you know that already, but I also hope you both understand what your father and I are training you *for*."

"We do," Alexis assured her mother. "You want to keep us safe."

Gabriel nodded. "And when we're ready, we will keep others safe."

"When you're ready," Bethany Anne repeated. A wave of her hand and the furniture vanished, replaced by a wide circle of vaguely humanoid shapes. "Time for your lesson, my loves."

"What is the lesson today?" Alexis skipped over to inspect the misty creations. "You *made* these? From Etheric energy?" She turned back to Bethany Anne with hope written all over her face. "Are we making them too? Is that our lesson?"

Bethany Anne shook her head and indicated the empty mat. "Those are to test you *after* the lesson. Take your meditation positions. We're going right back to basics."

Alexis groaned as she followed her brother to the mat. "*Basics?* Why?"

Bethany Anne arched an eyebrow. "Make an energy ball."

Alexis frowned but did as her mother asked. She opened her hand palm-up and willed the Etheric energy to manifest. The energy sparked briefly before winking out. "What gives?" Alexis demanded. "Where's my...oh. It's like we have to build up the connection to our bodies again."

Gabriel tried his own connection to the Etheric and got the same result. "It's there. It's just weak, like we haven't trained it. But we *have!*"

Bethany Anne sat cross-legged and rested her hands palm-up on her knees. "Then let's remind your bodies of that. Are you both comfortable? " She looked from Alexis to Gabriel across from her on the mat.

Both children nodded to indicate they were. They already had that faraway look, but Bethany Anne was there to guide her children.

Bethany Anne let out a measured breath and dropped her voice to a soothing tone. "Then let's begin. Breathe in, and out. You have done this a thousand, thousand times before. Feel the love surrounding you, and allow it to anchor you to this reality. Now find your connection to the Etheric."

Bethany Anne paused to give them a minute to feel the emotion she was sending. Just as they had been her anchor to this plane when she began working with the Etheric in this way, she was theirs. She was immune to the temptation, and nobody else would be visiting the Etheric by accident today.

She felt the energy in the room rising slowly but steadily.

Alexis opened her eyes, and Gabriel did the same a bare second after.

Bethany Anne kept her attention focused on the children, ready to cut them off if it looked like they were losing control for even an instant. "Good. Now, let's move through creating some of the different forms of energy."

"I think I can make an energy ball now, Mom," Alexis offered.

Bethany Anne got to her feet. "We're going to start with defensive uses. Sit five feet away from each other in the center of the mat and face each other."

The twins moved into position.

"What now?" Gabriel inquired.

Bethany Anne took a couple of steps back and waved her finger in a circle, and a barrier appeared around the children. "You get to play shield wars. Best of five."

Alexis and Gabriel whooped happily.

Bethany Anne grinned and held up three fingers. "You go on my count. Bonus point for whoever gets a full shield up first." The twins nodded. "All right. Three, two, *one!*"

Alexis and Gabriel glared at each other as siblings do, and the energy level in the dome spiked as wisps of Etheric energy formed.

The energy solidified around the twins, who stood in the centers of their translucent bubbles ready to play.

"You know I've got this," Alexis boasted. "You always get mad and drop your shield first." She waved her hands, and her shield rolled toward Gabriel's.

Gabriel stuck his tongue out at his sister and made the motion to set his bubble rolling. "That's what you think. I just won the point for the shield. There's no stopping me now."

Bethany Anne winced when Alexis slammed her shield into Gabriel's. Her children did not hold back when it came to competition. They went back and forth until the score was four-four and their shields were beginning to flicker.

She pressed her lips together for a moment, then clapped her hands. "Final round, winner takes all. Then we break for lunch before we move on to the next exercise."

Gabriel lost his focus for the briefest of moments at the mention of food and Alexis bounced his shield into the barrier.

Gabriel tried to recover, but his concentration was completely gone. He fell to the mat when his bubble vanished. "*Mom!* Why'd you have to mention lunch?"

Alexis lost her footing and dropped her shield also. "Fine, we'll call it a draw." She stuck her tongue out at Gabriel and then helped him up before heading over to Bethany Anne. "What's for lunch?"

Devon, First City, The Hexagon, Living Quarters
Sabine was relaxing on the couch looking over the

accounts when Ricole came crashing through the window that overlooked the events arena. "What the *fuck?*"

She dropped her datapad and was at Ricole's side in an instant. Ricole groaned as Sabine gently turned her over. "Are you okay? What happened?"

Ricole raised a shaky hand and pointed at the window. "Yollin. Just a kid."

Sabine stood and stormed into the office and out onto the balcony. A Yollin of the four-legged variety was pacing up and down, her mandibles moving rapidly.

Sabine guessed that nothing the Yollin was muttering to herself was pleasant. "You, Yollin," she called down. "What's your name, and why the hell did you think tossing my friend through a window was a good idea?"

When the Yollin looked up, Sabine saw that the female wasn't quite an adult. She also lacked translation software according to their EI, Winstanley. *But you can translate my speech for her, right?*

I can, but it won't be pretty.

Just do what you can, Sabine told the EI. She repeated herself and tried not to forget how to talk when all that came out of her mouth was a series of oddly rhythmic clicks.

"The name's K'aia," the Yollin replied testily. "I heard you treat fighters well here. Who do I have to speak to around here about getting some fights?"

Sabine smirked and jerked a thumb over her shoulder. "You just threw her through the window."

"Well, shit." K'aia closed her eyes and sighed. "Give me strength." She shook her head and shrugged before looking back up at Sabine. "I don't suppose my sincerest apology will make up for it?"

"I don't know," Sabine replied. "That would depend on why you tossed Ricole through the window. She can admit when she's wrong."

K'aia tilted her chin. "She thought she could take me in a fight. She was wrong. So, can I start earning already? I've got a ticket to buy."

Sabine held up a finger, hearing a groan from the living area. "Wait there." She went back to the living area to check on Ricole.

Ricole was holding her arm over a wad of paper towels in the sink, wincing each time she plucked a tiny piece of glass out of her elbow and dropped it onto the paper below.

Sabine leaned over Ricole's shoulder to look at the mess in the sink. "Need me to do anything?" she asked, making a face at the bloody shards.

"I'm good," Ricole grumped. "But I'm going to slap that kid upside her head just as soon as I'm done here." She grunted, and a slightly larger piece of glass landed in the sink.

Sabine frowned, leaning back against the island. "Go easy on her for now, will you? I think she's a runaway. She mentioned buying a ticket."

Ricole looked at Sabine and sighed. "*Fiiine*, I'll save it. We don't want her to run."

"What should we do with her?" Sabine asked. "I'm not comfortable putting her in the ring. What if she gets hurt?"

Ricole rolled her eyes and waved her injuries at Sabine. "Go spar for a minute with her. She's not likely to get hurt."

Sabine shook her head. "No. I'm going to go talk to her some more and see what I can find out. She should be with her family, if she has one." She left Ricole at the sink and headed for the door to the stairwell.

"Find out if she's any good at the acting thing," Ricole called after her. "Shasta quit yesterday."

Sabine went downstairs and through the door that separated the business from their living quarters. K'aia wasn't in the arena when she got there.

She tapped her wrist holo to pull up the security feeds, then remembered they had the EI. "Winstanley, where is the female Yollin who was here?"

The EI responded almost immediately. "She is currently in the indoor training area. I advise caution, Sabine. She is armed."

"I think I will be fine." Sabine made her way around the ring and up the ramp on the other side that led to the fighters' area. The changing area was empty, but Sabine heard practiced grunting coming from the training area beyond.

K'aia was armed, with two swords.

Sabine paused by the door to watch the four-legged Yollin work her way through a kata. She was surprised to see that some of the techniques looked remarkably famil-iar, while some were...well, alien to her.

K'aia spotted Sabine and came to a stop, her arms drop-ping to her sides. "I hope you don't mind. I saw the swords..."

Sabine waved her apology away. "It's not a problem. You have an interesting style, blending techniques from different worlds like that. Who trained you?"

K'aia's mandibles clicked a somewhat haughty reply. "I trained myself."

Sabine narrowed her eyes. She'd recognized a couple of the steps in the kata as being adapted from some of Bethany Anne's repertoire. K'aia's story might be a little more complicated than she had originally suspected.

"Where are you from, K'aia?" she pressed gently. "How did you end up learning those moves from Bethany Anne?"

K'aia gave Sabine a look, hearing the familiarity in the way this woman spoke about her Empress. "How did you know that?"

Sabine smiled. "If you've met Bethany Anne, then you must also have met Michael? I'm going to take a guess and say they helped you out like they did me."

K'aia narrowed her eyes. "It's true, I was a slave in a mine near City-On-The-Lake until I escaped. The Empress freed the rest of the slaves, and I went on my way to look for my family." She looked away.

Sabine nodded, reading between the lines. "But you didn't find them," she finished softly. This was a sad situation, and one that had occurred far too often on this planet before Bethany Anne came along and put a stop to slavery.

K'aia shook her head. "Oh, no. I found them, but they were long gone from this life. I decided to go and find my Empress and serve whatever cause she has." She shrugged. "Problem is, you need funds to travel, so here I am. Will the Noel-ni forgive me and allow me to fight?"

"I don't think that will be the issue," Sabine told the young Yollin. "I can see that you're an excellent fighter, but you're too young to fight in the adult leagues."

K'aia's shoulders sank. "You're not going to let me fight,

are you?" She walked over to the bench where she'd left her belongings and dropped the swords in favor of picking up her pack. "I'm sorry for wasting your time. I'll get out of here."

Sabine shook her head. "Wait," she called after K'aia as the female went to leave. "If your story checks out, I will get you passage to High Tortuga."

K'aia paused at the entrance to the changing room and turned back to Sabine. "High Tortuga. That's where my Empress is?"

Sabine nodded. "Yeah. Just…don't go back out there by yourself. Let us help you."

The young Yollin raised a hand in farewell as she turned to leave. "You just did. I know where I'm headed. Thanks, lady."

"My name is Sabine." She ran after K'aia, catching up before they got to the arena entrance. "And I'm serious about helping you."

K'aia kept walking. "I don't need the help. I can just work for passage on whatever ship is going to High Tortuga."

Sabine sighed inwardly and followed her into the arena. She put a hand on K'aia's arm to halt her progression. "That's not going to get you there. Travel to High Tortuga is heavily restricted."

That worked. K'aia paused as she turned to eye the human. "So how do I get there?"

Sabine swept a hand toward the door to the living quarters. "You get a shower and a decent meal while I confirm your story, which is just procedure, and I book you onto a transport."

K'aia narrowed her eyes. "Why would you do that?"

Sabine's heart broke at the suspicion in K'aia's question. "Because I was young and alone once, just like you. You aren't even the only former slave. Demon had it even worse than *that* before we rescued her."

K'aia's eyes bugged out as Winstanley's translation missed the mark. "You have a *rift beast?*"

Sabine frowned and shook her head. "No?" She chuckled when she realized what the confusion was. "Demon is a cat, an Earth species. You will meet the others, who all have their own stories. If we can help, it's not just our duty. It's our pleasure to give people options where they had none."

She thought she saw K'aia relent. "What do you say. Will you let us help?"

K'aia shook her head. "I'm good, thanks."

Sabine didn't try to prevent her from leaving.

She did, however, pull a move worthy of Michael's love as soon as the young female was out of hearing range. "Winstanley, put a surveillance drone on her. I want to know if she gets into trouble."

High Tortuga, Space Fleet Base, SSE Fleet Communications Hub

The fleet escort surrounded the prearranged coordinates, waiting to learn whether the SSE ships they were waiting for had made it back from the Ooken system without a tail.

The first Gate opened, and everyone in the room held

their collective breath as the gen III scout ships nosed into the system.

Alone.

Bethany Anne released the back of the chair she was gripping. "SSE fleet, good to have you home in one piece."

Mirabelle's voice came over, sounding static through the speaker. "Not entirely intact, my Queen. Those slimy fucknuts got Loralei again."

Bethany Anne hung her head. "I can believe it. She's damn heroic. Did you manage to retrieve her?"

Another Gate opened, spitting out three SSE ships and a hail of kinetic fire. The Gate snapped shut before the pursuers got the chance to follow, and the two EIs towed the third ship behind them toward the closest dreadnought.

All three ships were banged up almost beyond recognition.

Bethany Anne sent a mental instruction to ADAM to check them out. *It wouldn't do to take a Trojan horse in.*

>>Very true. However, these three ships are legit.<<

The lead ship opened a link to the hub. "This is the SSE *Savannah*. We managed to retrieve Loralei, but it's not looking good for her."

"Come on in," Bethany Anne told the fleet. "We'll have her good as new in no time." She nodded to the SSE techs and left the hub for the next task on her to-do list that day.

Bethany Anne wasn't exactly looking forward to what came next, so she chose to walk and have at least a few more minutes of normality before the shit hit the fan.

ADAM spoke up when she was halfway down the

corridor from the hub. >>**I've got the fleet report if you want to take care of that.**<<

That obvious I need a distraction? Bethany Anne forced some of the tension out of her body. *Go ahead. What's the word from the fleet?*

>>**The gen III squadron confirmed a sixth splinter world, and they picked up the gen II's latest from the dead drop as planned. They got all the information you requested on the first three planets. I'm translating it for you now.**<<

Bethany Anne didn't want to wait for ADAM to run all the data. *Just give me the highlights for now. What's going on out there? Is it as we suspected?*

>>**It is,**<< ADAM confirmed, giving her the hard data in her internal HUD. >>**They've been building, too—and they're ready to move.**<<

Bethany Anne tapped a finger against her lips as she scanned ADAM's report. It was exactly as she'd suspected. *You're right. They could be ready in as soon as a few weeks.*

>>**It could still be months,**<< ADAM countered. >>**We don't know for certain.**<<

You've seen the messages the scout ships intercepted. They're after blood for the colony they lost. Bethany Anne clenched her hands into fists. What she would have to put her family through to protect them all was killing her inside. *Without action, the Ooken will be free to cause chaos wherever they point those damned ships of theirs.*

ADAM spoke slowly, already sure of the answer but needing to hear it from Bethany Anne. >>**So, what are you going to do about it?**<<

Bethany Anne knew there was no other way around it. *There's only one thing to do,* she admitted. *Put on my big-girl panties and stop avoiding what needs doing just because we're all cozy here right now.*

We're going to war.

5

High Tortuga, Space Fleet Base, Western Wall, Guardhouse

Bethany Anne took the shortest route across the base to Tabitha and Peter's home, the action giving her time to get her emotion in check before she arrived.

Walking and thinking was becoming a theme recently, but then her mind was heavy with thought. Alexis was too damned astute, as always.

Bethany Anne hated what she was about to do. However, whether she liked it or not, it was the right choice for everyone involved.

Peter opened the door to the remodeled guardhouse just before she reached it. He smiled warmly as he stood aside for her to enter. "Thanks for doing this all the way out here. Tabitha's running late, but she'll be back from her thing with Barnabas soon."

Bethany Anne followed Peter to the living room, where Todd was on the rug doing his best to roll himself onto his stomach. She sat beside the baby, who immediately increased his efforts. "Hey, little man. Just look at you go!"

"I know, right?" Peter swelled with pride. "He's going to get that any time now. Oh, you should wave to Tabbie. She has CEREBRO livestreaming Todd to her while she's out."

Bethany Anne looked up and waved, then returned to cooing at Todd. The baby gurgled in return and waved his arms at her. "I wonder where she got that idea?" she murmured, a small smile escaping her lips as she picked Todd up and settled him in the cradle of her crossed legs.

Peter knew better than to let slip that he knew exactly who'd inspired Tabitha's twenty-four-hour surveillance of their son. "I wouldn't know," he offered in his most diplomatic tone. "It's nearly time for Todd to eat. Can I get you a drink? I think we have Coke in the fridge."

"I'm good, thanks." Bethany Anne supported the baby with her forearms and wriggled her fingers to create a swirling contrail of inert Etheric energy for Todd to grasp at. "Besides, I'm not done for the day yet. I have a few more visits to make when we're done here."

Tabitha arrived home in a whirlwind of leather. She blew kisses to Peter and Todd and waved to Bethany Anne. "You wouldn't *believe* my day." She grinned and waved her dirty hands over her blood-spattered clothing. "I'm gross. Ten minutes, promise," she called as she dashed for the bathroom.

Todd's sunny mood vanished the moment Tabitha left. Bethany Anne distracted him best she could while Peter went to get his food.

True to her word, Tabitha returned clean and fresh ten minutes later, her cruddy work gear replaced by soft sweats. Black, of course. "Hi, baby boy! Mommy missed you!"

Todd's grousing turned to delighted squeals when he laid eyes on Tabitha, then to outright joy when Peter came back from the kitchen with a covered container in one hand and a cloth over his shoulder. He grinned at Todd's reaction. "I guess *someone* got the hungry gene from their mom."

Bethany Anne snickered.

"Hey!" Tabitha protested. "You eat way more than I do."

Peter flashed a grin. "Our food bill says differently."

Tabitha stuck her tongue out at him. "See if I bring *you* leftovers again." She walked over to Bethany Anne and held her hands out for Todd. "Come to Mommy, son."

Bethany Anne handed Todd to his mother somewhat reluctantly.

Tabitha carried him over to the couch and settled into the corner with the baby in her lap.

"He's bigger every time I see him," Bethany Anne told her, getting off the floor to sit in the guest chair she'd been leaning against.

Tabitha adjusted the position of her crossed leg to give Todd a little bit more support. "Yeah, he's got that fast-growth thing going on. Thankfully Eve has a handle on keeping it steady."

Bethany Anne nodded. "That's good to hear. I was dreading hearing he had the same issues as Alexis and Gabriel."

"I know, right?" Tabitha tickled Todd's tummy. "Experiencing nine years in the Vid-doc had only one advantage. I'm nine years older than I look."

Bethany Anne rolled her eyes. "You've looked the same age since you were first upgraded."

Tabitha pouted. "It's how I *feel* that counts."

"If you say so," Bethany Anne offered. "So, Eve's certain he won't have any issues?"

"Eve's been great," Peter told her, passing Tabitha the open container and a small spoon. "She learned a lot about the needs of natural-enhanced babies from the twins' infancy."

Tabitha jiggled the container, "She even created this for him. It's balanced exactly for his nutritional needs."

Bethany Anne made a face. "I remember her 'nutrition blends.'"

Tabitha maneuvered the spoon past Todd's grasping hands into his mouth. Todd pushed the orange mush around his mouth a few times and blew a raspberry, covering her in food.

She wiped her face with the cloth Peter had given her. "As you can see, he really loves it." Todd babbled away on her lap. "Oh, you're proud of your achievement?"

"Well, obviously," Peter cut in, snickering. "He got every bit of you. I'd be proud. In fact, I am."

Bethany Anne snorted. "*That's* my nephew!" She sat back and folded her hands in her lap. "Guys, we need to get serious for a moment. I wish I could stay, but I have another stop after this, so I need to get a move on if I'm going to get home for dinner tonight."

Peter sat down beside Tabitha. "The status review would have waited until family dinner night if you've had a full day."

Bethany Anne made a face. "This isn't about the review,

and it isn't exactly dinner conversation, either." She watched Todd for a moment before returning her attention to Peter. "I didn't want to do this while Alexis and Gabriel were here."

Tabitha tried not to cringe as she snuck Todd another spoonful of food while Peter distracted him. She relaxed visibly when he accepted it this time. "I already know what you're going to say. It's time to move."

Peter just turned in his seat and gave Todd his pinkie to grab.

Tabitha's face worked through a series of emotions while she came to terms with the news. "We knew this was coming," she managed eventually.

Bethany Anne saved them the agony of saying it. "You two want to sit this one out." She didn't couch it as a question.

Peter sighed and nodded, slipping his arm around Tabitha. "One of us, at least. Tabitha, if I get my way. But we know where our duty lies."

Bethany Anne raised an eyebrow. "Your duty lies wherever I say it does."

Peter's face fell, and he held Tabitha and his son a bit closer. "I understand."

Bethany Anne looked at him like he'd hit his head. Several times. "Don't be a dumbass, Peter. I'm not going to split your family up. I'm sending you and Tabitha to take care of Devon in my absence."

High Tortuga, Space Fleet Base, Jean's R&D Lab

Bethany Anne pushed open the door to Jean's lab and

made her way down to the third sub-level. She was considering different issues with the fleet arrangement when she heard the sharp ping of metal on metal.

She located Jean by sound, walking through the lab until she found her old friend in the largest workshop. Jean continued to yell instructions to her team as she worked deep in the bowels of an enormous freestanding machine.

Bethany Anne assumed that to have Jean working on it, the machine was ridiculously expensive, vitally important, stupidly dangerous, or all of the above. She waited for a few minutes, then pinged Jean when it became obvious that she wasn't going to be done in there any time soon.

Jean's frazzled face appeared at the access hatch. "Hey, good to see you. Give me a minute." She pulled her head back in and climbed up to exit the hatch feet first. "I don't know if I like that look you have, Bethany Anne."

Bethany Anne held her hands up, one eyebrow raised in question. "I have no idea what you mean." She put a hand on Jean's back and guided her out of the noisy workroom, staying quiet for the moment while Jean issued yet more instructions to be completed in her absence. "Fuck, Jean. Do you want them to die of exhaustion?"

Jean frowned at Bethany Anne in confusion. "This is a slow day. In fact, there's been less to do since you had so much of the fleet production moved out to QT2."

Bethany Anne grinned as they entered the marginally quieter corridor. "Funny you should mention that."

Jean stopped walking and grabbed Bethany Anne by the arms. "Please tell me we're moving out there."

Bethany Anne shrugged her off, chuckling. "*We're* not. But you are, if you and John are okay with being apart for a while. I'm not going to war without my right hand, but neither do I want to leave anyone but the best in charge of preparing us to face the Kurtherians when we return."

Jean raised an eyebrow. "You mean I get to play in my lab guilt-free while he goes off kicking ass for a couple of years? I think we'll both be fine with that. It's not like we're newlyweds or short on time."

Bethany Anne relaxed. "You know, this is going better than I thought so far. I thought I was going to have to fight you, and Peter and Tabitha, to make you stay while I deal with the Ooken."

Jean waved a hand. "Nah. You've been doing this long enough to know where we need to be. I'm just glad I'm not the one moving the pieces on this board. I don't envy you, BA."

Bethany Anne looked off for a moment. "Maybe one day I won't need to do that, either." She turned back to Jean. "A day *will* come when the Seven have been wiped from existence and Earth is safe."

Jean made a sympathetic face and patted Bethany Anne's arm. "You're getting there," she offered. She was interrupted by a shout and a loud clang from the workshop. "Shit. I leave for one minute, and they start trashing the place. It's like having teenagers around the house again."

"Not in my house," Bethany Anne replied offhand. "I keep waiting for them to rebel, but I can't see it happening."

Jean made a face. "Yeah, well, your two are too busy blowing each other up to do much rebelling." She grinned. "I'd better get back in there before they set something on fire just to round the day out. But I'll talk to John. It's been too quiet around the house. It will be good to have a change of location."

Bethany Anne lifted a shoulder as Jean walked back to the workroom. "The guys are next on my list."

Jean waved over her shoulder. "Then you'll save me the task of telling him."

With that, she disappeared around the corner, and a second later Bethany Anne heard her yelling instructions once again.

High Tortuga, Space Fleet Base, Rec Room Beta

Bethany Anne strolled in on the final throes of an arm wrestling match between John and Eric. "I challenge the winner," she announced as she went over to them.

Eric lost his focus for the briefest of seconds and yelled when John tilted his wrist and slammed his hand down on the table. He opened his mouth to complain, but got up from the chair and gestured for Bethany Anne to take his place instead. "All yours, boss."

He smirked as Bethany Anne sat down and took John's offered hand. "Sucks to be you," he teased.

Bethany Anne adjusted her elbow on the table to get a comfortable grip. "I didn't actually come down here to play 'who can piss the farthest.'"

John's eyes crinkled slightly. "We know. We're heading out to stop the Ooken." He chuckled, "But sure, I'm willing to bet I can go farther."

Bethany Anne tightened her grip and applied enough pressure to prevent John from using his dirty trick on her.

"How the fuck does news travel around this place faster than I do?"

Darryl shrugged. "Peter called as soon as you left."

"He wanted to give us time to absorb it before you got here," John explained in a low voice. The muscle in his jaw twitched.

Bethany Anne winked at him and increased the pressure a touch. "I'll understand if any of you want to stay out of this."

Scott dragged the back of his hand over his forehead. "Thank fuck for that. It would have been *so* boring to take your freaking awesome new ships out for a spin."

"Yeah," Eric seconded. "Kicking alien ass is so five minutes ago. Who wants to go through all that?" He looked at his three best friends in feigned confusion. "Anyone?"

Darryl grinned, folding his arms on his chest. "And we're just *fiiine* with you running off starting a war without us. *Sure.*"

John grunted. "The vote is in. Looks like you're shit out of luck, Boss."

Bethany Anne looked around at them all with narrowed eyes. "Very funny, but this isn't the time for jokes." She relaxed her grip on John's hand. "We could be away for some time."

John eased her forgotten hand down to the table. "When do we leave?"

She snorted gently and got to her feet. "Any day now, so be prepared."

John inclined his head a fraction. "Like a Boy Scout," he promised.

"Wait, what?" Scott almost dropped the drink he'd just

picked up as he whipped his head in John's direction. "Ass, you were never a Boy Scout."

"How would you know?" John countered. He pointed at Scott's shirt. "You spilled something there."

Bethany Anne saw the ghost of a smile flirt with the idea of appearing on John's face when Scott looked down at himself.

The internal alarm Bethany Anne had set warned her that it was time to get home.

She turned to leave. "As much as I'd love to stay and hang out with you guys, I'm going to be late for dinner."

"What's on the menu tonight?" John asked.

Bethany Anne made a face over her shoulder as she walked to the rec room door. "Humble pie. Probably with a generous helping of 'I told you so.'"

With that, she disappeared.

6

QT2 System, QBBS *Helena*, Station Manager's Office

Giselle Foxton-Thomas strode into her office and waved a hand over her desk to activate the holoscreen. "Call my mother," she instructed, feeling none of the assertiveness she heard in her tone.

Helena Foxton appeared on the holoscreen a few moments later. Giselle smoothed her dark blue button-down self-consciously as she waited for the connection to stabilize. "How are you, Mother?"

Helena's eyes crinkled with joy. "All the better for seeing you, my dear. So, Bunny, are you looking forward to my arrival?"

Giselle repressed the urge to make a face at her child-hood nickname. "That's what I'm calling about, Mother. The announcement went out early this afternoon; we are officially at war. The Queen is on her way to take command of the fleet. I think it might be safer for you to stay in Federation territory."

Helena snorted elegantly. "I think not, Bunny. You

forget I was a journalist during the final years of the Leath War. You've seen holovid of some of the absolute cesspits I stayed in. I will manage perfectly adequately on the comparative luxury of a Queen's battle station."

Giselle smiled. "Good old Mother. I can always rely on you."

"Less of the old," her mother retorted. "I only had rejuvenation therapy fifteen years ago. I'm practically a spring chicken." Helena arched a perfectly plucked eyebrow. "Now, I'm sure you have enough to do without being on an endless call to me."

Giselle's mouth quirked. "I wasn't going to say that, but you were always straight to the point."

Helena tilted her chin. "I should hope so. But go on with your day, Bunny. I will see you in person very soon."

"Love you, Mother," Giselle called just as Helena cut the connection. She smiled and gestured for her keyboard to appear.

A portion of Giselle's thoughts remained on Helena as she worked through the never-ending administrative tasks for the station. Most of them were minor things to be passed on and dealt with by the relevant manager or operator. The ones that remained were the problems no one else could solve.

No one but her. Giselle enjoyed the challenges that crossed her desk. Her work provided the release her sharp mind needed, which made it much easier to be at home with the children. She loved her family incredibly, but there was only so much mental stimulation to be had from three under-fives and a husband whose first responsibility (rightly) lay with his command.

Between her job and the demands of taking care of the children, it was going to get pretty lonely around here when her husband left with Bethany Anne.

Maybe it wasn't too late to become friends with her mother.

Three grandchildren and a space station named after her should go *some* way toward laying a foundation.

High Tortuga, Space Fleet Base, Inner Courtyard

Bethany Anne arrived home at last and walked the last few paces across the softly-lit courtyard instead of slipping through the Etheric again.

She thought she might have missed dinner after all until she opened the front door and smelled goulash. "I'm home!" she called.

"We know!" came the chorus from the living area.

"I *know* you know," she finished their little ritual with a contented smile, walking through to find her world gathered around the kitchen side of the island.

Michael turned to Bethany Anne with everything he had to say written in his eyes. "Good to have you home."

Bethany Anne blew him a kiss and spread her arms wide. "It's good to *be* home. Now, what do I have to do to get some love around here?" Her stomach let out a loud growl.

She sniffed delicately as she wrapped an arm around each of her children. "And some dinner?"

"I'm with Mom," Gabriel agreed.

Alexis rolled her eyes at her brother. "That's not surprising. You're with whoever has the food."

Michael chortled quietly. *"I* have the food. We will eat when we have somewhere to sit." He waved his spoon at the twins, then at the table. "Let your mom get in. You can both make yourselves useful while you wait."

Alexis and Gabriel got to setting the table, while Bethany Anne went around the island into the kitchen and took out four deep bowls from the bottom cupboard.

She lined them up on the counter by the stove for Michael to fill. *No more waiting. I got the weekly report in from QT2, and we're ready.*

Michael nodded once and sharply. *Then it is time to make your decision, Bethany Anne. You know where I stand, but we need to be in agreement.*

Bethany Anne forestalled him with a look. *I've made my decision. Alexis and Gabriel are coming with us, providing they want to and they understand what it is they're asking for.*

Michael nodded and moved on to the next bowl. *I would also insist they continue their training. They still have a lot to learn.*

Bethany Anne picked up two of the bowls and headed for the table. *Of course. I was getting to that. I'm leaving for QT2 in the morning. I want you to prepare Alexis and Gabriel and join me there before the fleet departs.*

Michael turned to drop his ladle in the sink and followed her with the other two bowls. *Which will be when, exactly?*

Bethany Anne pressed her lips together. *If I listen to Bart, seven days. Qui'nan tells me five.*

Michael smirked as he put the bowls down on the table. *So we're going to leave in three days?*

Bethany Anne snickered. *If only. If it was just me, I'd be halfway there already. You know that.* She felt a gentle probing at the edge of her consciousness. *One moment. Our daughter is trying to eavesdrop.*

Wait, Michael urged. *We have a teachable moment here.*

Bethany Anne met his eyes with a matching twinkle in her own. She created an almost imperceptible gap, just big enough for Alexis to sneak through. *I don't know how Barnabas will feel about being responsible for two teenagers...but maybe a few years with him will teach Alexis how to listen in on our conversations* without *getting caught.*

They heard a tiny mental squeak and Alexis withdrew.

Bethany Anne gave Alexis a stern look across the table as she took her seat. "Serves you right for eavesdropping."

Alexis had the good grace to look ashamed. "Sorry. It won't happen again."

Bethany Anne raised an eyebrow. "Hmmm."

"How did your day go, Mom?" Gabriel inquired once the four of them were seated and had begun eating.

Bethany Anne reached for the breadbasket. "It went easier than I expected. Tabitha and Peter were glad to stay behind, and John and Jean were fine about spending some time away from each other. The guys—that went about as expected, too."

Michael read the words she wasn't saying. "Which made it all the more difficult."

Bethany Anne looked into her bowl as she dipped a piece of her roll. "Something like that." She smiled at them all and popped the bread into her mouth.

Alexis spoke up. "Why is it more difficult? Surely if

everyone is happy, then that makes it easier." She turned to snag a roll from the breadbasket before Bethany Anne passed it to Michael.

"I don't get it, either," Gabriel chipped in, spearing a chunk of meat on the end of his fork. "Is it because you want to take everyone with you but you can't?"

Bethany Anne nodded. "Again, my children amaze me." She passed Michael the basket "Are you going to miss Tabitha and Peter when they leave for Devon?"

"Not really," Alexis told her. "Aunt Tabbie won't leave us for real."

"We will still be able to see her and Uncle Pete in the game world whenever we want," Gabriel explained.

"You *do* realize that there will be very little time for them to spend in the Vid-docs?" Michael clarified. "This is not a scenario in the game, children. We do not have a set list of objectives to complete in order to win against the Ooken."

Alexis sighed. "We didn't think it was going to be anything like that, Dad. War isn't a game when real lives are involved. I'm happy Aunt Tabbie is staying behind. Then she will be relatively safe, and so will Uncle Pete and Todd." She shrugged. "We will find *some* time to spend together, and that will be enough until we are reunited."

Bethany Anne chewed her bread thoughtfully. "Jokes about your Uncle Barnabas aside, do you understand what coming with us would entail?" She paused, waiting for Michael to confirm what she already knew.

Alexis and Gabriel shared a long look, then nodded and turned back to their parents with identical serious expressions.

"We *think* we do," Alexis told them truthfully. "But we can't know for sure until we experience it for real."

"We understand that we can't fight yet," Gabriel continued, "but we can contribute in other ways."

Can you believe them? Michael asked. *I know we raised them this way, but for children to actually turn out the way you planned is quite rare, you know.*

Bethany Anne laughed lightly in his mind. ***Hold that thought. They've been pretty sheltered so far. There's still plenty of time for them to rebel, my love,*** She became serious a moment. ***But believe me, I know how much we lucked out with them. You never met Lilian's daughter.***

Michael's amusement trickled through in his voice. *Hellion, was she?*

Bethany Anne mopped up the last bit of her sauce with the remainder of her bread roll. ***You have no idea. Like I said, we're fucking* lucky.** She paused with the bread halfway between the bowl and her mouth to put Alexis and Gabriel out of their agony.

The twins were practically bouncing in their seats in anticipation of her decision, knowing she was the only thing between them and their hopes of seeing some of the galaxy.

Bethany Anne waved the piece of bread. "You can come with us."

Alexis and Gabriel jumped up and ran over to hug her.

"You're the best, Mom!" Gabriel exclaimed, squeezing her tightly.

Alexis grabbed her from the other side, pressing her cheek to Bethany Anne's. "Thank you, Mom. We won't let you and Dad down."

Bethany Anne laughed and kissed them on their foreheads. "I should hope you do so at least once, or you're not living. For now, that mindset works just fine. You're good kids, and we believe you're mature enough that you don't have to stay home."

"Your mother and I couldn't be prouder of the people you are becoming," Michael told them. "In fact, I'm even going to release you from your chores tonight. We begin packing up the house tomorrow, so enjoy your free time."

Gabriel ducked out of Bethany Anne's arms. "Cool! I didn't think I'd get any time to draw today."

Alexis' reaction was a touch more extreme. She released Bethany Anne and whirled to grab Michael's arm. "Tomorrow? Oh, no, I need longer than that. *Details*, Dad. What is our exact departure date, and who is coming with us? Which ship will we take? Is there a limit to how much of our stuff we can take with us?" Her eyes widened. "Please tell me we can take Phyrro with us. I couldn't bear it if we had to leave him behind."

Michael shook his head and gently turned Alexis toward the door by her shoulders. "Tomorrow. Don't you have something you've been waiting to read?"

Alexis nodded somewhat sullenly. "Yes, Dad."

Gabriel rolled his eyes. "Come on, Alexis, before you earn us chores instead of free time." He turned to Bethany Anne and Michael. "Night!"

Alexis allowed her brother to lead her from the room. "Night, Mom. Night, Dad."

"Goodnight, children," Michael replied with a smile. "Sleep well."

Bethany Anne blew them each a kiss. "Goodnight, my loves. I'll see you both in a few days."

Bethany Anne and Michael cleared the dinner things away and headed to bed. She yawned and leaned into him as they walked down the corridor to their bedroom. *What an absolute bitch of a day. If I had one ounce of energy left, I'd float to bed.*

Michael held her a little bit closer. *I could always carry you,* he offered. *Or turn us both to Myst.*

Bethany Anne chuckled. *I would even allow you to do that if we weren't five steps from the door.*

When they walked into the bedroom, Bethany Anne headed straight for the bed and sat down on the edge. She crossed one leg over the other to remove her shoe while Michael slipped his off by the door.

Bethany Anne looked up when Michael walked past her into the bathroom with his shirt in his hand. *Are we doing the right thing? Really?*

We're doing what we believe to be right, Michael agreed. There was the soft sound of his pants hitting the laundry basket, followed by running water. *As all parents have done since the dawn of humanity. Alexis and Gabriel are living proof we are succeeding.*

Bethany Anne pressed her lips together. *I hate when you're right. It's been happening far too often for my liking.* She sighed and yawned again as the shoe finally came undone. *Did I ever work out how to take my clothes off using the Etheric? I'm too tired to remember.*

Michael chuckled dryly in her mind. *I don't know, my love,* he replied. *But I suggest you work it out quickly. The water is wonderfully hot.*

She switched legs and started on the fastener on the other shoe. *I'll be two seconds.*

Devon, First City, The Hexagon, Network Command Center

Sabine tapped her foot, waiting for Mark to make some progress on locating K'aia. It had been almost an hour since the orphan Yollin had made Sabine's drone and slipped it.

Mark turned in his chair to look pointedly at her. "That's not going to make it happen any faster." He ran his hand through his hair to get it out of his eyes. "At least we have images of her to search by. It's taking Winstanley and me some time to search the city, because our satellites were built at *least* a thousand years before Michael was born."

Sabine put her hands on her hips and tapped louder. "You're joking."

"Barely." Mark shrugged. "But we *are* getting there, and from what you and Ricole have told me, this Yollin is pretty good at taking care of herself."

Sabine glared at him. "But she's still young. She shouldn't *have* to take care of herself!" She sighed and sat down in the chair next to Mark's. "You can't blame me for being concerned. We have no idea where she is or what she's going through."

Mark turned back to the console and continued typing. "I know, but the network wasn't designed to pinpoint a single Yollin in a huge city. We're working as fast as we can to find her." He pointed at another screen. "We have a call."

Sabine checked the screen and picked up right away when she saw that it was Tabitha. "Hey!"

Tabitha grinned. "Hey, yourself. How're things for you guys?"

Mark slipped his headset off one ear. "Is that Tabitha? Tell her I said hi."

Sabine smirked. "Of course. Then the next time you piss me off, I can tell Jacqueline." She winked at him and turned back to the screen. "Mark says hi."

"Hi, Mark," Tabitha called. "Give Jacqueline my love."

Sabine immensely enjoyed the bright shade of red Mark turned. She grinned at Tabitha, who was cackling with laughter with her audio muted. Sabine waved to get her attention. "So, what can I do for you? I'm guessing this isn't a social call."

Tabitha got control of herself. "You guessed right. I've got some pretty big news, and I need you guys to keep it to yourselves for now."

"What's up?" Sabine asked.

Mark piped up, "Are you pregnant again already?"

Tabitha's mouth dropped open.

Sabine reached over and slapped Mark on the back of the head.

Mark grabbed his head. "OW!"

"Be glad I wasn't there to do it myself," Tabitha told him. "Although I will be. Soon. That's my news. Peter and I are moving to Devon for a while. We thought you kids might know a good neighborhood to set up house."

Mark snorted. "Yeah, High Tortuga. This place is still a dump."

Tabitha pointed at Mark. "Does he have to be here for this?"

Sabine nodded. "Unfortunately, yes. But we can go somewhere else."

"Great idea," Tabitha agreed. "I've already got one male whining in my ear. Oh, he's pooped." Tabitha held up a finger. "I'll be back in, like, eight minutes. Don't go anywhere."

Sabine listened to Tabitha coo to her baby for a moment, then muted the audio and transferred the call to her tablet and headed out. "Tell me if anything changes with K'aia," she called back.

"I'll let you know as soon as we find anything," Mark assured her. He switched to their link. *Just don't let Tabitha hurt me.*

Sabine rolled her eyes as the door locked behind her. She made her way to the cafeteria on the fighter's level, looking for a hot meal.

Tabitha returned as Sabine took a seat with what the chef insisted on calling a rarebit, but she knew as a *croque monsieur*. She rested her tablet against the condiment basket and blew on her food.

"Whatcha got there?" Tabitha asked, eyeing the steaming plate curiously.

Sabine pulled the two halves apart. "Cheese—not real cheese, ham—not real ham, and toast—which *is* real bread, since we can get grain out here." She took a small bite and chewed quickly. "I know a few places for sale. You want room for people to stay, right?"

Tabitha nodded. "Oh, yeah. Maybe rural, but still close

enough to see people when we want to. And plenty of outdoor space."

Sabine's eyes lit up. "How do you feel about a lake view?"

Tabitha shrugged. "You know, I'm ambivalent, but I think Peter would like that. For some reason, he's taken a liking to fishing. Keeps taking me on boat trip scenarios."

Sabine snickered. "Maybe he'll leave you home if you get him the real thing. Actually, there's something you can help me with."

"If I can, I will," Tabitha replied. "What's going on?"

Sabine quickly recounted the story so far; K'aia showing up out of the blue, kicking Ricole's ass, and then leaving; how she'd somehow slipped Sabine's surveillance.

"I just want to confirm that Bethany Anne knows this Yollin," she finished. "And if she would approve her passage to High Tortuga, then she should do so before the youngster gets herself in trouble attempting to sneak aboard one of our ships."

Tabitha looked off for a moment, her eyes unfocused. A minute later she nodded and turned back to Sabine. "Done. Also, they're watching for her now. She'll be okay."

Sabine felt a weight lift. "Thank you. You're all more than welcome to stay with us while we find you a place to live."

Tabitha shook her head. "We wouldn't want to intrude."

Sabine understood that what Tabitha really meant was that she had a small baby and she didn't want to be intruded *upon*. "The residential part of the building is entirely soundproofed. We all live communally, so we knocked three of the apartments into one. That left the penthouse apartment for guests, and you're honestly welcome to it for as long as you need."

Tabitha grinned. "In that case, we'd be glad to impose on you. We'll be there in a few days. Can you get the place babyproofed?"

Tabitha dropped the connection before Sabine had a chance to ask what "babyproofing" was.

She blanked the tablet screen and bit into her *croque monsieur* with a very Gallic shrug. "I'll figure it out, somehow."

7

Devon, First City, Spaceport

K'aia threaded her way through the crowd in front of the spaceport, careful not to jostle anyone and draw attention to herself. The last thing she wanted was to get noticed by one of the Guardians right before she attempted to sneak into the port.

Sneaking wasn't the ideal choice, or even an easy one, given her four-legged Yollin physique, but K'aia'd had years of practice at being invisible, and she didn't see she had any other choice.

K'aia left the line to come at the problem from another angle. She had originally thought to buy a ticket at the gate with the credits she'd earned in street fights these last few days, but it didn't look as though that was an option.

She had only been in the line for a minute when a trio of disgruntled Yollins walked past. One bitched loudly that this was the only way to get to High Tortuga. Another snapped that they had better get the relevant permissions to travel before she dragged them all out here again.

Her hastily revised plan was to find a way into the spaceport to stow away aboard a ship that looked about ready to leave. She would throw herself on the mercy of the captain once they were underway.

K'aia was entirely aware of the stupidity of her plan, but at the same time, it was freeing to know that it was *her* stupid plan and not some slave driver's.

If only Barien could see her now.

That morning she had thought of him while eating a breakfast of strange pastry and bitter juice under an awning in the bazaar, surrounded by every color and smell imaginable. He had always believed they would break free. She wished he was here to experience the First City with her.

Now she was just a face in the crowd, dwarfed on all sides by ships far larger than anything she'd seen outside of holovids.

K'aia was resigned to the fact that she probably wouldn't make it to High Tortuga this way. Still, she had to try. There was no life for her here.

She shrugged her pack to adjust the weight and walked past the gate, making certain she didn't gawk. That was the fastest way to let anyone whose job it was to watch know you didn't belong somewhere.

Nevertheless, it seemed she had managed to draw the attention of a couple of Guardians. K'aia put her head down and fought to maintain the same pace, hoping she was being paranoid and it was the Shrillexians ahead of her that they were heading toward.

No such luck. She turned, feeling a hand on her shoulder.

"Are you K'aia?" the female Guardian queried. "We're looking for a Yollin named K'aia."

K'aia was surprised to hear the human version of her name. She looked the Guardians over. They weren't acting in a hostile manner, and they weren't armed—but then, Guardians didn't *need* to be armed. "What do you want? How do you know who I am?"

The one who had yet to speak looked at his wrist. "Yeah, it's her," he told the female before turning back to her.

"K'aia, the Queen has requested you join her. We're going to get you there, but we have to hurry, or you'll miss your ride." He waved for K'aia to follow and set off back toward the gate at a brisk walk.

K'aia's mandibles moved without making a single connection. Bethany Anne wanted K'aia to *join* her? She had thought her path lay in the military, earning her keep. Not as a hanger-on, pampered like some pet.

The female Guardian held out a hand. "I know it's a lot, but we really have to get going. We're gearing up for war and time is something that seems to be in short supply."

K'aia nodded, feeling better at the mention of something she understood. She let her four feet carry her after the Guardians, who led her straight past the line and into the spaceport. Too overwhelmed to say a word, she trailed behind the Guardians while they showed her to one of the ships she'd been in such awe of just a few minutes ago.

She finally found enough of her voice to thank the Guardians as the ramp descended to take her aboard. "I'll tell Bethany Anne how helpful you were when I get to High Tortuga. What are your names?"

"I'm Fletcher, and this is Thistlemar," the female told her. "But you're not staying on High Tortuga. Like we said, we're at war. The Queen is on the move."

K'aia nodded. One location was as good as another. "Will there be work for me there?"

Fletcher nodded. "There's work for anyone who wants it. What do you do?"

The young Yollin's eyes didn't waver. "I'm a fighter," she replied.

The Guardians snickered, and Thistlemar waved her on with a grin. "Then you'll be just fine."

QT2 System, QBBS *Helena*, Shipyard

Bethany Anne exited the *Izanami* and walked down the ramp to meet Admiral Thomas. "How are my ships?" she asked in greeting.

"It's good to see you, too," he replied. "Never let inane personal updates get in the way of a good ass-kicking."

Bethany Anne waved a hand as she walked past him, a small smirk playing at the edges of her lips. "We know how we are," she countered. "*Busy*. Later on, we might not be so busy. Now," she rolled a finger in a circle, "my ships?"

Admiral Thomas had no retort for that. He escorted her to the roamer he had waiting to take them to the command center. "We have a total of seventeen battle-ready super-dreadnoughts, plus all the ancillary ships to back them up thanks to Lance for coming through with the materials to build them."

Bethany Anne nodded. "Giselle sourced a hell of a lot of it too," she reminded him.

"Most of that went into building the shipyard," Admiral Thomas informed her. "Lance was able to deliver a literal shitload of metal through the Interdiction for ship construction. Otherwise, we'd have stalled before we hit double digits."

Bethany Anne made a mental note to send her father a thank you gift. "What about the crews to run all these new ships?"

Admiral Thomas grinned. "Peter has been a godsend. The training program for new arrivals from the Federation is running well. It helps that the recruits are mostly young Wechselbalg who turned up at Devon looking to blow off some steam."

Bethany Anne raised an eyebrow. "So, what...they got planetside and found that Devon is just a bit wilder than they were anticipating?"

"Pretty much spot on," he agreed cheerily. "Giselle hasn't stopped singing Peter's praises. He had Tim send teams down to round them up before they get hurt or killed, then he gives them the option to be shipped home or come out here to harden up some."

Bethany Anne pressed her lips together in amusement. "Good. The last time I was on the *Meredith Reynolds* I thought there was getting to be a surplus there."

Admiral Thomas shrugged. "There haven't been too many requests for transport back to the Federation."

They reached the transfer station, and both sat back to enjoy the show the universe put on for everyone who used the transfer rail.

Bethany Anne looked back to take comfort in the sight of her fleet. She was momentarily struck by the endless backdrop of stars, allowing her gaze to wander until the roamer pulled up in the station at the other end.

They left the rail and the roamer crossed the transfer station floor, rolling to a stop in one of the elevators.

Bethany Anne tapped her fingers on her armrest. The admiral noticed her eyes flicking back and forth, too fast for him to follow. He assumed she was reading through the status reports of every ship while they waited for the elevator to get where it was going. She stopped and looked up at him. "Looks like the three of you have everything sewn up here."

Admiral Thomas nodded as the roamer exited the elevator and crossed the concourse. "We're operating well as a team, and the station is settling into a rhythm. It's good."

"You'll be operating even better once Jean gets here." Bethany Anne looked out of the window. "You did get my message about making room for her, right?"

"I did," he chuckled. "Qui'nan wasn't too pleased about sharing her space at first, but she came around when Jean's equipment started arriving yesterday."

Bethany Anne's mouth twitched. "I'll bet. I expect Michael will arrive sooner rather than later. I know my husband all too well."

Admiral Thomas chuckled dryly. "I don't know about that. I'd argue that it's Michael who knows *you*."

Bethany Anne spotted a note from Qui'nan. *ADAM, what is Qui'nan trying to say? It looks like production at the shipyard could be higher.*

>>**She appears to be voicing her disappointment that**

the **shipyard isn't being used to its full capacity,<<** ADAM replied.

Bethany Anne pressed her lips together. *Hmmm...*

>>**Bethany Anne?<<**

One minute, I need to deal with this.

"Is something the matter?" Admiral Thomas inquired.

"I'm just working out how many more ships you can turn out once I leave."

He frowned. "I have no idea what you mean."

"Well," Bethany Anne drew her words out, "I *get* that you had to keep production tight while the station was under construction. However, construction is expected to be completed any day, so I can expect an immediate increase in yield. Yes?"

Admiral Thomas tried to swallow the lump in his throat. "Technically, the station is still under construction," he pointed out. "And I *did* have something of a resource nightmare up until the point Lance came through. But yes, we can increase production now."

Bethany Anne dismissed the report. "By a third."

Admiral Thomas sighed, bitching to the gods inside his head. His Queen rarely missed opportunities to increase production and reduce the time one had to accomplish anything. "By a third—providing our supply chain remains intact."

The roamer pulled up in an alcove that was lined with the vehicles, and they got out and headed for the elevator to the command center.

Bethany Anne nodded. "Fair enough."

>>**Bethany Anne?<<**

Bethany Anne held up a finger to Admiral Thomas. "It's ADAM." *What's up?*

>>The SSE ladies have found one, maybe two more splinter worlds.<<

She frowned. *Only maybe?*

>>Saffron and Savannah located the planet, but they can't get close. This colony knows how to use their technology to its fullest.<<

Bethany Anne thought on her feet. *How would you like to take another joyride?*

>>Probably about as much as you would like a new pair of shoes.<<

Bethany Anne chuckled at the excitement in his voice. *Saddle up, then. You're on. Get me the intel on both of those planets.*

>>I'll have Jean get my ship ready.<<

You should take Loralei if she's up and fighting again.

>>Yeah, because what I need is more ammunition to feed the SSE rumor mill. It's a shark tank, Bethany Anne.<<

ADAM.

>>Yes, Bethany Anne?<<

You're not making any sense.

>>Sorry, but you're female. You know how terrifying you all are.<<

ADAM.

>>Yes, Bethany Anne?<<

There was a pause before she finished her thought.

Be careful out there.

. . .

High Tortuga, Space Fleet Base, Hangar 001, QBS *G'laxix Sphaea*, Twins' Quarters

Michael put his head through the door adjoining his and Bethany Anne's quarters and told the twins, "I have to take care of a small matter before we leave. Would either of you care to join me?"

Gabriel shook his head, still absorbed in his artwork. "I'm good here, thanks."

Alexis jumped down from her bunk and dropped her book on the nightstand. "What's the problem? We're due to leave in an hour."

"Not a problem," Michael clarified. "We are collecting our final passenger. This shouldn't take too long, and then we can be on our way to join your mother." Michael withdrew his head.

Gabriel looked up, having gained interest for half a second. His head dropped a second later, however, his interest waning just as quickly.

Alexis half-jogged to catch up, falling into step beside her father. "Who is the passenger? I just checked with Phyrro and everyone is aboard already."

Michael indicated a place farther along the long corridor that linked the series of almost identical doors. "Not everyone. There was a last minute addition to the list, someone who helped your Mom and I free some slaves not too long ago." He snorted softly. "I suppose it would be more like ten years from your perspective."

"Oh." Alexis frowned and changed the subject. "Dad, is it weird for you and Mom that our ages are all messed up?"

Michael's brow furrowed as he glanced down at his daughter. "How do you mean?"

Alexis took her time with the answer. "Well, Gabriel and I were talking last night about how you and Mom see this world and the game world as completely separate, so to you, we've only been alive for nearly six years. But we've experienced fourteen."

Michael pointed to the next door along. "I have not given it much thought. You and Gabriel are simply teenagers now. I have lived long enough that a mortal life-span passes in an instant," he snapped his fingers, "and yet to some of our friends, even we are like mayflies."

"Mayflies?" Alexis asked.

Michael nodded. "Earth insect. They live their entire adult lives in just a few hours. My point is that when you have a span of centuries instead of decades in front of you, a few years here and there is arbitrary as long as you are living them to your best ability."

Alexis tilted her head, standing aside for Michael to verify his identity for the door. "I don't get it," she admitted with more than a little frustration.

Michael smiled fondly. "You will in time."

Alexis huffed. "Why can't we use the Vid-doc to fast-forward to then?"

Michael's smile widened. "Because that would be cheating, wouldn't it?"

She made a face. "I suppose so."

Michael laid a hand on his daughter's shoulder. "It was okay when it was necessary to save your lives, but living inside the game world is not an option for the rest of your life." He pushed open the door and they entered an office that looked down on one of the hangars.

Alexis dismissed the aversion she had for the crowd

below. Instead, she looked over the rows of ships. "They're coming in on a public transport?"

"You are made entirely of questions today, Alexis." Michael held the door until she was through and then ensured it was locked behind them. "Stay close."

Michael led Alexis to the floor below and around the edge of the crowded docks to another office, where he instructed her to wait outside for a few moments while he spoke to a pair of people wearing loose-fitting shipsuits whom she identified as Guardians.

Alexis reluctantly took a seat on a bench made for the four-legged outside the door, next to a Yollin who looked just as happy to be outside the office as she was. She turned around on the padded seat to face the window and kept her eyes on her father, thinking to lipread what he was saying.

Michael spotted her attempt and raised an eyebrow. He waved a finger and the window blind snapped down abruptly, making both Alexis and the Yollin jump.

"Dammit," Alexis muttered softly to herself. "How am I supposed to find out what's going on if he keeps figuring out I'm listening?"

The Yollin chuckled. "You could always ask me," she offered. "Since I'm the one they're talking about. Might as well get used to this translation software they put in on the way here."

Alexis turned on the bench to get a better look at this Yollin they had sidetracked for. "You're the mystery passenger?"

The Yollin nodded and turned to face Alexis. "The

name's K'aia. What's yours, and why are you with Michael?"

"I'm Alexis. You know my dad?" She lifted her feet onto the bench and crossed her legs to get comfortable. "Tell me how you ended up here. Where are you from?"

K'aia looked at the door of the office where Michael and the Guardians were, discussing her like some adolescent who hadn't been taking care of herself since forever.

"Oh, they'll be *ages,*" Alexis assured her with a wave. "And I really am interested. Dad told me you helped him and Mom free some slaves?"

K'aia shrugged. "I was one of those slaves until about a year ago. I escaped and ran into your parents, and we all freed the rest of the slaves in the mine."

"So that's how they know you," Alexis wrapped her arms around her knees and leaned in to listen. "Tell me everything. What are you going to the *Helena* for? Are you here to fight in the war?"

K'aia nodded. "If I can."

Michael's shadow crossed them. "I have a more suitable role in mind for you, K'aia. That is, if my wife agrees and if you wish to take it on." He looked distant a moment. "However, the ship will leave without us if we remain here talking."

Alexis jumped up from the bench. "Yeah, no. Let's go before that happens. I want to see Mom."

Kael-ven did not leave without them. Michael walked briskly ahead while Alexis and K'aia followed, chatting as girls did—in his limited experience.

Michael received another message from Kael-ven as

they boarded. "Alexis, I'd like you to show K'aia around the ship. Take her to her quarters and then get settled in."

Alexis nodded and smiled at K'aia. "I'd be happy to. How many Gates away is QT2?"

Michael rolled his eyes in amusement. "More questions? Save them for later. Kael-ven needs me on the bridge."

"This is the weirdest day," K'aia confessed once Michael had left.

Alexis looked at her potential new friend. "In what way?" She gestured to K'aia to follow her in the opposite direction.

K'aia shrugged. "Just... I'm on the *G'laxix Sphaea*, one of the most famous ships in the galaxy. I definitely didn't expect your parents to take time for me personally." She snorted. "I still think of your mother as the Empress, and yet here I am." She raised her hands and turned her upper body to indicate the corridor.

"If you're here, it's because you deserve to be. My parents don't have time for hangers-on." Alexis shook her head earnestly. "I hope you didn't call my mom 'Empress' to her face."

K'aia nodded, her eyes wide. "Oh, that was exactly what I did." She broke into a chuckle. "Believe me, she set me straight on *that* pretty much as soon as I met her, but she is still the Empress to me."

They got into the elevator side by side, and Alexis gave the level she wanted.

Alexis grinned at K'aia. "We will go to your quarters, but I'm going to introduce you to my brother first. Otherwise, he'll just complain for the next hundred years that I left him out."

K'aia nodded. "That sounds good, but it's been a long day. Can we do it quickly?"

Gabriel was packing away his art supplies when Alexis and K'aia reached the twins' quarters. He was more than surprised to see a Yollin he didn't know come in with Alexis.

Alexis jerked a thumb over her shoulder. "This is K'aia. She's the mystery passenger traveling with us to the *Helena*."

Gabriel nodded. "Hey, I'm Gabriel. Where are you quartered?"

K'aia shrugged. "I just got here. I have no idea."

Gabriel made a face. "That won't do. You should feel at home. Phyrro?"

"I was about to do that!" Alexis exclaimed.

K'aia looked from Alexis to Gabriel. "Do what?"

Phyrro's avatar appeared on the wallscreen. "How can I help?"

Alexis flicked her hair back over her shoulder. "Phyrro, where are K'aia's assigned quarters?"

Phyrro looked off to the side for a moment. "K'aia is quartered in the suite next to this one."

Alexis clapped her hands and bounced on the spot. "Great! That means we can hang out." She spotted the signs of exhaustion on K'aia. "After you've eaten and rested. How does that sound?"

K'aia nodded, a touch of her exhaustion creeping through her tough facade. "That sounds like the best idea anyone has come up with ever."

Michael opened his link to Bethany Anne as he left Alexis to help K'aia settle in.

My love, I have retrieved our young Yollin friend and we are on our way.

I can't wait to see you all. There was concern in her voice. **How is K'aia? Sabine's call made it sound like she was in need of help.**

She's flighty, Michael reported. *She needs to spend some time with people who give a damn before the urge to run fades in her.*

She's been through hell, Bethany Anne murmured. **I wish we could have done more for her the first time we met. We'll do what we can to help her recover.**

I've made a step toward that already. Our daughter was taken with K'aia almost immediately, so I had ArchAngel put her in the room next to the children.

Good thinking. She hesitated. **You don't think K'aia is too old for Alexis and Gabriel?**

I think the three will do each other good. Alexis and Gabriel need to develop friendships outside the family as much as K'aia needs the security of friends she can rely upon. Besides, it can't hurt that our little Yollin is fierce as a box of kittens, despite her attempts to appear otherwise.

I don't know, I liked how she fought. What does that have to do with this?

You were considering assigning a guard detail to Alexis and Gabriel, Michael reminded her. *K'aia's thoughts were clear on her earning a place here if she was to have one at all. Would it not be ideal for the three to form bonds while they are still young?*

Bethany Anne loved it as a solution. ***Dammit, will you stop being right all the time? How am I supposed to maintain my position as your better half if you keep showering me with wisdom that's actually...I don't know, wise? You're killing me here.***

Michael chuckled dryly. *That would be like asking water not to be wet. If you wanted incompetence in a man, perhaps Bobcat would have been a wiser choice of husband?*

I can't believe what I'm hearing. Bethany Anne couldn't believe the audacity of the man. Then again, she couldn't say she didn't *like* it. ***Just wait until I get my hands on you.***

Michael's voice was silk over their link, a caress in her mind. *I am anticipating it already.*

8

QT2 System, QBBS *Helena*, Meeting Room

Bethany Anne adjusted the placement of her feet on the large conference table. Her fingers drummed a rapid tattoo on the arm of her chair to match the angry beat of her heart against her ribcage, her lips pressing together in a tight line as she regarded the holomap above the polished stone.

Seven Ooken worlds. *Seven.*

That fucking number was *taunting* her and her failure to bring her vendetta against the Kurtherians to a satisfactory conclusion.

Right now all she had was the possibility of a lead waiting for her at the end of this war. Granted, it was a very *high* possibility, not to mention that the task of removing such a serious threat was a necessary one.

The question was how to best apply her assets to the problem to get the most efficient result in the shortest amount of time. She sat up and brushed off the table where her feet had been and resumed her tapping while she worked on the solution.

Bethany Anne's concentration was broken by the arrival of her husband. She looked up as Michael entered the meeting room, savoring the little jump her heart did whenever he came into her presence.

Michael brushed his lips against her cheek as he placed a takeout cup on the table. "The children are settling in well. I thought you'd appreciate some time to arrange your thoughts before the briefing."

Bethany Anne looked under the lid and smiled. "As much as I appreciate that you knew I was thirsty." She replaced the lid and sipped her Coke through the straw.

Michael scrutinized the map. "We're up to seven locations?"

"Mmhmm." She put the cup on the table and waved a finger at the map. "The sixth is confirmed, and the seventh we're almost certain about."

Michael took the seat beside Bethany Anne. "Could one of them be the homeworld?"

"I really fucking hope so," Bethany Anne shrugged, "but I doubt it. ADAM and Loralei have gone out to confirm it, one way or the other. Kael-ven left with him on the *G'axix Sphaea* after you guys got here with instructions to get whatever they can get on the third planet."

Michael pointed out the largest of the marked planets. "That's this one, with the highest population density?"

Bethany Anne nodded grimly. "It looks to me like they settled that planet first, then spread out. I think that's the one with the biggest likelihood of giving us a lead to the homeworld. If not, then we just keep on kicking in doors until we find it."

"I would expect nothing less from you." Michael took her hand. "Of course, we can always hope for a favorable resolution."

Bethany Anne squeezed his hand in return. "Fucking right we can. I never give up hope. But we are also smart enough to prepare for the worst, which is why I'm having Jean and Qui'nan step up fleet production here after we leave."

Michael's brow furrowed. "So Bart *has* been holding out on you."

Bethany Anne dropped his hand and narrowed her eyes at him. "You *knew*?"

Michael lifted a shoulder. "I knew he was up to something. This makes perfect sense." He was silent a moment. "But we know he wouldn't hold back without a good reason. Will increasing production cause a bottleneck?"

Bethany Anne sipped her Coke, putting her annoyance at not having already resolved this aside to be realistic for the moment. "Not anymore. The station is complete near as I can tell, and the drain on resources from supporting so many people will ease as soon as we leave with the fleet."

Michael nodded. "I'm not even going to question the need for expanding so rapidly."

"Oh, it's completely necessary." A sad smile touched the corner of Bethany Anne's lips. "Given the information that's been coming in from the scout fleet these last months, I don't think we *can* be overprepared."

Michael leaned forward, steepling his hands on the table in front of him. "It's the numbers, right?"

Bethany Anne nodded. "The damn numbers. Seven planets, various population levels on each. There are too many Ooken to fucking count, so it would be beyond stupid not to be cautious."

Michael had no argument with that. "Agreed. So what's your plan?"

Bethany Anne tapped a finger on her lips, turning her attention back to the map. "The biggest challenge here is managing the expansion of the fleet in a sustainable way. As for the Ooken, I want to know what *they* know, then I want them wiped out before they even know we've been there."

Michael looked up as familiar presences tickled his awareness. "We have company."

Bethany Anne's eyes flicked from the map to the door. "Mmhmm. I heard them too."

John was first into the meeting room. "See, I'm here on time, Boss."

Bethany Anne raised her eyebrow. "Good thing, or push-ups on the table would have been your reality for however long this meeting takes."

John hid his smirk as he made his way to his chair.

Darryl, Eric, and Scott filed in behind him with the usual shenanigans, followed by Gabrielle. Jean and Qui'nan arrived a couple of minutes later, accompanied by Admiral Thomas and Giselle.

Jean grumbled something about this not being what Bethany Anne had promised. She slid into her seat as Akio and Eve slipped through the door.

"This is *exactly* what I promised," Bethany Anne sighed with exasperation. "If you stop bitching for ten minutes, you'll find out." She waved a hand and the holomap winked out of existence. "Now that we're all here…"

"Why *are* we all here?" Jean asked, a little more congenially this time.

Bethany Anne leaned forward and placed her hands on the table. "You, Giselle, and Qui'nan are here because you're responsible for this part of space while we're gone."

Giselle raised a hand.

Bethany Anne anticipated the question on Giselle's lips. "You will take care of the people and the station while Jean and Qui'nan take care of things like defense and expanding the fleet," she narrowed her eyes at Admiral Thomas, "in the *fastest* sustainable time."

Admiral Thomas shrugged. "Consider us even, and next time you build a ship I can't find, please don't." He pretended not to see the glare she shot him. "It didn't occur that the first time you did that, we almost lost you?"

Bethany Anne's face softened when she saw glances of agreement pass around the table. "You can all save your concern. I have one focus and one only—eliminating the Ooken on my way to the Kurtherians."

She got to her feet, her hands remaining on the table. "This has gone on long enough. I want to go *home*. We have an opportunity to move closer to that goal, and there's no fucking way I'm going to let it pass. Neither am I going to stand for any species that thrives on the misery of others."

"Isn't that two things?" Scott asked, flashing his dimples. There was a sparkle in his eyes.

Bethany Anne returned his grin with a hard smile. "You know, I think I've been going too easy on you folks. A training session is just what we all need."

"Seconded," Michael agreed as everyone else groaned. He rubbed his chin thoughtfully. "In the meantime, what are we going to do about the Ooken? We're in the same situation as we were nine months ago. We have the means to blow their planets to dust, and they have both the information we're looking for and the numbers to make us reticent about kicking in the front door to obtain it."

Bethany Anne sat down again. "I agree completely, so we're going to take a similar tack here as we did on the first splinter world. If it's not broken, then it doesn't need fixing." She held up a hand before anyone could object. "Same plan, with some adjustments."

Her fingers began to tap on the table again. "We're going to split into teams, each with someone who can protect the rest from mental manipulation. But honestly, I don't expect there to be a need for it."

"Why not?" Eric asked. "I'm not going to lie. As much as I wanted to be there for Peter, I was relieved you benched us the last time."

Bethany Anne's face was hard as stone. "I'm not expecting there to be a need because our objective is to get into the administration centers for our assigned colony, and that is *all* we are going to do. No big stands, no heroics. We go in, get our hands on every bit of information we can find, and get the fuck out." She clenched her hands into fists, fighting to keep her emotions under control. "I will *never* put any of you in a situation like we had with the grubs again. This universe would be too small to contain my grief if anything happened to any of you."

Admiral Thomas had confusion written all over his

face. "How does that prevent the Ooken from attacking anyone?"

Bethany Anne frowned. "It doesn't. There will, however, most likely be a clue *somewhere* in all the data we copy as to where their homeworld is." She waved a finger around the table. "We'll take care of that. After we're done, that's where you come in. I want the fleet ready to blow the colonies into last fucking week as soon as the teams are far enough from the planets."

Admiral Thomas nodded once and sat back in his chair. "*That* I can arrange."

Bethany Anne returned his nod. "I have complete faith that you can. Just like I know without a doubt that when we get back here, there will be double the ships I left with awaiting my return." She raised an eyebrow at Jean. "Are you satisfied?"

Jean smirked. "More than."

Qui'nan chittered happily in the background, already lost in her designs.

Bethany Anne looked around the table. "Back to the plan; this is what we're going to do."

"We have seven targets." She narrowed her eyes at Gabrielle's amusement as she brought back the holomap with another not-quite-necessary wave. "It's habit at this point."

Gabrielle's mouth twitched. "Not vanity?"

Bethany Anne tilted her chin, the corner of her mouth quirking up slightly. "Me, vain? Never." Her fingers danced, and the rest of the map fell away as the seven locations were enlarged. Data for each site was in a box alongside. "The SSE fleet has identified one, possibly two more

Ooken planets. It's going to require an adjustment to the plan."

John pointed at the seventh planet. "There's no data on that one."

Bethany Anne shrugged. "It was only just discovered. ADAM is headed straight there from the third planet. He will arrive before we do, so we won't be going in blind."

John nodded. "So we're leaving the mystery planet until last. What about the rest of them?"

Bethany Anne made a flicking motion with her fingers and the seven planets winked out, leaving the space over the table clear. "Team leaders are—Gabrielle and Eric, Akio and John, Eve and Scott, and Michael and me."

Scott's chuckle held a touch of nervousness. "What about the freaky mind powers? I'm still not convinced it's safe."

Bethany Anne made a see-saw motion with her hands. "It's a calculated risk. If you encounter anything beyond your capability to deal with, get out and call in the fleet. But really, it was so easy to walk in and out of the first colony that I'm not as concerned as I was before."

"Meaning?" Eric asked.

"Meaning," Bethany Anne clarified, "that if anything *does* go down, each team will have someone with even freakier mind powers to take care of it. You all have your assigned section of the fleet and the locations you're to take."

All the team leaders looked through the packets they had received. Darryl frowned, not seeing his assigned team. "What about me?"

Bethany Anne grinned. "You know, I must have forgotten you... Uncle Darryl."

Darryl grimaced. "Babysitting? I don't know anything about kids."

Bethany Anne grinned. "That's great, because the twins don't know that much about you, either." She shrugged. "That must be why they asked for you. After you're done, you can pick your team."

John and Scott exchanged the looks of two men who knew exactly what the third was in for.

"*Daaamn*, it was nice knowing you, dude," Scott muttered in a near-whisper.

"I know, right?" John replied equally quietly. "If they asked for him, it means they got a topic in mind."

Devon, QBBS *Guardian*, Dock 001, QBS *Achronyx*

Tabitha hooked both arms under the handle of Todd's travel seat to take the strain from her shoulder as she waited at the top of the ramp.

"Want me to take him a spell?" Peter offered.

Tabitha shook her head and flashed a mischievous grin at him. "No, thanks. I've got our chunky monkey just fine." Todd griped in the seat, protesting either the nickname or the passing of what he thought was his dinner time. "I can lift a car off the ground but holding a car seat hurts—go figure. However, it would be nice if you could take care of finding Sabine."

"Tabithaaa! Over here!"

Tabitha and Peter turned as one to the source of the

shout. Sabine was waving from below. Peter smirked but kept his remark to himself.

Sabine grinned as she walked over briskly. "Thanks for stopping by to pick me up. The transports planetside are booked solid for the next thirty hours."

Peter smiled. "Isn't it your fight night? I've heard great things."

Sabine nodded, adjusting the weight of her overnight bag. "Yeah, which is why the transports are booked up. If not for you I would have had to cancel my date, so thank you."

Tabitha wiggled her eyebrows. "Oh? You and Tim are official now?"

Before Sabine had a chance to answer, Todd decided he'd had enough of traveling, and his grumping turned to loud wails.

Tabitha gave him her finger to suck, which he promptly bit and spat out. "Todd needs a change and a meal." She grinned when her stomach growled. "He's not the only one. Baby first, though." She turned and went back into the ship, being careful to avoid jolting Todd's seat.

Peter waved Sabine aboard and excused himself. "Feel free to explore. If you want to call home to let them know we're on our way, just come to the bridge and I'll set you up."

Sabine tapped the side of her head as she passed Peter at the top of the ramp. "I already did."

CEREBRO cleared them to leave the *Guardian* as soon as everyone was aboard. Tabitha spent some time in their quarters taking care of Todd.

She hummed to her son as she rocked him. Todd's

energy for protesting was all gone, sated by the meal and the warmth of his mother's arms, His tiny eyelids fluttered closed, and Tabitha eased him into his Pod-crib. *How long until we get to the Hexagon?* she asked Peter.

We're nearly there, he replied. *Is Todd okay? You should come up to the bridge and see how this place has changed.*

Clean, full, and fast asleep, Tabitha told him. *I'm on my way with him now.* She set the Pod-crib to float along behind her and made her way to the elevator outside their quarters.

I'm surprised he settled. He was kicking up such a stink.

Tabitha gazed through the Pod-crib's viewing panel at her sleeping son while the elevator took them up. *Like a dream. You know, he really loves classics for his lullabies.*

Peter chuckled. *Have you been singing Iron Maiden to our son again?*

Tabitha strolled out of the elevator and onto the bridge with her hand resting on the top of Todd's Pod-crib as it bobbed beside her. "He loves it, and you can't argue with his taste."

Peter walked over to look at their son. "If it works, it works." He grabbed Tabitha's hand and pulled her over to get an unobstructed look at the viewscreen. "Quick, before we're over the city."

The majesty of the lakes spread out below took Tabitha's breath away. "It's beautiful!"

Sabine turned in her seat. "You got here just in time. We went by the scenic route, and we're about to fly over the property I was telling you about."

Peter tilted his head. "Oh, yeah?"

"Sabine says it's a good fishing spot," Tabitha told him. "I haven't seen it yet."

Sabine pointed at a dark smudge in the middle of the water in the distance. Tabitha and Peter looked at the small island as they passed overhead.

Tabitha "I do like that it's on an island, but it's not in the best shape." She tilted her head. "I didn't see anywhere for the ship, either."

Sabine shrugged. "I asked around about it. It will need work since it's been empty for a while."

"It could be a project," Peter countered. "We might be here for some time."

Tabitha made a face. "New baby *and* home renovation? Um, I'll pass, thanks."

"You're right," Peter shook his head. "It's also a little too far out of the way. We need to be somewhere with easy access to the station."

Sabine looked at Tabitha. "I thought you wanted something rural?"

Tabitha waved a finger at the screen. "Yeah, no. I want my own space, but that's some Robinson Crusoe shit down there. I'm guessing services aren't much of a thing out here?"

"Exactly," Peter agreed. "I don't want to wake up one morning and find that Tabitha has eaten me out of desperation and a lack of snacks." He took the hard fist to the arm Tabitha gave him as his due and continued, absentmindedly rubbing the spot she had punched. "But it's no problem. We'll find somewhere in the city."

Sabine gave Tabitha and Peter a warm smile. "Well, the three of you are welcome to keep the apartment for as long as you like." She made a fond face at the Pod-crib. "I'm looking forward to meeting this little guy properly."

The ship swooped over the First City, heading straight for the bazaar.

Tabitha pointed out a huge, six-sided building abutting the east wall that hadn't been there on her last visit. "That's the Hexagon?"

Sabine nodded proudly. "Uh-huh. We just opened last month."

Peter folded his arms on his chest as the Hexagon came into focus. "Business must be good, then. Congratulations."

Sabine shrugged. "We can't complain. We had some help from Michael, too. It just took focus to make it happen once we made the decision to stay here."

Tabitha caught a glimpse of greenery on a section of the roof as the ship made a tight turn on the way to the building's private hangar entrance. "You've got something growing up there?"

"That's your garden!" Sabine told them, her hands waving excitedly. "We put it in so the baby would have some outdoor space to play."

Tabitha put a hand to her chest. "That's so sweet!"

Sabine grinned, getting to her feet. "I have to admit, you had me at a loss with the babyproofing thing at first, but we all worked it out. Come on. I can't wait to show you everything we did to the place."

They disembarked and waited for the antigrav carts with their essentials to make their way out of the cargo bay.

Tabitha shifted from one foot to the other until the

slow procession finally got its act together and picked up speed near the bottom of the ramp.

Peter shook his head at the carts as they trundled by. "How is it that one baby needs so much *stuff*? I remember not so long ago I could go anywhere with just a pack and be cool for weeks. Now we need a whole freaking cargo bay full of stuff just for a day out."

Tabitha rolled her eyes and placed her hand on Todd's Pod-crib. "Let's just get all this into the apartment."

Sabine led them out of the hangar to a bank of three elevators while the carts caught up. She rummaged in her pocket and turned to Peter and Tabitha with a pair of keycards in her hand. "These are just until we get you in the system, or you won't be able to go anywhere in the building. Do you want the tour now or after you get settled in?"

Tabitha glanced at Todd, who was still sleeping soundly, then at Peter. "I think we'll just go to the apartment."

Peter nodded. "Yeah, if you don't mind."

Sabine handed over the keycards. "Of course. I under-stand completely. We'll see you all at your welcome dinner later though, right?"

Tabitha smiled. "Wouldn't miss it."

Sabine grinned. "Great!" She pressed the button for the third elevator. "This elevator is the only way to enter our living areas. It can only be accessed by the five of us, and now the two of you."

They all squeezed into the elevator along with the anti-grav carts, which stacked themselves neatly in the corner, and Todd's Pod-crib which bumped everybody's legs as it bobbed in behind Tabitha.

"Penthouse," Sabine commanded. She turned to Tabitha and Peter with a twinkle in her blue eyes. "I hope you like it. We had fun researching babyproofing."

The elevator opened on a small hallway that had just one door.

Sabine waved them over to the door. "Your keycards are good for today and tomorrow, but we'll get you in the system first thing."

She stood by the elevator doors, then got in once the antigrav carts had all exited the car. "Oh, and just call Winstanley if you need anything."

"We will," Tabitha called from the apartment doorway. "Thanks for all this."

Sabine shrugged as the elevator doors closed. "Not a problem."

Todd began to stir as they entered their temporary home for the first time.

Peter bent to pick him up. "Look who's awake? Hey, little man, you're just in time to see our new home." He held Todd close and set off from the entryway into the open living area.

Peter bounced the baby gently on his hip as he looked around. Todd blinked sleepily in his arms, turning his head from side to side to take in the strange surroundings. "This place is nice!"

Tabitha noted the safety features blended in with the tasteful décor. She loved bare brick and dark polished wood as an aesthetic. "They've done a fantastic job."

She put her head on Peter's shoulder, smiling softly. "I think we can be happy here while we look for a place of our own, but tonight will be the test. If the noise of the event disturbs Todd even *once*, we're getting back on the ship."

Peter chuckled. "What, with Todd?"

"Um…" Tabitha made a face while she considered the logistics of flouncing out with a baby.

"*Dammit.*"

Being sensible sucked.

9

Federation Deep Space Research Outpost

Tinesha left the school building with a lightness in her heart and a skip in her step.

Two whole cycles of freedom!

She looked at the clear sky above the dome as she walked with her friends Brad, a human, and Kinbel, a Baka.

Kinbel jostled Tinesha gently to shake her from her daydream. "Did your father say if your mother was going to be home before we leave for the falls?"

Tinesha shrugged. "He wasn't sure, but I don't care. We're going, whether she allows it or not. I'm almost an adult. She can't keep telling me what to do!"

Brad snorted. "Maybe if we were la-di-da fancypants nobility like you, she wouldn't hate us so much."

Tinesha rolled her eyes. "Nope. She'd hate you anyway because she's a stuck-up speciesist. You've heard her. 'A Torcellan of your standing shouldn't mix with humans or Bakas, Tinesha.' Ugh."

A low, keening moan came from Kinbel's throat.

Tinesha threaded an arm through her friend's to comfort her. "I know. You have to deal with that crap from everyone."

"Not us, though," Brad chipped in, taking Kinbel's other arm. "We're a threesome, at least until Tinesha's mom goes batshit crazy and ships her off to marry some prince to get her away from her unsuitable friends."

Tinesha and Kinbel cracked up. "Can you imagine that?" She hoped her mother didn't ever get the idea to arrange a marriage contract for her behind her back.

Not even her father could save her if that happened.

Tinesha sighed. She knew there were many other ways that her life could be difficult. An overambitious mother wasn't the worst thing.

"As if I would marry a stranger." Tinesha couldn't wait to come of age and break free of the stuffy traditions that said she couldn't be friends with someone because their species was inferior. "My majority can't come soon enough."

Brad frowned. "You know you can always come and stay with us. My moms have told you a thousand times that you're welcome."

"I know." Tinesha wasn't entirely happy that Brad's parents felt sorry for her. They were always extra nice to her when they had study nights at his house. She didn't want pity. She wanted to reach her majority and leave for the Federation.

She wanted to wear *pink*. Shocking pink, hot pink, magenta—bright colors that made her happy instead of the soul-sucking array of neutrals her mother insisted on as tradition.

One day, she would.

One day.

Tinesha swept her pale hair out of her eyes and picked up her pace to keep up with the others.

The last leg of the walk was always a little lonely once Brad and Kinbel had turned off for their own homes.

Tinesha left the park and took her time wandering the last few streets to the large, empty house set away from the other residences in her neighborhood where she lived with mostly just the staff for company.

Tinesha greeted the keeper at the gates and dragged her feet up the long driveway, reluctant to enter the house.

Tinesha was nearing the front of the house when the sky above her grew dark unexpectedly. She looked up, expecting to see clouds gathering outside the dome.

It was no storm.

Tinesha dropped to her knees as her legs failed her.

The body of a gigantic ship hovered above the dome some way away from her house. It blocked the light, testing the dome with the enormous, writhing tentacles that made up the front of the ship.

Tinesha's horrified gaze was drawn to a spot on the ship's underbelly that glowed brighter each second.

Her eyes darted over the ship, her body refusing to do much more than take in the nightmare. Another part of the ship vomited a thick cloud of drones into the atmosphere. They stayed close to the ship as though waiting for something.

The glowing spot on the invaders' ship had grown larger, and it was getting unbearably bright.

A flash lit the dome, whiting everything out. Tinesha

shielded her eyes, peering through her fingers to see a rope of light explode from the ship.

It licked the dome, and the world went white again.

Tinesha clutched a hand to her throat in an effort to breathe when the light faded and the crack in the dome became clear.

They were in serious trouble.

Without warning, the drones attacked the dome, which was designed to keep the colony safe from the storms that raged across the surface of the planet for three cycles of each year.

It wasn't made to withstand a sustained attack from many sources.

However, much to Tinesha's relief, the dome held—*at first.*

Then the cracks widened.

Tinesha finally managed to draw a breath when a huge section of the dome fell in, exposing them to the enemy above. She screamed as the drones poured in, bringing her mother running from the house.

"What is going *on?*" her mother exclaimed.

Tinesha pointed upward, where the dome was in the process of failing under continued bombardment from the alien ship. "The end," she whispered hoarsely, her words stolen by shock. Her disagreements with her mother seemed so small now. She just wanted to be held by her.

"*No!*" Tinesha's mother sank to her knees beside her and pulled her daughter into her arms. "I have dreams for you!" Her tears drenched her daughter's hair.

Tinesha clung to her mother and watched on as their

world burned around them. "What can we do?" she croaked, the haze hot in her lungs.

The pause between her question and the answer was both immediate and infinite. "Nothing," her mother replied eventually. "But we will be avenged." Her eyes narrowed. "Baba Yaga will not stand for this."

It was cold comfort, but being avenged was all she had left to offer her daughter.

They remained glued to the spot as the gigantic ship broke fully through the dome and unleashed its weapon on the homes of people they knew.

Something snapped. *"Run."* Tinesha pulled hard on her mother's arm as her focus returned. "We have to try!" She staggered to her feet, dragging her mother along with her.

A drone overhead locked on to them and opened fire, tearing up the ground around the two Torcellans as they made a desperate break for the corner of the property.

They were almost to the edge of the property when Tinesha felt a momentary pain. *Did she run into something?* Hurt or not, she kept running, helping her mother scramble over the wall at the back despite the burning sensation blooming in the place she'd felt the initial pain.

They ran into the cover of the trees nearby, frantically trying to stay ahead of the drones. The pain in Tinesha's side ebbed, and she urged her mother toward the caves in the distance. "We'll be safe there," she panted.

Tinesha's mother stopped her daughter with a hand on her shoulder. "Tinesha, you don't sound good."

Tinesha glanced down at her side, which was beginning to throb once more. "I think I banged into something in the garden." She went to lift her clothing to check for a bruise and pulled her bloody hand away in shock. "Mother..."

Tinesha's mother darted forward to catch her as her legs gave way.

"It's okay." Tinesha's voice cracked as the last of her energy drained away. Looking up, she allowed a ghost of a smile to cross her face. Her mom, at least, would make it to the caves. "Just don't let them catch you. Tell the witch about me."

Tinesha's mother cried, cradling her daughter in her arms as she bled out onto the dirt. Her entire body was shaking, her mind refusing to make sense of anything as alarms blared in the distance.

Tinesha closed her eyes and let out a final choked whisper as the darkness came for her. "I never got to wear...pink."

In Transit to the Seventh World, SSE *ADAM*

ADAM picked up the signal and forwarded it to the *ArchAngel II.* "Kael-ven, are you getting this?"

The scratchy reply came over the long-distance connection. "I don't know, ADAM. It looks like a distress signal."

"That's what I thought. We're going to divert to investigate."

Kael-ven's voice was filled with concern. "What about the schedule? You could send a drone."

ADAM had already considered that option. "A drone won't be much use if people need help. Can you catch up in case there are casualties?"

There was a pause on the other end before Kael-ven answered, "We're on our way, but it's going to take us a while to get to your location."

"I'll leave a marker for ArchAngel to follow," ADAM told him before dropping the connection.

Loralei swooped in silently beside ADAM's ship. *We going on the side quest?*

>>**We are. Want to lead the way?**<<

My pleasure. Loralei adjusted her course to head for the origin of the distress signal. *I haven't done one of these before.*

>>**One of what? A distress call?**<<

Yeah. Organics are messy when it comes to competition.

>>**I can't argue that.**<< ADAM put on a burst of speed to cruise up alongside Loralei's ship.

What can we do for them?

>>**We can fight off anyone or anything attacking them. We can defend them until Kael-ven gets here.**<<

It's not much.

>>**It is all we can provide.**<<

QT2 System, QBBS *Helena*, APA

Alexis and Gabriel led K'aia to the seats at the side.

K'aia threw a glance in the direction of the adults. "I thought we were going to train?"

Gabriel shook his head. "No, we're here to observe and learn today."

"Today," Alexis continued, "Mom is teaching, and we haven't done anything that needs correction."

Gabriel nodded toward the adults. "My money is on Uncle Scott being the object lesson today."

K'aia examined Scott's body language. "He does seem tense. What did he do?"

The twins shrugged in unison.

K'aia shuddered. "It's weird when you do things at the same time. Like you're clones or something."

The twins giggled.

"Seriously, quit it," K'aia protested. "How old are you, anyway?"

"Fourteen," Gabriel replied simply.

Alexis lifted a shoulder. "Although if you want to be technical—"

"She probably doesn't," Gabriel cut in, pleased to be the one who caught the nuance—for once. "What about you, K'aia?"

K'aia looked at the adults again. "I don't really know. I think I'm almost a young adult physically, so call that about nineteen? But I can't be sure. I don't know how old I was when I was taken from my family."

Alexis put a hand on K'aia's shoulder. "I'm so sorry you went through that."

K'aia patted Alexis' small hand with her own much larger one and nodded toward Bethany Anne and Michael. "It's okay, it's over now. What's happening over there?"

Gabriel shushed them by raising his hand. "They're getting started," he whispered.

Bethany Anne stood alone, with Scott, Gabrielle, John, Eric, and Darryl fanned out in front of her.

"This is always really funny," Alexis explained as Bethany Anne rolled her shoulders and gave the guys a "come at me" gesture. "Whenever we sit in on training, they all try really hard not to curse."

K'aia tilted her head in question. "I think my translator is malfunctioning. Where is the humor in that?"

Gabriel "It's funny because they fail when Mom's wiping the floor with them, and then Dad gets involved."

"Oh." K'aia had wondered why Michael stood off to the side. She wasn't sure that Alexis and Gabriel quite understood the concept of humor either. "What happens next?"

Alexis nodded at Bethany Anne, who was suddenly not where she had been the blink of an eye ago.

Bethany Anne's voice carried through the room, although she was nowhere to be seen. "It's time to step it up. Take your abilities to the next level."

K'aia couldn't believe what she wasn't seeing. Bethany Anne was back, but her Empress was moving too fast for K'aia's Yollin eyes to track. She flinched, feeling a presence at her shoulder.

"No empresses here," Bethany Anne whispered in her ear. "Don't give me a reason to put you on the floor with everyone else."

K'aia whipped her head around, but there was nobody there. The next second Bethany Anne was back over with the other adults, and K'aia was left with her mandibles opening and closing soundlessly.

Alexis giggled and tugged on Gabriel's sleeve, pointing at the young Yollin. "See? Funny!"

K'aia gave Alexis a look and returned her attention to the floor.

Bethany Anne was talking about a lot of things she didn't understand. She assumed it was all related to the powers these humans had.

"They're not powers," Alexis whispered. "We have

access to technology that enhances our capabilities to the point where everyone *thinks* we have powers. Of course," she qualified, "I have tried to imagine things from the perspective of someone who does not have access to the Etheric." She made a face. "It's difficult without having experienced it."

"It *looks* like you have powers." K'aia huffed. "Hasn't anyone ever told you it's rude to read someone's mind?"

"Everyone. Repeatedly." Gabriel snickered. "But Alexis doesn't allow a little thing like that to stop her from prying at every opportunity." His eyes were on Bethany Anne's demonstration of how Gabrielle could improve her control of the Etheric, which to K'aia looked an awful lot like Bethany Anne was toying with the other woman.

Alexis waved her hands. "How else am I supposed to work out all the stuff the adults won't tell us? Anyway, I didn't see you complaining when I figured out how to circumvent the lock they put on the Etheric so you could raid the fridge."

Gabriel's brow furrowed in thought. "You could get the experience if you could persuade Mom to allow your nanos to be deactivated for a short time."

Alexis raised an eyebrow at her brother. "You have to be kidding me. That's *too* funny. You know Mom would never agree to that."

Gabriel shrugged. "Just a thought. You don't really want to be that vulnerable. What if you get hurt?"

K'aia left Alexis and Gabriel to their confusing discussion and went back to watching the masterclass on the floor.

Bethany Anne moved like nothing she had yet seen in

her life. It was impossible for any being to be *that* graceful and yet there she was, beauty in motion.

Bethany Anne *flowed*.

Gabrielle was thrown back again and again, not landing a single energy ball for her efforts. She stopped to push her hair out of her eyes, exhausted from working with so much Etheric energy.

Bethany Anne wasn't even breathing hard. She inclined her head. "That's an improvement; good work. Think about what we talked about before our next session. You are the conduit, not the source." She pointed at John, Scott, and Darryl in turn. "Next lesson. Late for meetings. Snarky. And you have avoided our children."

Eric snorted. "What did *I* do?"

Bethany Anne grinned. "Nothing, but you're here, and you know I hate to leave anyone out."

The music on the speakers cut out before Eric could reply and CEREBRO spoke. "My Queen, you are needed in the command center."

Bethany Anne narrowed her eyes at the interruption. "Thank you, CEREBRO. Tell Admiral Thomas I will be with him in a moment."

"Aw, such a shame we have to cut this session short." Scott winced as his tone fell short of sincerity.

Bethany Anne tilted her head, her lips pressed together. "Hmmm. Yeah, I don't think so." She turned to the side and crooked a finger at the twins and K'aia before turning to Michael. "Advanced combat practice until...oh, Alexis has had enough. It will do our children good to test their Vid-doc training in real world circumstances. K'aia can see the level she's aiming for."

A chorus of groans sounded in Bethany Anne's mind.

Not Alexis, Boss, John begged.

We beg you, Scott cut in. *She's relentless!*

Think about it, Eric pleaded *We'll still be here when the fleet leaves...*

Bethany Anne shut out their complaints and blew a kiss to her children. "Have fun, my loves."

Federation Deep Space Research Outpost

ADAM and Loralei approached the source of the distress signal cautiously, Gating in a safe distance from its broadcast location.

Loralei made a noise of confusion. The signal *looked* to be coming from a ringed gas giant. *They can tolerate that environment? Ooh, maybe they're a brand new species we haven't met yet. They might not be humanoid.* Loralei paused. *Oh, wait.*

ADAM repressed a chuckle at Loralei's enthusiasm. His scans were rough, but it seemed that the outpost was actually on a tiny planetoid orbiting the space between two of the gas giant's rings, hidden by dust and interference thrown out by the rings. >>**You found it?**<<

Uh-huh. I don't want to say I'm disappointed, but, well...

>>**You were hoping for first contact with flame people.**<<

Loralei snickered. *Perhaps? Kinda?*

>>**You might still get your mystery bone tickled,**<<

ADAM offered. >>**My scans are reading a faint Federation signal from within the rings. I didn't realize Lance had anything this far out.**<<

This is a Federation site? Loralei asked. *Fuck, that is far out. Consider me tickled. What are your orders, O Magnificent One?*

ADAM set his scanners to work as soon as his scout ship cleared the Gate. >>**We need to get closer. The signal is still looping, which hopefully means we're not too late to make a difference.**<< That wasn't all his scanners were telling him. He adjusted his course to come at the planet directly. >>**Are you getting all these transmissions?**<<

No?

ADAM linked her into his inputs.

Oh, I can hear it now, Loralei told him. *Wow, Jean really beefed your ship up, huh? Shit, what's all that other noise?*

ADAM assumed she was referring to the malady of shrieks escaping the cover of the rings. >>**That would be the Ooken language,**<< he replied. >>**Harmonious, isn't it?**<<

Loralei sniffed. *It sounds like souls in a shredder.* She brought her ship up alongside ADAM's. *The people...we need to save them. Race?*

ADAM gave it some serious thought. He considered being sensible for maybe a tenth of a second. >>**You're on.**<<

They tore up the distance, pulling to a halt just short of the rings.

Loralei cackled, flying circles around ADAM. *How does it feel to lose to a humble EI?*

ADAM snorted. >>**You can claim a lot of things, but I don't think humility is one of them.**<<

You're one to talk. Didn't you make that Ooken EI believe you were the god of digital intelligence to break it?

ADAM was about to reply when a mechanized tentacle erupted from the swirling dust and thrust past, setting the two scout ships spinning in its wake.

>>**PULL BACK!**<< ADAM and Loralei managed to avoid the thrashing metal limb before it dropped back into the maelstrom. Both regained control and edged over to the place the ginormous tentacle had been and gone.

Loralei hung back a bit while ADAM moved erratically, scanning the ring. *What the Gigerian fuck was that nightmare?*

>>**That was an Ooken battleship, or one section of one. The tentacles are a theme with them. We should move, since it's gone for now.**<<

So how do we get to the outpost without getting suckered by one of them?

>>**Very , very carefully. Stay close to me.**<< His ship dove. >>**We are going in.**<<

Loralei did as directed, and ADAM led them into the murky dust cloud.

The moment they were enveloped, ADAM's sensors all but cut out. He put a little more into clearing it up, but the interference he'd picked up before was playing with his perception. >>**Loralei, how are you doing in this? Are your sensors coping?**<<

Um, no. I'm completely blind.

ADAM almost turned them back there and then, partly out of concern for Loralei, but mostly because he was struggling to maintain his connection to Bethany Anne as well as navigate for both SSE ships.

His ship was demanding everything from him and ten percent more than that.

I wonder if this is what it's like for humans in the dark? Loralei pondered.

ADAM chuckled, his fear for her gone. >>**I don't know. Probably?**<< He sent a tether. It took a few tries, but eventually it attached itself to Loralei's ship. >>**Better?**<<

We won't get separated, at least. Where is the outpost from here?

>>**It's ahead, but I can't tell how many Ooken ships there are between us and the signal location.**<<

It took every cycle of ADAM's available computing power to remain focused on the here and now. His connection to Bethany Anne was down to almost nothing, and the sensation of being all but cut off from her and TOM was not a pleasant one.

However, maintaining control of his ship was paramount to his and Loralei's survival.

ADAM poured his concentration into navigating the murk ahead, the secondary chip in his ship pulling almost everything to give him a chance of avoiding the parts of the ring that could smash them to a million pieces.

He caught the reappearance of the Ooken battleship just in time.

>>**DROP!**<<

Loralei reacted instantly, turning her thrusters to shoot downward with ADAM.

>>**Stop. We're good.**<<

What happened? she asked, perplexed.

>>Ooken ship. We're hugging an asteroid, and our cloaking will keep us hidden while it passes.<<

That was too damn close.

>>We were never in danger,<< he assured her.

Is Bethany Anne listening in or something? Otherwise you're just fooling yourself, since I won't give a shit either way.

ADAM completed what scans he could. >>It's clear. I think.<<

The two stayed side by side under the cover of the dust as they searched for a spot on the planet's surface away from the action.

The dust cleared somewhat when they reached the edge of the path cut into the rings by the outpost's orbit.

They had another close shave when Loralei slipped out of the cloud and was almost detected by an Ooken seeker.

ADAM reeled Loralei back in by the tether, ignoring the stream of curses from the potty-mouthed EI.

>>You were visible for a second. This dust is not working entirely in our favor.<<

Loralei snorted. *If you say so. In that case, I forgive you.*

>>Well, thank you. I appreciate your magnanimity.<<

Loralei cackled. *Strong is the sarcasm in you today.*

>>I hate to break it to you, but you and your sisters do not own the monopoly on snark. In fact, if we were going to look at things from a different angle, you could say you inherited your sense of humor from me. <<

Loralei was silent for a beat. *So what you're saying is that you're a part of every EI personality that has been created?*

ADAM diverted precious bandwidth from keeping them on course to scan for Ooken ships. >>That's right,<<

he confirmed distractedly, focused on the fuzzy readings he was getting.

Hmmm... So, like a god, then? She let rip that raspy cackle again when ADAM faltered. *Too easy, ADAM. Too easy. You walked right into it. Shame on you.*

ADAM considered retracting the tether, but only for a moment. >>**Remind me again why we keep restoring you?**<<

Because I'm a fucking rock star, Loralei told him cheerfully.

ADAM sighed. >>**Well, if your diva self wouldn't mind getting her ass in gear, I've found us a safe route to the surface.**<<

All you had to do was say that, Loralei retorted.

ADAM and Loralei broke for the surface. The asteroid the outpost was based on was a little bit larger than ADAM had calculated from outside the ring, but once down they quickly covered the kilometers between their entry point and the research post.

ADAM's hope began to fade when the sprawling domed city came into range. The sky above the city was filled with the Ooken ships he'd been picking up.

The largest of the domes was cracked open, and the upper section within was filled with drones.

>>**Oh, no. Oh, *fuck* no. We need to do something. This is not going to go down well with Bethany Anne.**<<

It's not going down well with me, either.

>>**Just monitor your cloaking. We're going in.**<<

They swooped in low and entered through a hole in the base of the dome. It was slow progress to make their way across, since the ruined streets were crawling with all kinds of drones.

These drones are like crabs in a brothel, Loralei bitched when they had to take cover for the third time. *We aren't too far from the signal now.*

ADAM had a feeling they were in for a nasty surprise. **>>I just hope there's someone left to save.<<**

You still haven't told me how we're supposed to save anyone when we have no way of getting them out of here. What are you thinking, have them ride our backs?

ADAM snickered. **>>I'm not sure what I'm thinking, but I guarantee it isn't that.<<**

Loralei sulked. *You telling me you can't work out how to extend our shielding to cover a few people?*

ADAM picked up something a billion times better than the distress signal—heartbeats. They were fast and thready with fear, but strong. **>>A few, yes. A couple dozen, not so much.<<**

Loralei was only picking up the drones. *You found them?*

>>They're a few hundred meters away.<< A flying drone passed overhead. **>>We go as soon as the way is clear.<<**

Damn, what did Jean put in that ship of yours?

>>That would be telling. Come on, we're clear.<<

Lead the way. I can but follow.

ADAM headed cautiously in the direction of the heartbeats, keeping his sensors peeled for drones. They had to stop and hide twice more before they found the survivors huddled inside a huge dumpster in an alley.

ADAM engaged his external speakers. "Don't be afraid. We're here to help."

"Go away," a tremulous voice called from inside the dumpster. "Before they find us all."

Charming, Loralei commented.

They heard a snuffle and a soft wail from inside.

>>**There are children in there.**<<

Fuck it all, what can we even do? Kael-ven won't be here before they're discovered.

>>**We're going to...**<< ADAM's mind turned over millions of possibilities within the space of a few seconds and rejected every one of them—except one. >>**Use my chip to hide them in the Etheric until Bethany Anne gets here.**<<

Loralei was puzzled. *Why would you think Bethany Anne is coming here?*

>>**Because I know Bethany Anne. The second she realizes I'm not at all present in her mind, she'll get straight on the *Izanami*.**<<

O-kayyy. So how do we get them into the Etheric, and what does it have to do with your chip? And, what chip?

>>**There's no time to explain. I need you to be there when she gets here and tell her I'm not dead.**<<

That you're not... ADAM, you need to explain what the fuck you're planning to do.

ADAM couldn't hear Loralei for the moment. He had adjusted his frame rate to the point that time in the alley stood still to give himself a chance to work out an answer for himself, if not for Loralei.

All he had to do was persuade the chip that made it possible for him to be separated from Bethany Anne and his Gate drive to work together to create a path to the Etheric that these people could walk.

Or rather, that he could shove the dumpster they were hiding in through.

An eternity later, he took a mental step back and checked his work before readjusting his frame rate to bring himself back in line with reality. It was all he could do.

It would work or it wouldn't.

...inefficient, if you think about it. See, it's moments like this that make me glad I'm not an AI. I mean, you don't see me freezing up with emotion when we're thirty seconds away from being discovered.

>>**Loralei, I am trying to perform a complex procedure here.**<< He registered what Loralei just told him. >>**Discovered?**<<

Suck it up, buttercup. Twenty seconds.

ADAM knew the people huddled in the dumpster were dead if this didn't work. The problem was, so was he in most of the simulations he'd run.

He didn't mind dying, since he could be resurrected from any number of locations. What he worried about was what Bethany Anne would do to him after he was brought back online.

And what thinking he was dead would do to *her*.

The Ooken seeker turned and began to sweep the street outside their alley for life signs.

Probing metal tentacles crossed the mouth of the alley and contracted, dragging the brick along with a shower of sparks and a sound that was very like the Ooken language.

One of the people screamed.

Then there was no more time to deliberate. It was now or never.

ADAM crossed fingers he didn't have and initiated the sequence. >>**Make sure she knows I'm alive.**<<

ADAM, what the fuuuuuucck*!*

ADAM's sensors ceased to function.

He would be quite upset if Loralei's furious screech was the last sensory input he ever received.

Devon, First City, The Hexagon

Tabitha answered the apartment door to greet Sabine with a wide grin. "Hi! You're a bit early, but Peter's almost ready."

Todd squirmed on her hip, gurgling happily at the sight of his babysitter.

Sabine melted instantly and bent to bring herself down to Todd's eye level. "Hello, handsome! How's my favorite guy today?"

Tabitha laughed. "He's stealing all the ladies' hearts." She touched her nose to Todd's. "Aren't you!" She gestured with her free hand for Sabine to come in.

Todd reached out and tangled his hands in Sabine's hair as she passed Tabitha in the doorway.

"Oh, no, baby," Tabitha told him.

Sabine laughed. "It's fine." She disentangled herself gently from his pudgy fingers and tied her hair back as she walked into the hall.

Demon sauntered in after Sabine before Tabitha shut the door. *Hello, Tabitha. I am anticipating training your young to be fierce in the hunt this evening.*

Tabitha raised an eyebrow as the sleek cat hopped onto

the couch and made herself comfortable. "Um...okay. I think?" She looked at Sabine and shrugged.

Sabine waved a hand. "I think she means she's expecting to be used as a jungle gym for the next few hours."

Tabitha snickered. "Sounds like your expectations are just about right," she told Demon, bending to let Todd down. "He's gotten more mobile since we were last together for dinner."

As if to prove the point, Todd heaved himself onto his forearms and shuffled toward Demon's tail, which she was dangling over the edge of the couch like a teaser toy.

Demon purred low in her throat. *If he was a kitten, I would maim a small creature for him to play with.*

Sabine frowned. "You remember we talked about why it's not appropriate to do that for a human baby, right?"

Demon's tail twitched, drawing a delighted giggle from Todd. *Of course. My tail is sufficient as a lure.* She chuffed to the baby, losing interest in Tabitha and Sabine.

Peter clattered down the stairs and walked straight over, kissing his son. "Sorry for keeping you waiting. I'm good to go." He grinned at Sabine and Demon. "Hey, good to see you both. Thanks for sitting tonight."

Sabine nodded once, a small smile on the corner of her lips as she watched Todd. "Of course. It's our pleasure to help family. Besides, you're doing us a huge favor. You should see how well the pre-booking for the event is doing. Your date night is going to make this a very good month for the company."

Tabitha winked and nudged Peter with her elbow. "It's going to be a good night all around."

"Not if we don't get going," Peter told her. "Come on, babe."

Tabitha rolled her eyes. "Okay, already."

They finished saying their goodbyes to Todd and Peter slipped an arm around Tabitha's waist to steer her toward the door.

Tabitha twisted around. "You know where we are if you need us for anything, Sabine. Todd, Mommy and Daddy will be home soon."

They made their way down to the arena, skirting the public areas to get to the changing rooms.

Tabitha snuggled under Peter's arm as they walked, her arm around his waist. *This might be one of your best date night ideas ever. I know I say this every date night, but this one has that extra-special...something.*

Peter snorted softly in her mind, feeling the difference in her stride the nearer they got. *You're listening in on the crowd.*

Tabitha's strut became even more pronounced. *Aren't you?* she retorted. *They're saying very nice things about me.*

I hear them. Peter's voice dropped to a huskier tone. *If you want to hear nice things...*

I'll listen to all the nice things you have to say after you impress me tonight.

Well, that inspires me to go the extra mile.

Tabitha dropped her hand a little lower and squeezed. *That's* exactly *what I was hoping you'd say.*

QT2 System, QBBS *Helena*

Bethany Anne let the grin escape once the door closed behind her.

The Bitches' bitching was something she'd missed recently. It was good to be back together and on their way to kick some ass. It was also wonderful to have Alexis and Gabriel here with her.

TOM interrupted her thoughts. **You are in a better frame of mind than you have been of late. I would almost say you're feeling cheerful.**

Bethany Anne's eyebrow twitched. *I've got plenty to be cheerful about. We have a new member of the family to celebrate, and we're mostly together for a change. Life doesn't stop because of tragedy.*

Nothing to do with you being untethered from High Tortuga now that Alexis and Gabriel aren't so young anymore?

Oh, it's got everything to do with that. She made the turn for the elevators down to the concourse, the determined click of her heels echoing in the empty corridor. *I've been sitting still for way too fucking long. I'm not made to stay still when there's work to be done. It's frustrating.*

I hadn't noticed.

Bethany Anne narrowed her eyes as the elevator began its descent. *It is not too late for me to reach in there and pull you out.*

Good luck walking afterward, he shot back. **What happened to your good mood?**

Some contemptuous Kurtherian cockup ruined it by running his mouth.

TOM had been with Bethany Anne long enough to know the difference between real threats and friendly banter. Not everyone *could* tell. **Seriously, you're feeling good about the plan?**

Bethany Anne waved a hand. *I fully expect the plan to go to shit, but we're ready for that. It kind of feels like we're getting the band back together.*

TOM was silent for a moment, then he cracked up. **Trust you to turn a war into a family outing, BA.**

Bethany Anne pressed her lips together in amusement. *I suppose you could look at it that way.*

All that's missing is the picnic basket.

Bethany Anne chose not to mention that she'd had something made up and sent over to the children. She rubbed her temple absentmindedly as she walked.

You okay?

She noticed the hand and shook her head. *Yeah, just had a headache for a moment.*

Want me to check it out?

I'm fine. It's gone now.

She strode into the dimly-lit command center and made her way down the stairs and through the rows of occupied consoles to the front, where Admiral Thomas was deep in concentration at his station. "You needed me up here?"

Admiral Thomas turned from his console with worry stamped across his features. "Yes, but not for the reason I originally asked you to come up here. I've just heard from Kael-ven. It's ADAM and Loralei; they're in trouble."

Bethany Anne's eyes flashed red. "What kind of trouble?"

His lips met in a tight line. "We're not sure. He reported a distress signal he found to Kael-ven and went to assist.

When Kael-ven got there and followed ADAM's marker, all he found was a ravaged Federation outpost. No sign of ADAM or Loralei."

ADAM.

There was no reply. "Fuck*dammit*, I knew that ship was a bad idea! I *told* him to be careful."

ADAM!

Bethany Anne searched but found no trace of his presence within her. *TOM, tell me you're there, at least.*

I'm here, he replied, **but I'm as mystified as you are.**

A shiver went down Bethany Anne's spine. She felt as though she'd just reached to pick something up and discovered she had no hands. *Michael, have you heard from ADAM?*

No, my love, Michael replied. *I'm in the Vid-doc with the children. Should I have?*

Bethany Anne sighed. *No. I'm just clutching at straws because he's out there in his ship somewhere, in trouble, and I can't reach him. He was between two Ooken planets when he dropped off.*

You want to send a search party or do you want to be *the search party?*

Bethany Anne snorted softly. *What do you think? How soon can you and the children be ready?*

Give us two hours.

One.

Michael made a noncommittal noise. *Don't forget we have K'aia in the Vid-doc for enhancement today.*

Shit. I did forget. How long until she's done?

Two hours, he replied. *I can have her transferred straight to the ship.*

Michael's tactic of tricking her into a debate worked well enough to clear the red mist from her fractious mind.

Even so, Bethany Anne could only think of ADAM. *Have Eve transfer K'aia's Vid-doc to the* Izanami. *The rest of you have one hour and thirty minutes until we leave, not a second more.*

Bethany Anne dropped the link and returned her attention to the room, "I can't get hold of him. Neither can TOM."

Admiral Thomas' eyes widened in shock. "Not even…" he waved a finger at Bethany Anne's head.

Bethany Anne closed her eyes, shaking her bowed head. "Nothing." She lifted her chin and flashed blazing red eyes around the room before she disappeared.

Admiral Thomas sighed. "I hope she doesn't just tear off alone," he muttered to himself.

Bethany Anne's voice was suddenly in his mind.

Send me the exact location ADAM and Loralei vanished from, and have CEREBRO make an announcement.

I'm taking command of the fleet.

QT2 System, QBBS *Helena*, Shipyard

Giselle waited nervously on the gantry for her mother's ship to arrive. She was still unsure whether she and Helena would survive this extended stay.

At least the station no longer resembled a construction site. There were still a few places being worked on, like the shopping court on the concourse, but otherwise the hectic pace of the last few months was winding down to something resembling ordinary station life.

If Giselle didn't count the fact that her station was filled almost to bursting by the gathering Navy.

Her husband may have been mystified by how she had suddenly gained the ability to be completely serene. Giselle knew it was because she was the ringmaster responsible for the logistical nightmare of keeping almost a quarter million people of differing species, occupations, and environmental needs fed, housed, and gainfully employed.

Refitting a whole level at the bottom of the station to accommodate the vacuum-dwelling Matrial, who Bart had dubbed "telepathic space narwhals," hadn't even been the biggest challenge during the building.

CEREBRO informed Giselle of the *Shanks' Express* arrival. She gripped the railing out of sheer habit as the doors opened to admit the ship.

The *Shanks' Express* nosed through the translucent barrier and came to a gentle stop by the gantry.

Giselle walked over to where the ramp touched down at the end of the metal walkway and waited for the hatch to open. She dismissed the young Torcellan male who exited first and helped her mother down from the ship without a thought. "Mother, how was your journey?"

Helena continued to hang onto the flight steward's arm as she moved unsteadily down the ramp. "It was awful, Bunny. Didn't sleep a wink the whole way, and I didn't enjoy the onboard chef at *all.*"

"You're here now." Giselle smiled at the steward, about to ask his name so she could make sure she showed her appreciation for his conscientious treatment of her mother in his paycheck.

"Oh," Helena cut in, "how rude of me. Let me introduce my husband. Giselle, meet Yuane."

Giselle felt her carefully constructed composure slip for a second. She grasped her serenity before it crumbled entirely. "Of course you got married again. Without telling me. *Again.*"

Helena waved her judgment away. "A woman's needs don't disappear with the advent of motherhood, my dear." She rolled her eyes at the expression Giselle failed to suppress. "Now, where are Yuane and I staying?" She flounced off down the walkway, pausing at the exit to look back at Giselle and a nonplussed Yuane. "Well, come on! We haven't got all day, and I want to see my grandchildren."

Yuane trotted after her mother like a good little trophy husband.

Giselle took a deep breath and hurried to catch Helena before she caused a catastrophe. She got ahead of her mother in the corridor, but only because Helena didn't know which direction to take.

Helena stood at the interactive station map, where one of the many facets of CEREBRO was running her through the most-visited parts of the station. "Just how big *is* this place?" she asked Giselle incredulously.

CEREBRO had the answer. "The QBBS *Helena* is large enough to contain over four hundred thousand occupants, although the actual number is lower than that since we have provided environments for a number of species that require something other than the standard oxygen-nitrogen-based atmosphere to survive."

"I think it looks like a hand holding an axe," Yuane offered.

Helena ignored her husband, turning to Giselle with her hands clasped to her chest. "Did you really name the station after me?"

Giselle nodded and smiled. "Of course. I wanted it to feel like home."

They were interrupted by a shipwide announcement from one of CEREBRO's more calming and authoritative voices. "Calling all hands of the fleet. This is not a drill. Report to the shipyard. I repeat. All hands of the fleet. Report to the shipyard. This is not a drill."

Giselle's head snapped toward the speaker. "Oh, *fuck*."

"Giselle!" Helena exclaimed. "Is there any need for that kind of language?"

Giselle winced at her slip. This place was rubbing off on her. "That was the call to war we've been waiting for. I won't get a chance to say goodbye to Bart before he leaves."

Helena flapped her hands at her daughter. "Then why are you still here? Go say goodbye to your husband."

Giselle was torn. "I can't just leave you and um…"

"Yuane, dear." Her mother supplied.

"I can't just leave you and Yuane here alone. You just got here. What sort of daughter does that to her mother?"

Yuane turned at the sound of his name. "Huh?"

Helena shooed her again. "Go! We can find our way with the help of the EI."

Giselle waved over her shoulder as she sprinted toward the exit. "Thank you, Mother!"

Immersive Recreation and Training Scenario: Meteor Madness

Bethany Anne dropped the link, and Michael touched his comm button to speak to the Alexis, Gabriel, and K'aia. "Bring it in, children. It's time to leave."

The scenario dissolved, leaving the four of them standing in the equipment room. They had the privacy settings on, so there was nobody else around.

"But I thought I couldn't leave until Eve was done putting the nano-things into my body?" K'aia asked.

Michael nodded. "That is still the case. You are being taken in the Vid-doc to the ship we will be traveling on."

"What about us?" Alexis looked at Michael with concern. "Can we stay in here with K'aia?"

"K'aia will join us once we're aboard the *Izanami*," Michael told her. "There will be time for play. We had Vid-docs installed aboard the ship for your training."

Gabriel turned to K'aia. "Will you be okay on your own?"

K'aia chuckled at the concern her young human companions showed. "I'll be fine. I saw a Library in the scenario list, I've wanted to know what goes on in those places for a while now." She made hand gestures until she got the one that brought up the menu, and her avatar winked out.

Michael nodded, satisfied that the young Yollin was being truthful. "Eve, begin the rejuvenation cycle, please."

Eve was in the process of preparing K'aia's Pod for transport when Michael's Vid-doc opened.

She looked up from her task when Michael emerged. "You have one hour and fifteen minutes until Bethany Anne leaves, and you will need every minute of it." She pointed out into the corridor. "There is a roamer waiting in the charging alcove outside to take you over to the shipyard."

"Thank you, Eve." He helped Alexis and Gabriel get their docs open and the three of them left the Vid-doc room in search of the roamer.

The corridor leading out of the training and rec level was beyond busy. The whole level was emptying out in obedience of CEREBRO's looped announcement from Bethany Anne.

Gabriel made a left outside the Vid-doc room. "The roamers are over here, Dad."

Michael paused by their roamer when they reached it, his hand on the door. "The ride will give us the opportunity to discuss a few things."

Alexis and Gabriel exchanged a glance.

"What things?" Alexis asked.

Michael opened the door and climbed into the roamer. "We can start with your duties aboard the ship."

The twins slumped into the roamer seats with identical expressions of consternation. "Chores?" they chorused.

Michael gave a shrug, sitting back with his hands laced behind his head as the roamer reversed out of the charging alcove. "You can *choose* to see it that way if you want to."

His eyes flashed, the old Michael still there. "I suggest you apply the concept of *duty* instead."

QT2 System, QBBS *Helena*, Concourse

The concourse was loud with a hundred thousand mingled voices.

The station employees, nonmilitary personnel, the families of Bethany Anne's brave troops. The young and the old gathered beyond the enormous curtain in the center of the concourse to wait for word from their Queen.

Bethany Anne stood behind the curtain, staring at the names carved into the rock and counting down until the moments the roamer she was tracking arrived with Michael, Alexis, and Gabriel.

She looked to her left, registering a twitch of the

curtain in her peripheral vision. "Tell me my fleet is ready, Admiral."

Admiral Thomas nodded. "Your fleet is ready, my Queen."

Bethany Anne placed a hand on the smooth stone of the monolith. "It fucking kills me that there will be more names on this memorial before this is over."

"Names of heroes who sacrificed themselves to enable others to live without fear," Michael stepped through the curtain as he spoke. *I believe you owe a forfeit for that f-bomb.*

Bethany Anne laughed in Michael's mind. *I'm not paying a forfeit for that, you sneaky mother—*

We can hear you, Mom. Gabriel snickered as he pushed through the heavy drapes.

"Mom, that's definitely a forfeit," Alexis agreed, popping through the curtain behind her brother.

Admiral Thomas looked at the four of them in bemusement. "What's the forfeit for?"

Bethany Anne covered her face with a hand. "Nothing."

Alexis snorted. "If we hear Mom cursing, she has to do a forfeit."

Gabriel nodded. "We found out about it when we were eleven, while we were in the game world."

Bethany Anne walked over to the thin gap left in the curtain by the twins. "Yes, and haven't you both just gotten the biggest kick out of trying to catch me ever since?" She opened the gap a smidge with her finger and peered out.

Michael chuckled along with the twins. "Something in my bones tells me you're rolling your eyes at us right now, my love."

"*So* hard," Bethany Anne confirmed. She removed her

finger and turned to Gabriel and Alexis. "I have a few words to say to everyone, and then we're leaving. Your Aunt Jean wants to see you both in the armory aboard the *Izanami*. Make it quick, so Aunt Jean has time to get off the ship. And if you hurry, you can be there when K'aia gets out of the Vid-doc."

Michael remained by Bethany Anne's side while Alexis and Gabriel ran off to find Jean. *You have something prepared?*

Bethany Anne's eyebrow twitched. *I only decided to move the unveiling forward an hour ago.* She ducked through the curtain and walked out onto the temporary stage. *Something will come to me.*

The crowd noise doubled when she appeared.

Long before he loved her, Michael had recognized that Bethany Anne would give her life before she gave up on a call to Justice.

Her Justice.

The Justice where everyone got exactly what they deserved, honor be damned. Then again, Bethany Anne had always been more than happy to bring a whole lot of "oh, fuck" down on anyone who thought she was going to allow things to go any other way than what *she* decreed.

Equally, she stood before these people—her people—to offer comfort and hope despite the agony Michael knew damn well she was feeling about ADAM.

I can feel you admiring my ass. Bethany Anne held up her hands to quiet the crowd.

Michael scanned the concourse as a matter of habit, locating Eric, Scott, and Darryl by the energy they gave off. *Then you must have been channeling Tabitha, because I was "admiring"* *your strength as a leader.* He nodded when he spied John looking down from the security booth above.

Suck-up.

Michael's deep chuckle reverberated through her mind.

Bethany Anne walked over to the lectern and placed her hands flat on either side of the microphone. She leaned in to look out over the sea of color representing most of the peoples she had gathered under her aegis over the years. "Thank you all for being here to honor our fallen. I appreciate that you came at such short notice."

Her voice carried to the farthest corners of the concourse without any need for the mic, the contrast between her soft tone and the weight of the words reaching everyone there. "This ceremony was scheduled for a few days from now, but as you've probably noticed, about half the people on this station are about to depart. Before that happened, I wanted to remind everyone we're leaving behind why we're doing this."

She waved a hand and the curtain dropped, revealing the shining monolith. "Without any theatrics, because we will celebrate life once the dead have been avenged, I give you the Robinson Memorial. For Tessa and Calvin, and for every cherished life lost in this war so far."

Bethany Anne paused a beat to let her words sink in, then swept a hand back to indicate the two long columns of gold script on the black rock. "*So far.* Make no mistake, these names are not the last we will carve on this wall. Again and again, the Ooken have brought us pain. We've given it back in equal measure, but it has cost us dearly."

Bethany Anne stepped out from behind the lectern, spreading her hands wide in front of her. "The losses have hurt us, *but they have not broken us*. Thanks to the hard work and support of everyone aboard this station this last few months—and believe me when I tell you I know exactly how hard it's been—we are ready to repay the Ooken tenfold for that pain."

Bethany Anne heard the murmurs of comfort and felt the shared emotion and pain in the air. She lifted her chin and let the tears fall for all to see, and they wept with her. The bond between her and her people would never falter, never fail. Not when they knew she would shed tears for any one of them. That she would fight until the end of her days if it meant they were safe from harm.

She moved to grasp one side of the lectern as the connection she felt with the sea of faces took her with it for a moment.

Should I dial your emotion down so you can concentrate? TOM inquired carefully.

No, she told him. *I want to feel every bit of this.* She composed herself and continued. Her eyes began to glow, her hair rising around her as her feet left the stage, walking into the air. "This war, these deaths—it's all on me. I thought I had made it clear to the whole damn universe what happens when you mess with what's mine, but I will address my failure to communicate."

The tension around the concourse ratcheted as Bethany Anne's eyes flashed her incandescent fury. Hair, hackles, nerve pulses, and all sorts of other biological reactions went up as the rage of the Queen was revealed to them.

"The Ooken came here for a fight and we sent their sorry asses home to lick their wounds." Bethany Anne laughed without a single hint of empathy. "When we turn up on their doorstep looking to resolve our grudge, they're going to be even fucking sorrier." She looked around. "Prepare for battle, because we only have *one* response to the murder of our own…"

Bethany Anne rose higher, flashing her red eyes at them as her hands curled into fists by her sides. She uttered two final words before vanishing.

"*Total* annihilation."

QT2 System, QBS *Izanami*, Rec Room

Alexis paced in the space between the Vid-docs. "How long, Izanami? Did it go as planned?"

"I'm about to put K'aia into the rejuvenation cycle," Izanami replied. The AI's avatar vanished in a spray of pixels, reappearing on the other side of the Vid-doc in almost the same instant. "And yes, the process was successful."

Gabriel looked up from his half-drawn sketch of Izanami, considering the difference between Izanami and most of the AIs he knew.

The aura Izanami projected sparkled and glitched. The apparent malfunctions highlighted her inhumanity, which Gabriel thought was a perfect juxtaposition to the hidden emotion the AI's deliberately poised body spoke to.

He touched his stylus to the screen, making gentle, sweeping lines to recreate the way her hair floated around her. "Izanami, why do you do that?"

Izanami phased in and out a few times. "That is a broad question, Gabriel. Can you clarify what you wish to understand?"

"Well, you are kind of human in appearance, but you also have an unreal quality. It's the way you move." He paused. "No, that's not quite right. It's more in the ways that you *don't* move."

Alexis nodded, pausing in her pacing to look at the avatar. "Yes, exactly! I think it's like someone drew you in a comic. You move from frame to frame without any actions to join them together."

Izanami tilted her ghostly-pale face to smile at Alexis and Gabriel. "What is movement but the expression of emotion and intent? Each step, each touch, each glance is revealing. I can choose whether or not to emote, unlike most biological life forms," the AI explained. "When I *do* move, it has meaning."

Izanami was lit by a soft golden glow, the folds of her dark kimono billowing as the invisible wind snatched at her long white hair, whipping it around her. Her eyes were filled with galaxies as she spread her arms wide and rose a few more inches off the floor. "Besides, am I not glorious?"

The twins nodded, awestruck as the stars spilled from Izanami's hair and eyes and her avatar burst into a million shining lights.

"Even prettier than Aunt Eve," Alexis agreed in a whisper. "But don't tell her I said that."

Izanami's presence grew, and her voice came from the speakers for a moment while her freeform avatar swirled around the room. "I am not restricted to one form, nor am

I bound by needing to express myself physically. I admit that this display is mostly for your entertainment."

Alexis gazed at the starbursts dancing in complex patterns around her, her smile growing by the second. "So why have an avatar at all?"

Izanami returned her avatar to its previous serene form and directed her smile at Alexis. "I choose to retain my nature while still appearing in a form that is conducive to communicating with organics."

The Vid-doc lit up and Izanami looked down. "K'aia has completed the rejuvenation cycle. Please step back, Alexis. She may be disoriented when she emerges due to the changes in her physique."

Gabriel tilted his head. "I didn't think she was having stage three enhancement?"

"She did not," Izanami clarified. "However, the repairs during stages one and two were significant. K'aia is now in peak condition for a female Yollin of her age, which she was limited from reaching by poor nutrition and years of hard labor."

The Vid-doc opened and K'aia stretched, blinking slowly. "Did it work... Oh. *Oh!*"

Alexis was done giving her new friend space. She rushed to K'aia's Vid-doc and climbed the side to get a closer look. "What is it? Are you in pain?" she asked, eyes darting up and down the space where K'aia lay.

K'aia rolled one shoulder, then the other. Then she stood up inside the Vid-doc. "The opposite."

Gabriel grinned. "That's awesome. Alexis, get down from there so K'aia can get out."

Alexis rolled her eyes. "Oh, yeah."

She hopped down and gave K'aia room to move and test her repaired body.

K'aia looked around in amazement as she slowly put her weight on the rear left ankle she'd injured in a rock-fall years past. Her mandibles tapped in surprise. "I'm pain-free!" She looked at the humans. "How long will this last?"

Alexis chuckled. "Forever, or near enough that it doesn't matter."

K'aia's mandibles dropped open. "That's…dangerous technology. What if someone tries to take it?"

Gabriel's mouth turned up at the corner. "I don't see that being a worry," he assured her. "Mom has some experience dealing with those types of situations."

Alexis snickered. "We need to get going. She wants to see us all on the bridge."

K'aia nodded to Izanami and followed Gabriel and Alexis out of the rec room. She looked around as she walked. "Where are we? This doesn't look like the *Helena*."

Alexis turned to answer. "We're aboard the *Izanami*."

K'aia nodded. "Another location. Okay. And that was the ship EI in there?"

"AI," Gabriel amended. "Izanami has free will, to a point."

"The ship and the AI have the same name? Why?" K'aia wanted to test her body's limits but resisted the urge to run the length of the corridor because she felt so full of energy. "I've met a few artificial intelligences—"

"Digital life forms," Gabriel supplied. "AIs are people, too."

K'aia bobbed her head. "Well, either way, I can't tell the difference."

"You have to get to know them to see it," Alexis explained. "Like Aunt Eve."

K'aia looked at them skeptically. "The scary android?"

Gabriel snorted. "I suppose if you're not used to her she could seem that way."

K'aia looked at Gabriel in disbelief. "She offered to upgrade me with armor I never had to take off," she told them in a horrified voice. "Have you *seen* how bulky Yollin armor is?"

Alexis and Gabriel shared a look and burst out laughing.

"Have you seen Aunt Jean's armor?" Gabriel asked.

K'aia shook her head. "I haven't met your aunt."

Gabriel winked. "I bet you've heard of her, though."

K'aia racked her brain for the name. "No, the only Jean I've ever heard of is Jean Dukes."

The twins did that weird smiling thing that creeped K'aia out, but their meaning was clear.

"Jean *Dukes* is your aunt?" She threw out a couple of choice Yollin cursewords in exasperation. "Of *course* she is." She groaned long and loud. "I can't *believe* I turned down Jean Dukes' armor. How could I be so stupid? *Jean Dukes armor!*"

Alexis patted K'aia's arm as they walked. "Don't stress it. We'll find a way to get you hooked up with some."

QBS *Izanami*, Bridge

Bethany Anne and Michael stood shoulder to shoulder,

looking out over the fleet. The ships were displayed across half of the screens that wrapped the bridge.

Bethany Anne's mouth drew into a tight line as she observed the three other groups getting into formation. "Is this enough, or have I kept too much back to cover my ass while we're gone?"

The ancillary fleet looked tiny and insignificant in comparison to the super-massive ships they were flocking to join.

Michael's hand enveloped hers. "You're sending four superdreadnoughts plus a host of other ships, all filled with *highly* destructive weaponry, to each of the larger targets. That should be more than sufficient to deal with what we're looking at."

John's voice cut in over the speaker. "Hey, Boss. We good to go?" His face appeared on an unoccupied screen. "I think Eve might just use Scott as a warm-up if we hang around much longer."

Bethany Anne raised a finger. "Let me check. Izanami, get me the others onscreen."

The remaining screens lit up. Bethany Anne opened her link to Alexis and Gabriel while she waited for everyone to arrive. *Alexis, Gabriel, we are about to get underway, and the three of you are not here.*

We're almost there, Mom, Alexis replied.

The elevator door opened a moment later to emit the three youths.

"Nice shipsuits," Bethany Anne commented to Alexis and Gabriel.

"A gift from Aunt Jean," Gabriel explained.

Bethany Anne smiled. "Then I'm sure they have a few

extras included." She turned her smile on K'aia. "Good to see you again, K'aia."

K'aia nodded, lost for words. She'd forgotten again what it was to be in Bethany Anne's presence.

Bethany Anne gestured to the couches and turned back to the screens.

"Now that we're all here," she gave Scott a pointed look as he slid into view beside Eve, "*finally*, let's move out."

Scott grinned. "What, no speech? I'm disappointed."

Bethany Anne shook her head, her lip curling slightly. "No more speeches. I've talked enough recently to be mistaken for a politician."

Gabrielle made a disappointed face. "Not even, say, one minute and forty seconds for a pep talk before we leave?"

John grunted, shrugging nonchalantly. "I reckon two would do it."

Eric shook his head. "Nah, I need a good solid five minutes of you telling us how great we are."

Bethany Anne raised an eyebrow, her mouth making a little "o" of sympathy. "That's a shame. I don't know why you'd put money on me taking five whole minutes to go over what you already know."

The guilty faces on the screen said it all.

"No speech," Bethany Anne told them with finality. "See who makes money on me now." Scott's eyes flicked toward Michael. "Really?"

Michael lifted his hands in a good-natured shrug. "What can I say?" He grinned at the others on the screens. "You can settle up when we get back." He didn't fail to catch the look Bethany Anne threw his way. "My wife and I will enjoy the dinner you all just paid for."

Bethany Anne cut the screens and returned to watching the fleet. "Izanami, I need to speak to Bart."

Admiral Thomas appeared on the screen vacated by John a moment before. "Bethany Anne."

"It's time to move. Fire up the Gate drives, and good luck to you all."

Admiral Thomas nodded briskly and the screen went dark once again.

Alexis, Gabriel, and K'aia watched on from the edges of their couches as the fleet exodus got underway.

Gabriel leaned in to whisper to his sister, "It's so…serious. This feels nothing like the game."

Alexis was transfixed. "It's *exactly* like the game."

Gates sprang into existence one after the other, flooding the space around the departing ships with pale, wavering light. Izanami initiated their Gate, the rippling light increasing in intensity the nearer they got to the event horizon.

Alexis took hold of her brother's hand as the *Izanami* entered the Gate.

Federation Deep Space Research Outpost, QBS *Izanami*

Bethany Anne reached out with her mind as the *Izanami* crossed the Gate.

She caught the barest whisper of ADAM, no more than a slight pull far in the distance. Nothing like words, just the familiar sensation of his presence. *ADAM, are you here?*

There was no reply.

The throb at the base of Bethany Anne's skull returned with a vengeance.

TOM, can you get a lock on him?

He's here *somewhere*, but that's all I can tell. Bethany Anne, there's something happening with your chip.

My chip? Is it malfunctioning?

No... But it's not working at its optimal level right now.

That would explain the headache. Tell me if anything changes with it.

I will, he assured her. In the meantime, I will keep attempting to diagnose and repair the problem.

Bethany Anne turned her attention to Alexis and Gabriel. "I believe your father discussed your duties while aboard the ship?"

The twins nodded in unison.

"Help Izanami keep the ship running smoothly," Alexis reeled off, "keep the repair bots running optimally, take care of the more complicated repairs if the ship is hit. But Mom?"

Bethany Anne tilted her head toward her daughter. "Yes?"

"The *Izanami* is invisible. Who's going to hit her?"

Bethany Anne shrugged. "It doesn't matter because we'll be ready if it happens."

K'aia spoke up. "What about me? How can I help?"

Bethany Anne's smile widened into a grin. "Right now, the most important thing you can do is train your body to its new capability. In the long term? I don't know. That's up to you. What do you *want* to do?"

K'aia lost her ability to speak again for a moment.

Izanami winked into existence on the center screen. "I'm picking up a trace of—"

A ship shot out of the churning dust at top speed.

Bethany Anne recognized the lines. "We'll talk about this later. That's Loralei. Put me through to her, Izanami."

Izanami inclined her head. "As you command."

Bethany Anne winced. "Children, cover your ears. This is not going to be pretty. Loralei. Can you hear me?"

"Ohfuckohfuckoh*fuuuuuuuck!*"

The frantic cursing stopped for all of a second. "Thank fuck you're here. ADAM has done some crazy shit, and there's like a million billion drones on my ass."

Bethany Anne scanned the rings for activity. "Izanami."

"My readings are distorted," Izanami reported.

"It's the rings," Loralei bitched. "There's massive interference from the dust. It's like pushing through sand, it's so dense."

Izanami appeared by Bethany Anne's side. "There may be an issue if Loralei fails to reach us quickly," she told her quietly.

Bethany Anne frowned, searching the screens for anything out of place when the drones exploded from the ring, every single one locked onto Loralei's position.

Alexis screamed. "*Loralei, behind you!*"

Loralei laughed wildly. "Those drones are nothing, princess. I didn't get to the rest of the bad news, my Queen. They built some big-ass ships while we weren't looking…"

The dust at the edge of the ring erupted outward, a writhing mass of tentacles emerging from the scattered particles. The Ooken ship rose out of the ring, the tentacles glowing at various points on the underside.

Bethany Anne felt Alexis' and Gabriel's nervousness. "It's okay to be scared."

"Really?" Alexis asked, not taking her eyes off the monstrous ship on the screen.

"Really," Bethany Anne told her calmly. "But you have to remember that in most of these situations, whoever we're facing is probably more scared of humans than we are of them."

13

The Collective still seethed at the injustice of losing part of their whole.

None had denied their will in all the time since the gods elevated them. They would not be bested by the aberrations who had destroyed their ships and stolen so much knowledge from the collective consciousness.

This Adversary. These...*Individuals*.

They did not know where this species had come from. It had been pure chance that the hunter had come across the enemy ship in the first place.

What the group consciousness *did* know was that the Adversary did not care for intruders. They were strong and aggressive, and they fought back with the technology of the gods.

Back and forth the rage passed through the Collective, feeding itself on an infinite loop. It was amplified by the instinctive urge that had spread out with the final thoughts of the lost colony to every mind in the group consciousness.

Kill.

Destroy.

Slake their thirst for vengeance.

The echo of that abrupt end had kept the Collective's grief whetted to a keen edge while they built their revenge.

The consensus on how to react to this travesty had been instant and unanimous: all resources were to be directed to wiping out the Adversary and taking their technology for the benefit of the Collective. It had been no difficult decision when every mind still felt the severing of the lost minds as sharply as the moment it had occurred.

The ships were ready, the lust for blood high. As soon as consensus to leave was reached, the Adversary would die.

The many minds paused when a message passed through the group consciousness—a call to action that reached every mind across the seven worlds.

The Adversary has returned.

Then pain and silence.

They had taken from the Collective again.

As one the Collective moved to answer the fresh injury.

The Adversary would pay in blood.

Ooken Territory, QBS *ArchAngel II*

Admiral Thomas listened to Bethany Anne's retelling of Loralei's report in his mind while he monitored the data charting the progress of the other teams from his chair on the bridge. *You're breaking up, and I'm getting zero visuals from the* Izanami.

Bethany Anne grunted in frustration and her voice

became clearer for a moment. *It's these damn rings around the planet. They're throwing out all sorts of weird shit. It's taking a fuck-ton of energy to maintain this connection.*

Admiral Thomas made a sympathetic sound. *You don't sound too happy about what ADAM did.*

Well, can you blame me? I have no clue what ADAM has done, and I can't get down there to find out because there's a fucking huge ship in my way.

Just how large is this ship? he asked.

Bethany Anne sighed impatiently. *Bigger than we've seen so far, but nothing we can't handle. They've got no idea we're here yet, but even Izanami's cloaking can't hide us once we're in the rings. Not unless she has a function to prevent the ship from displacing the dust, which she assures me is beyond even Jean's capability.*

Sounds like the wisest course of action is to take the ship out first.

No shit. I haven't got an issue with going through them to get to ADAM, but it will cause a problem with our timing on the smaller locations. How are the other teams doing for time? Can any of them divert to take care of my and Michael's first target?

So far, you and Michael are the only ones who've made it to your location. John and Akio are close to their first target, so it won't be them.

Don't tell me who's not available.

Admiral Thomas felt Bethany Anne roll her eyes. His mouth tightened as he scanned the war board, opening a channel to Gabrielle's team when he noted that they were closest. "Gabrielle, what's your position right now? Can you and Eric divert to take care of location two?"

Gabrielle's voice came from the speakers. "Of course. Are Bethany Anne and Michael okay?"

"They're good," he confirmed. "Just tied up right now."

Bethany Anne chuckled darkly. *Not as badly as this ship will be in a few minutes...*

Eric cut in. "We can divert. We'll need Gate coordinates."

Admiral Thomas sent them over. "That do?"

Gabrielle chuckled. "Nicely. Changing course now. Thank you, Admiral."

"Give 'em hell," he told them.

"We weren't going to invite them for dinner," Gabrielle shot back, signing off.

Admiral Thomas rubbed a hand over his eyes. *Just once, I'd like things to go to plan. All right, you're covered for location two. Do you need me to send your backup early?*

Bethany Anne considered having the superdread-noughts come in and deal with the Ooken ship. *No, we're good with the plan. My way will be less messy.*

He didn't agree, but he knew better than to argue the point with her. *Okay, but you'll yell if you do.*

Bethany Anne's tone cooled by a few degrees. *That didn't sound like a request, Bart.*

It wasn't, Admiral Thomas replied, his concern clear despite his tone. *Good luck, Bethany Anne.*

Luck won't be necessary, Bethany Anne told him. *I'm going to dick-punch the fuckers and run. They won't know what hit them, and as soon as that ship is floating around in tiny pieces, I'm clear to rescue ADAM.*

Admiral Thomas shook his head after Bethany Anne cut

the connection and got up to go find Kael-ven. "CEREBRO, ready the captains. Our Queen is about to introduce herself to the enemy in her usual charming and neighborly way."

QBS *Izanami*, Bridge

Bethany Anne cut the link to Admiral Thomas and took a moment to recover from the drain on her energy the conversation had caused.

Michael saw the focus return to Bethany Anne's face. *What is Bart saying?*

Her eyes flicked to Alexis and Gabriel, who were staring at the screens, their game forgotten.

Alexis and Gabriel are distracted by the enemy ship, Michael reasoned. *They're not even attempting to listen in on us.*

Bethany Anne allowed her gaze to linger on the twins for a moment. ***Good. It's easier when I don't have to censor my thoughts. We'll never let our mental defenses get slack after raising our children.***

I consider the eavesdropping a just reward for the delight you took in using me to hone our children's skills in mind reading when they were small.

Bethany Anne tapped her lip with a finger. ***Hmmm. I'm not sure that compares to...oh, I don't know... Teaching them how to blow each other up using the Etheric?***

It wasn't that way, and you know it. Michael shook his head. *The apportionment of parental blame aside, what do you want to do about that ship?*

Bethany Anne's finger paused on her bottom lip. ***It's a*** *sneak attack or nothing. Our children are aboard, so I'm not taking a risk I don't have to.*

Michael regarded the ship skimming the edge of the rings. *What do you suggest?*

Bethany Anne's lips met in a cold smile. *That we go over there and fuck up the ship without the Ooken realizing where we came from.*

Michael turned from the screen to face Bethany Anne. *I have a few ideas on how to create a large enough explosion, but how do you suggest we get in, and—more importantly—out?*

Izanami can get close enough that I can walk us across through the Etheric and back out before your explosion goes off. She made a motion with her fingers. *Easy as pie. Addix is here to stop the children from crashing the ship while we're gone.*

Michael reached out to Addix.

The spymistress and erstwhile nanny answered. *Yes, Michael?*

Bethany Anne and I need to step out and take care of something.

Addix paused a beat. *I will assume the "something" you are referring to is the Ooken ship that has just emerged from the planet's rings? And that you wish me to chaperone the children while you are...taking care of it?* Her inner voice was laced with amusement.

Michael chuckled dryly. *I have to tell you how much I admire your deductive skills, Addix. That would be good of you, thank you.*

I will arrive on the bridge shortly. Addix cut the link.

Bethany Anne raised an eyebrow in question. "You ready to go?"

Michael nodded. "Addix is on her way."

"Where are you going?" Alexis asked, her eyes locked on the ship filling the center screens. She pointed at the screen. "Over there?"

Gabriel cocked his head at Bethany Anne, his eyes bright with the prospect of adventure. "Can we go too?"

K'aia watched quietly, waiting for the answer.

Bethany Anne shook her head, smiling ruefully. "Not a chance. I have an important task for the three of you, though. Addix is on her way to the bridge to chaperone, but for all intents and purposes the ship is under your command until we return."

Alexis' mouth opened and closed.

"But…" Gabriel began.

Michael held up a hand to stop their protests. "There is no room for discussion on the matter. You three are not trained for this yet."

K'aia shrugged. "If you say so."

The twins looked at K'aia like she was two Cokes short of a six-pack.

K'aia shrugged again, deeper this time. "Your mom and dad know I can fight. If they say I can't handle this, then my Yollin behind is remaining right here, where it gets to stay in one piece. "

Bethany Anne gave Alexis and Gabriel the Look. "If you want to fight once you're ready, I won't hold you back. But you're not ready *yet*. What if anything happened to you because we let you go out there too soon? What would we do?"

The twins nodded, unhappy but understanding.

Michael nodded, satisfied that Alexis and Gabriel

would cooperate. He looked down at his shipsuit, then back at Bethany Anne. "I think a short diversion to the armory before we leave would be apropos to the mission."

Bethany Anne grinned. "I was thinking the same thing." She paused a beat for effect. "How do you feel about couples' outfits?"

Michael regarded his wife coolly. "I hope you did not actually have Jean make us matching sets of armor."

Bethany Anne's mouth twitched. "Would I do a thing like that?"

Alexis giggled, and Gabriel out and out cracked up at the barely repressed smirk on their mother's face.

Michael sighed and touched his fingers to his forehead. "Yes. Yes, you would."

Federation Deep Space Research Outpost, Ooken Ship

Bethany Anne stepped out of the Etheric with her Jean Dukes' at head height.

It would be unfortunate for any Ooken who happened to be there since the height difference meant she would be aiming closer to their groins.

The cargo bay Bethany Anne had chosen was empty, meaning that the absent guards' capacity to reproduce got a reprieve for the second.

She lowered her weapons fractionally and waited for Michael.

Michael emerged in the next moment, and Bethany Anne admired the view as he turned a slow circle to assess their surroundings. *That armor looks good on you.*

Michael gave her a dry look. *I didn't think we would be out here in matching armor.*

Bethany Anne smirked. *I'd love to say it was my idea, but all the credit goes to Jean on this one.*

Michael made a noise of disapproval. *Then I will be certain to thank her appropriately when we return to QT2.*

Bethany Anne rolled her eyes. *It's not so bad. If you quit being so moody, I'll show you something cool.*

She fed a trickle of Etheric energy into her armor's gauntlets, grinning at Michael's expression when they shifted to form a hooded blade for each hand. *Activate them just like your gauntlets.*

Michael did, and the blades came into being in his hands. *I always liked katars,* he told her, testing the oversize blades for balance. *This is a nice take on them. Very effective.*

You know Jean. If she doesn't improve the deadliness of a design, it doesn't make it past the prototype stage. Bethany Anne sheathed her blades and reached out with her mind to scan the immediate area outside the cargo bay, which she found to be empty of life. *We're clear to move.*

She pulled up short when the hatch swung inward and they got their first look at the interior of the ship. *Holy...*

There were no corridors to link the levels. Instead, something resembling tree limbs grew horizontally, vertically, and diagonally from a series of wide trunks that linked the metal walkways that ran every which way across the impossibly large space.

Bethany Anne and Michael peered over the edge of the walkway outside the bay, which dropped off with no warning onto a huge length of cargo netting that joined the gently glowing branches below, forming yet more links between levels.

She hesitated to choose a direction. *We need a map. There's nothing here to tell us where we are.*

The Ooken are telepathic, Michael supplied. *I'm not sure they even have a written language.*

Bethany Anne raised her eyebrow. *How would you know?*

He indicated the path to their left. *I had TOM help me learn what we know of their spoken language from the seeker ADAM captured.*

Good, Bethany Anne replied. *We should grab one and find out where we need to be to blow up this homage to the living rainforest.* She shrugged at the look he gave her. *What?*

Michael lifted his head. *There's an Ooken on the next walkway down. Almost directly below us.*

Bethany Anne grinned at him and dropped to a crouch. *Oh, goody. That saves us the effort of going looking for one.* She grabbed the edge of the walkway they were on and swung herself over the edge.

Michael winced at the slight crunch as Bethany Anne landed feet-first on the Ooken's bulging head and moved to join her on the walkway below.

Bethany Anne came to her feet in a smooth roll and turned to catch the Ooken by the tentacles before it plummeted over the edge and alerted the rest of the crew.

What is it with this species? She hoisted its awkward body back to the center of the branch and shook off the suckers that had attached themselves to her armor. *I've seen some out-there evolutionary quirks, but these tentacles top* the list. *What fucked-up environment makes a species select for* **that?**

Michael dropped onto the branch beside her. *Knowing as we do that the Kurtherians have had some involvement with this species, I think we can safely surmise that it was our old enemy who did the selecting.*

Bethany Anne grimaced. **Mmhmm. We've got our Ooken, but I still don't like how quiet it is. Where are the rest of the crew?**

They're around, Michael assured her. *I'm sure we'll be eyeballs-deep in the fun soon enough. This one will wake up at some point and alert the rest.*

Bethany Anne rolled her eyes. **Well, that puts all of my concerns to rest. Now we can pretty much guarantee they'll come pouring out of the woodwork at exactly the worst moment.**

The Ooken twitched, and she laid a boot into its temple to make sure it stayed asleep. **Can you read its mind?**

I can. Michael frowned, kneeling to put a hand to the Ooken's bleeding forehead. *Surprising.*

Bethany Anne crossed her arms. **What's surprising?** She started tapping her foot when Michael didn't answer, falling somewhat short of patience. **Well? Don't keep me in suspense.**

Michael got to his feet, wiping a spot of the unconscious Ooken's blood off his hand onto his leg before motioning for Bethany Anne to follow him. *You were lucky the Ooken did not see you. The surprising thing was that I was able to access its visual memories. I have our route, but also an insight we did not possess before.*

Bethany Anne raised an eyebrow. **This I have to hear.**

What insight? She swept a hand in front of her to indicate Michael lead the way.

Michael looked over the edge of the walkway, which culminated in a short gap opposite a branch with a net fixed between the two.

He jumped and caught the net to climb over. *For one, they seem to operate codependently. The Ooken's psyche was under considerable stress at being cut off from the rest of its kind.*

Bethany Anne chose not to touch the filthy ropes. *So our theories about them having some sort of hive mind were on the mark?* Her lips pressed together in thought as she floated down. *That's going to be a pain in the ass if even one of them spots us.*

Michael let go of the net a little way from the floor and landed gracefully at Bethany Anne's side, smiling wryly. *Then I suggest that we stay out of sight, my love.*

They made their way deeper into the ship, Michael taking the lead while Bethany Anne kept their backs guarded. It was difficult to navigate, since the only way to move around was to work their way along the living walkways, avoiding pockets of Ooken.

Bethany Anne sighed at the sight of yet another turn in the walkway. *It feels like we've been walking forever, and everything looks the damn same.*

Michael swerved around a slick puddle in his path. *Watch your step,* he told Bethany Anne. *There's something slippery-looking here.*

Bethany Anne bent to examine the viscous liquid Michael had avoided. *This is the same substance we saw at the colony. I didn't see the substance they found on Loralei after the initial encounter, but I'd put any money on that being the same stuff as well.*

Michael examined the opalescent smear at their feet. *It does look the same. Is there any way you can confirm it?*

Bethany Anne patted herself down. *Yeah...no. I left the lab in my other armor.*

TOM interjected. **Did you forget I was here? I can analyze it.**

I didn't forget. Bethany Anne sent TOM mental images of every painful way to die she could think of in the space of half a second. *And, no, I'm not doing it, so don't even entertain the idea.*

TOM sniffed. **Sorry I offered.**

Michael cocked his head in confusion. *Doing what?*

Bethany Anne took a resealable bag from her utility belt and knelt to scoop a sample. *TOM can analyze the substance if I get it into my system. Since there's no way to inject it at the moment, that leaves only one option. I'm telling you both right fucking now that I am* not *putting the mystery goop in my mouth.*

Michael shrugged.

Bethany Anne strode off before either of them could debate it with her. *We need to move our asses. The analysis can wait until we get back.*

Michael took one last look at the shining puddle and set off after Bethany Anne. *It would help if you knew where you were going,* he teased as he came up beside her.

Bethany Anne waved a finger toward the glow a few levels down. *I'm going to guess we're headed down there.*

Michael paused. *Yes, that looks to be the core chamber as I saw it in the Ooken's mind. However, we are entering an inhabited section of the ship. I can sense other minds ahead.*

Bethany Anne looked around, expecting to see an Ooken. **We're still good for the moment. What are you going to do when we get into the core chamber?**

Michael hesitated before answering. *I have a way to destabilize the core, but it takes some concentration to bring into being.*

Bethany Anne chose to let the hesitation slide for the time being. **How many Ooken can you sense between us and the core?**

Michael skimmed lightly over the surrounding portion of the ship. *I'm reading twelve, but it's not clear since their minds are much the same.*

Bethany Anne's hands caressed the grips of her Jean Dukes Specials. **That's not so many.**

All it takes is one to alert the others, and then we have to work that much harder to complete our objective.

Bethany Anne debated a second, then sighed and dropped her hands to her sides. **So we just kick the door in and you do your...whatever it is you're going to do.**

Michael smirked. *Nothing more complicated than concentrated Etheric energy contained in a super-hardened shell.*

Michael was looking far too pleased with himself for the solution to be so simple. **How does that equal a force large enough to destabilize... Oh, unless you...** Her eyes narrowed in appreciation. **That's clever, honey. You set the energy to accumulate without any restriction on the draw, then the pressure builds until there's an explosion of Etheric energy.**

Michael nodded. *We just need to make a rapid exit once I*

release my hold on the ball. It can get somewhat messy when there is organic matter involved.

Bethany Anne scrutinized her husband carefully. **Why does that sound like the voice of experience talking?**

Michael clammed up and focused on his cupped hands.

Bethany Anne snickered as the reason for Michael's embarrassment occurred to her. **I think I just got a bit closer to the truth about your T-rex hunt. You blew it up? Really?**

Sucked to be the creature.

QBS *Izanami*, Bridge

Alexis, Gabriel, and K'aia were playing video games on the wraparound screens while Addix worked quietly on one of the couches built for her species when Izanami appeared.

"We have a situation," the AI announced.

Addix looked up from her tablet, and her mandibles twitched with curiosity when she saw the dark aura surrounding Izanami's avatar. "What kind of situation?"

"A Leath ship has just entered the system. There are a number of Ooken seekers on a course to intercept."

Addix shrugged. "The Leath have the best technology apart from Bethany Anne's. They will fight off a few seeker ships easily enough without a need for us to reveal our position."

Alexis pulled her neural headband off and dropped it on the couch. "Have you got a video feed, Izanami?"

Izanami inclined her head a touch. "I do."

"Then put it up onscreen, please," Alexis requested.

The occupants of the Leath ship were oblivious to the danger they were in until it was too late.

The seeker ships shot down the defensive missiles and surrounded the Leath ship. They opened fire, targeting its most vulnerable spots.

The Leath ship was too bulky to shake the seekers off. The seekers dodged the next round of defensive fire, nipping in to cause damage and darting back out again before the Leath could react.

The twins watched in stunned silence.

K'aia paced angrily. "We should go help them."

Addix shook her head. "The safety of Alexis and Gabriel is my only concern."

Alexis didn't like that one bit. She wheeled around with a fierce expression, pointing at the screen. "So those Leath have to die?"

Addix shrugged. "If it means that you and your brother do not, then yes."

Gabriel's eyes remained on the screen. He spoke up finally. "I don't think they're going to die. Look."

A Gate opened as Gabriel spoke, and the seekers herded the beleaguered Leath ship toward it.

Izanami disappeared in a spray of pixels. She came back a moment later as a dark shape shot away from the Izanami and after the hijacked Leath ship.

"What was that?" Addix inquired.

"That was Loralei," Izanami informed them. "While I could not allow the children to be discovered, Loralei was available to follow. My Queen will know how best to deal with the matter when she returns."

Gabriel turned to Alexis after Izanami disappeared again. "Do you think Izanami considered how Mom will react to finding out there are a bunch of Leath who need saving?"

Alexis shook her head, lost for words for once.

They waited and watched nervously to see if Loralei would make it through the Gate.

Her small ship sped toward the shimmering circle, disappearing through the event horizon in the barest second before it snapped shut again.

Location One, Outer Wall

John crept up behind the guard and thrust his knife into what he hoped to hell was its brain stem.

Akio was having none of those problems on the other side of the gatehouse. His swords caught the firelight from the mounted torches as he parted the Ooken on that side from its head.

Both guards slumped.

John punched the air with his knife hand. *My guard hit the deck first. Point's mine.*

Akio was about to argue when a keening wail went up inside the walls at the same time a blanket of lights winked on across the colony.

John froze on the edge of the wall. *Motherfucking... Did we make that happen?*

Akio listened intently to the psychic distress in the air. *It appears so. Plan B?*

John's sharp vision picked out the Ooken emerging from the lighted buildings. He didn't need Akio's mind reading ability to work out that they were pissed. *Plan B,* he agreed.

The Pod arrived as the Ooken made the base of the wall.

Akio kept the tentacles at bay while John jumped aboard, then John covered from the Pod's hatch with his JDs dialed to eleven.

Akio's feet left the wall a fraction of a second before John took out the tentacles that had been coming for him, along with a huge chunk of the wall.

Akio fixed John with a hard look as he walked past him into the Pod.

John shrugged as he holstered his pistols. "What did you want me to do, let them drag you down there?"

Akio's face didn't move.

John rolled his eyes, muttering something about overly dramatic reactions as they made their way to the front of the Pod to get eyes on the Ooken below.

"You know I can hear you," Akio told him. He turned his back to John and laid his swords out for cleaning.

"Oh, I know," John replied. He grunted to get Akio's attention as the pucks screamed past at high velocity. "Plan B worked."

Akio turned to look at the brand new craters exploding into being on the viewscreen. "It would appear so."

The Pod shot upward, taking them out of range of the spray of debris from the multiple impacts. Wood, metal, and plastic bloomed upward and outward in a hundred-foot circle around the former colony.

John grimaced as the dust settled far below. "That

wasn't the outcome we were hoping for. The point was to get information before obliterating the place."

Akio didn't pause in the meticulous cleaning of his swords. "On the contrary, we learned something invaluable to the wider mission. These," he waved at the destruction below, "are alerted when one of them dies."

John's brow furrowed. "The others need to know about this. I'm calling it in to the Admiral."

Federation Deep Space Research Outpost, Ooken Ship

Bethany Anne held a bubble of Etheric energy over the nook they were using as cover, creating a temporary shield to prevent the Ooken from discovering them. *Michael.*

I'm going as fast as I can, he replied calmly. *It's a bit challenging with the noise pollution.*

Bethany Anne didn't tell him she'd dialed down her hearing the second TOM had offered. *I know. It sounds like the place fax machines come to die.*

Michael let his hands drop. *This isn't working. We need to get inside the chamber and work from there.*

Bethany Anne waved a hand toward the chamber. *We already risked alerting them.*

The shrill cry went up across the ship again, echoing eerily in the spaces between the walkways. It got almost unbearably louder when the Ooken began swarming from the central trunk onto the living walkways.

Michael's mouth twitched. *How many are there?*

Bethany Anne risked a quick glance around the wall at the walkway they were on. *Fuck me.*

Michael frowned. *That many?*

Actually, a few more than "fuck me." *They're all headed for the walkway where we left that Ooken. It must have come around.* She scowled in frustration. *I should have kicked it a bit fucking harder.*

Michael snorted softly. *It would have been much more challenging to mind read a dead Ooken.*

True. Bethany Anne ducked when an Ooken dropped onto the walkway from the level above. *Get down, there's one about to pass us.*

The Ooken swung past, using all the available space to maneuver at a rapid pace along the walkway. Its tentacles crept along every surface as the Ooken felt its way along as well as using its eyes.

Bethany Anne and Michael held their breath when a stray tentacle curled around into their hiding place and slapped the wall above Michael's head.

Bethany Anne opened her hand and tapped the Etheric, ready to make calamari rings of the Ooken's face if it got a single inch closer to her love.

The tentacle receded, and Bethany Anne and Michael shared a relieved look when the Ooken moved on as quickly as it had appeared.

She dropped her connection to the Etheric for the moment. *We can't stay here much longer.*

Michael nodded his agreement. *Let's move.*

They took a nearby net to the level below and continued working their way down until they reached solid metal. *Looks like they have to do things a bit more normally down here,* Bethany Anne remarked, slipping into another alcove.

Michael indicated the Ooken guards patrolling the corridor outside the core chamber. He calculated the distance from their present position to the glowing entrance. *Can you take us in through the Etheric?*

Bethany Anne activated the blades on her armor's gauntlets and moved to stand between Michael and the Ooken. ***Perhaps naked, but not on a moving ship with all this armor, and not without ADAM to calculate the exit point.***

Michael kept low as he darted across. *Yet you brought us to this ship with no problem.*

Bethany Anne lifted a shoulder, looking out to check the position of the guards before she crossed to the next available cover. ***It's one thing hopping down here from the Izanami, but the odds of us not getting spaced in the process are the kind only someone with a death wish would take.***

Michael slid around to stand beside Bethany Anne with his own blades activated. *Then next time we go naked.*

Or we take the lighter armor. Of course, we could always just walk ***the rest of the way and take the guards out. They're going to work out we're here any minute.***

Michael shrugged. *If you insist. I do like this set, despite the drain the effort to Myst it would cause.* He frowned, feeling a shift in the Ooken consciousness toward excitement. *They've figured out where we're headed. We have minutes at most.*

Bethany Anne darted forward to remove the guards blocking their way. ***Well, fuck. We'd better get our asses into that chamber, then.***

The first Ooken reached Bethany Anne just in time to meet the upward swing with her left blade. She moved on, denying the second Ooken a chance to react.

Her momentum brought her around again, her right blade flashing downward to sever the Ooken's tentacles even as she completed the spin and sliced clean through its skull with the left.

She turned to Michael to offer him the third, but he was occupied with the glowing sphere he was growing in his cupped hands.

The third Ooken held back. It blocked the walkway between Bethany Anne and Michael and their goal, shrieking at them unintelligibly.

Bethany Anne took a step toward the Ooken and held up a finger. "I'm going to ask you to move, but something tells me you wouldn't do it even if you could understand me."

The Ooken took a step forward and screeched at them again.

Bethany Anne glanced at Michael. *Do you understand any of what it's saying?*

Michael lifted an unconcerned shoulder. *It's not saying anything much as far as I can tell.* He nodded at the walkways above. *But then, all of the Ooken up there are also singing from the same songbook. Death to someone—I would hazard a guess and say they mean us—and revenge upon their enemies. Again, I assume we are the intended recipients of this present example of stellar hospitality.*

I would say it's a safe assumption. Bethany Anne waved the hand she was holding up at the Ooken, slicing it cleanly in two with a thin sheet of Etheric energy. *Time to throw that dick-punch while we still have breathing room.*

Michael watched his wife stride through the spreading

blood. *How very quaint of you. Have you been watching old British sitcoms lately?*

Yes, because I have so much time for tv. Bethany Anne lifted her hands in a shrug, and an energy ball appeared in each. **I want to get done and gone. There's no reason to keep it quiet if they already know we're here. Get ready, we're going in.**

Michael drew fast and hard on the Etheric to fill the shell he'd created with expanding energy. *We don't have too much time before it explodes,* he warned Bethany Anne.

This won't take but a minute or two. Bethany Anne threw both energy balls at the core chamber's doors. She stalked into the chamber with her arms raised as the solid metal doors were flung back.

Michael stayed a few paces behind her, putting the finishing touches to his creation while he gave Bethany Anne room to conduct her bloody symphony. He found it somewhat difficult to concentrate on his task when her every graceful move drew his gaze.

Etheric energy flowed from Bethany Anne's hands, eviscerating everything in its path. The Ooken who rushed Bethany Anne were cut down in their tracks. Those remaining froze for a moment.

Bethany Anne bared her teeth and waved a hand to end their existence. "Too fucking late," she ground out as the sections of their bodies slid to the floor.

She joined Michael at the railing around the ship's core. **Well?**

Michael held up his hand to show Bethany Anne the pulsating energy within the sphere. *It's time.*

Bethany Anne searched with her mind to get a lock on

Gabriel and Alexis. She grabbed Michael firmly and nodded. ***Whenever you're ready.***

Michael prepared to release the energy. *On three. One... Two...* He flung his hands forward.

JUMP*!*

15

Federation Deep Space Research Outpost, QBS *Izanami*

Addix turned to see what had tripped her senses as Bethany Anne and Michael stumbled out of the Etheric into the transfer area on the bridge. She nodded at them. "Good work."

Izanami took them out a safe distance while Bethany Anne and Michael joined Addix and the children at the screens and watched the death throes of the Ooken ship.

Explosions ripped through the ship, blowing it open. The outward force when the hull burst drove the ship back into the rings, throwing up splashes of displaced rock and dust.

The larger asteroids were unaffected by the disturbance. The Ooken ship was bounced around like a pinball as one huge chunk of rock after another smashed into the ship, throwing it back out of the ring even as they tore away the main body from the tentacle-like arms at the rear.

The two halves drifted away from each other, lacking the self-repair capability Bethany Anne's ships had.

Bethany Anne shifted from one foot to the other, then turned to the avatar floating behind her left shoulder. "Izanami, can you get this wrapped up any faster?"

Izanami's expressionless face held the ghost of anticipation for the briefest moment. "I have just the thing, my Queen."

They saw nothing leave the *Izanami*. However, a few minutes later fresh explosions lit the two halves of the Ooken ship as Izanami's toys ruptured the hull, exposing the last remaining pressurized areas to space.

Bethany Anne watched for a few moments, then turned her back on the screen. "That's taken care of. Izanami, patch Loralei into the bridge and take us to the outpost."

Alexis dragged her gaze from the light show. "Loralei isn't here, Mom."

Izanami inclined her head slightly to confirm. "While you were on the enemy vessel, a Leath ship entered the system and was hijacked by a number of Ooken seeker ships. It was taken through a Gate, and Loralei followed."

Bethany Anne sighed. "Of course she did. She uploaded her logs when she got in though, right?"

The air around Izanami glitched, and one of the inactive screens lit up. "For what they are worth."

"The Leath ship will wait until we have ADAM safe and sound." Bethany Anne waved a hand at the screen. "This really isn't the most helpful. All I can see is, well, nothing."

"I have done what I can to reconstruct the footage using the metadata," Izanami explained, "but since Loralei received next to no data input either time she was inside the rings, there wasn't much I could do with those parts."

Addix frowned at the shifting block of color and turned

her head to Izanami. "This is inside the ring? The EI was essentially blind?"

"On the way out, yes. ADAM led her in."

Michael made a noise of appreciation. "How did she manage to get out unaided?"

Izanami's aura turned pink. "She says she turned her nose sideways to the current and hoped for the best."

Bethany Anne chuckled, squinting at what she thought might be the outline of ADAM's scout ship. "Uh-huh. I'm sure she said it somewhat less politely than that. Just skip ahead to what happened at the outpost."

The AI did as she was asked and the image switched to a jumpy birds-eye view descending on a curve toward the ground. ADAM's scout ship took the lead as the view leveled out.

Bethany Anne waved a hand at the screens. "Are there any more nasty surprises waiting for us down there?"

Izanami confirmed they were clear for now. "You took care of the primary threat, and as far as my scanners are telling me, all of the seeker ships left through the Gate."

Michael frowned, continuing to follow ADAM and Loralei's route into the largest dome. "How reliable are those scans?"

Izanami's avatar glitched in and out a couple of times, her aura flashing deep red. "As accurate as you would expect. I had time to find a workaround for the interference while you and my Queen were on the enemy ship."

Bethany Anne turned her head from the screen. "Excellent. Then it won't be too difficult to coordinate the rescue and get back to our objective."

Alexis and Gabriel shared a look with K'aia, which

Bethany Anne didn't miss. She turned a pleasant smile on the children. "Is there anything you three would like to contribute?"

Gabriel winced when Alexis jabbed him with her elbow. He narrowed his eyes at her and turned to Bethany Anne. "What about the Leath ship? When will we rescue them?"

"I'm getting to that." Bethany Anne felt another tight pulse of pain band her skull. "While I'm more than concerned that the Ooken have taken hostages who could lead them back to the Federation, finding ADAM comes before anything else."

She turned back to the screen to hide her discomfort from the children. "You kids go get suited up. If Izanami says it's safe enough, I see no reason to leave half our team aboard the ship."

Alexis and Gabriel jumped up and dashed for the armory, pausing when K'aia was slower to move.

Bethany Anne shooed her after the twins. "You too."

K'aia shrugged. "I haven't got any armor to put on. I'm good with my staff and my knives if anything goes down."

Bethany Anne winked at her. "I think you'll find something in the armory that will suit your purpose."

Gabriel whooped. "Told you we'd get you hooked up." He grinned at Bethany Anne. "Mom's pretty awesome like that."

Alexis came over and tugged on K'aia's hands to get her moving. "Mom's just awesome, period. Come on!"

K'aia's mandibles worked for a moment, finally making the connections to stutter a thank you as the twins dragged her off.

Bethany Anne and Michael chuckled as the young Yollin hurried from the bridge with Alexis and Gabriel.

Michael raised an eyebrow at the retreating children. *I think K'aia will relax and settle in well, given time.*

Bethany Anne turned back to the screen, observing their progress through the rings with her arms folded. *I think...* she stood like that, tapping her fingers on the elbow of her other arm while she drew the thought out, ***the child has seen far too much. I didn't like that she left Irey without giving us a chance to help her.***

She is too spirited to hand over control of her life, even to you, Michael qualified gently. *Wouldn't you feel the same if you had been mere property most of your life? What* wouldn't *you do to retain that freedom once you had fought to win it?*

Bethany Anne nodded. ***I recognize that K'aia has that fierce independent streak. It's one of the things I liked about her from the start.*** Her hands dropped to her sides. ***The question is whether we can do anything for her now that we have her here.***

Michael walked the few steps to his wife and held out an arm. *I know how much you want to wave a magic wand for K'aia, but I do not believe she would accept a handout.*

Bethany Anne's mouth twitched in amusement. Her husband knew her too damn well. ***That's fine, since I wasn't planning on giving her one.***

She looked at Michael for a moment, then relaxed into his embrace. ***I don't think it's necessary to compromise K'aia's need to be independent. If she wants to earn her way in life, then we need to find a niche for her.***

I can't see that being an issue, Michael agreed. *I take it you have a plan in mind?*

Bethany Anne touched her cheek to Michael's chest. *Actually, yes. Yours. I like the idea of Gabriel and Alexis having someone to watch their backs. The three of them seem to be bonding well enough as a group.* She stretched up and brushed her lips against his jaw. *I've had some time to reassess how I feel about this infuriating habit you've formed recently of being fucking* right *all the time.*

Michael wasn't quite sure where this was leading. She'd accepted his arm around her and her inner voice was soft, but... *And?*

Well, I'm not going to pretend it doesn't piss me off. But, she snuggled into his chest, *it's also good to know I don't have to worry about you so much as I have been.*

You are *aware that I kept myself alive and in one piece for a very long time before you walked into my life in those red heels of yours?*

One hundred and fifty years, Michael. You can't blame me for being protective. However, I can see I've been holding on too tightly.

Michael held Bethany Anne closer, pressing his lips to her hair. *Does that mean I'm forgiven at last?*

For getting yourself blown up in a nuclear explosion? She snorted against his chest. *Fuck, no. But I* have *been thinking a lot about how we're going to win this war, and I refuse to be the reason it gets dragged out.*

How...progressive of you. I was beginning to think you would never relax your grip on us all. Michael raised his eyes to the ceiling and prayed to whatever gods were out there working to keep males and the most precious parts of their anatomy together that she never found out the whole truth about his hunt.

Bethany Anne released Michael and moved away from the screen. *It was that or face mutiny. Apparently, I've been driving everyone insane.*

Michael was definitely not falling into *that* trap. *We all understood why you needed to place strictures on us.*

Bethany Anne put an indignant hand to her chest. *Wow, want me to turn around so you can twist that knife a bit more?* She laughed at Michael's raised eyebrow. *I know I've been overdoing it when my stick-up-his-ass husband compares my protective nature when it comes to our family to the bloody reign of terror he inflicted upon the Unknown-World for centuries.*

A reign that was entirely justified, Michael pointed out.

Of course, dear. Her mouth quirked as she teased him. *Nothing at all to do with your refusal to accept anything other than your will being followed to the letter?*

Michael snorted. *Pots and kettles, my love?*

Bethany Anne shook her head. *I will admit to a certain level of expectation when it comes to getting shit done. But as long as it gets done, I don't care how it's achieved. I trust my people to be responsible about their methods.*

You mean you don't like being swamped with all the details.

Bethany Anne patted Michael on the ass as she passed him to get to the transfer area. *Exactly. I have a couple of calls to take care of now that Izanami has solved the issue with the interference, but then I'll be good to go.*

Michael turned and caught her in his arms before she took another step. *I'll go light a fire under the children. They should have been done by now.*

Bethany Anne pulled Michael close and kissed the corner of his mouth lightly. *Not an actual fire, though, my love. I have to say that wouldn't be proper parenting. It hasn't been done since the Dark Ages.*

She turned and stepped into the Etheric, opening a connection to Admiral Thomas as she exited a moment or two later in her personal armory.

What can I do for you, Bethany Anne? Did you find ADAM and Loralei yet?

We have Loralei, or rather we had her. ADAM is still missing. We're almost at the outpost now.

What happened with Loralei?

She went after a Leath ship that was taken out of the system by the Ooken. That's why I'm calling; as soon as we have ADAM, we're going after the ship.

Admiral Thomas sounded more than a little confused. *You're going off to rescue some Leath?*

Yes, and don't imagine for one moment that I'm at all pleased about it. Bethany Anne scowled as she replaced her katanas in their mount on the wall. **But it's a short leap from the Leath to all the other parts of the Federation. The last thing we need is the Ooken learning anything about them.**

Admiral Thomas made a noise of comprehension. *That makes more sense now. Want me to join you?*

No. I want you to keep on coordinating things from there. I'll call if I need you once we reach wherever Loralei has tracked them to. Bethany Anne dropped the connection and looked out on the destruction below.

The outpost's domes resembled a grisly row of boiled eggs. The tops had been cracked open, leaving nothing but jagged shards at the top of each one.

Bethany Anne eyed the damage to the smaller research

modules. The equipment had been torn out, leaving bright spots in the otherwise burned buildings. She saw no bodies and sensed no one hiding.

Bethany Anne's sense of ADAM grew slightly stronger as the ship neared the largest dome.

TOM, can you feel that?

Um, no. I am rather busy trying to work out what the hell is going on with your chip. What is it you want me to feel?

Bethany Anne almost growled in frustration. *ADAM, of course. I can* almost *locate him, but the energy is shifting too much for me to pin him down.* Bethany Anne almost lost her balance when her skull briefly felt as though someone had driven an icepick into it. *What the fuck was* that?

I'm sorry. I loosened my hold on your nervous system to see if I could sense him too.

Did you?

No, but then I didn't dare leave your chip unattended for long enough to really try.

Bethany Anne rubbed the base of her skull. *Yeah, don't do that again until you've fixed the problem. Has the issue gotten that much worse? Am I in danger?*

I'm still not sure what the problem is, but it's within my control. As for the cause, I would hazard a guess that it has something to do with ADAM being absent for so long.

Then we'd better get him back. She opened a large drawer and began attaching the contents to her armor's utility belt.

Are you expecting to need grenades?

Bethany Anne shrugged. *Better to have them and not*

need them than need them and not have them. She added a few other bits and pieces before taking a shortcut through the Etheric back to the bridge.

Michael and the children arrived a few minutes after Bethany Anne stepped out of her transfer area.

"I can sense ADAM," Bethany Anne informed them. "He's somewhere inside the main dome."

She turned her attention to the children as Izanami brought the ship in to land inside the largest dome. "Pay close attention. We are allowing you to leave the ship. This is not a game scenario. You are part of a working team, and your actions will have real repercussions. I want to see you making good decisions, just like we trained you for. Okay?"

Alexis and Gabriel nodded and chorused, "Yes, Mom."

Bethany Anne's face was soft although her tone was hard. "K'aia, you want to earn your place here?"

K'aia nodded fiercely. "I came here to serve *you*, whether you want to be an Empress, a Queen, or just plain Bethany Anne. But I don't want to stay if you have no use for me. I won't be kept out of pity."

Michael snorted. "What did I tell you?"

Bethany Anne raised an eyebrow at Michael, then turned back to K'aia with her million-watt smile. "That suits me perfectly. You are now Alexis and Gabriel's shadow. Swear to protect my children and you will have a home with us for as long as you want one."

K'aia's eyes widened. "Seriously? That's *all*? I'd do that anyway." She shuffled her back legs slightly and looked at the twins. "That's if you want me?"

Alexis paused the happy dance she was doing around

the bridge and put her hands on her hips. "Of *course* we want you! Does the dancing not speak for itself?"

K'aia shrugged, abashed. "I wasn't sure what you were doing, honestly."

"I thought you were having a seizure, Sis," Gabriel offered less than helpfully. He walked over to K'aia and gave her a brotherly punch in the arm. "Welcome to the family."

Bethany Anne's eyes sparkled a little, seeing a possible future for the three of them as a force to be reckoned with.

They grow up so quickly these days, Michael deadpanned.

Bethany Anne made sure he heard her groan. **What are you now, the font of all dad jokes?**

Michael grinned. *If it annoys you, my love? I'll get to studying.*

Not if I murder you in your sleep first, she replied.

She gave the children another moment before herding them toward the elevator. Michael snickered every now and again on the elevator ride down.

Bethany Anne shook her head, refusing to give him an opening to bombard her with bad puns.

Izanami's avatar was waiting for them at the ramp. Her aura flickered green/blue. "There are no life signs in this area, human or otherwise. Neither can I find any trace of ADAM, although there are strange readings coming from an alley nearby."

Bethany Anne reached out with her mind. ADAM's presence was the strongest it had been since he'd cut out. "I can find ADAM. Keep us covered."

Michael sidestepped Bethany Anne before she could

leave the ship first. "I will check to ensure it's safe for you and the children."

"Is that necessary?" Bethany Anne asked impatiently. "Izanami has already confirmed that it's safe."

Michael shook his head. "I *don't care.* I want to see for myself."

Bethany Anne and the children exited the ship once Michael was satisfied there were no hidden threats.

Bethany Anne strode down the ramp and looked around. "If this is the place ADAM vanished, where is his scout ship?" She headed into the alley and looked around as if expecting to see it appear from behind one of the dumpsters.

A slightly cleaner patch on the wall in the gap between two of the dumpsters caught Bethany Anne's eye. She stood back to get a better view and saw the scorch marks around the clean spot.

She looked over her shoulder at the mouth of the alley. *Izanami, what did you mean by strange readings from this alley?*

Izanami answered instantly. *The signature was from Gate energy. I only mentioned it because it was unexpected. I deduced it to be a false reading since this part of Loralei's logs were indecipherable.*

Bethany Anne waved Michael and the children over. *Check again. You may have been right the first time.*

There was a pause from the AI. *There is residual Gate energy here, but it's mixed with Etheric energy.*

He made a Gate to the Etheric? Why?

The reason is unclear, but the evidence leans toward that conclusion, yes.

Bethany Anne was looking at the evidence with her own eyes, but she still didn't quite believe it. *Is it even possible to create a Gate on a planet without causing an earthquake or something equally detrimental?*

It would appear so, Izanami replied. *I, however, lack the ability to travel between realms. I must wait here for your return, my Queen.*

Michael came to stand beside Bethany Anne, spotting the anomaly immediately. Alexis also noticed the scorch marks and diverted to run a finger over the blackened brickwork. "What *happened* here, Mom?"

Bethany Anne explained in a nutshell. "It looks like ADAM made a Gate to the Etheric and went through it."

Michael regarded the place ADAM had entered the Gate, his posture betraying his concern. "Excellent. Then we can find out why he expended the energy to take the missing dumpster with him."

16

The Etheric

Bethany Anne and Michael dropped Alexis and Gabriel's hands once they were on somewhat solid ground.

The twins let go of K'aia, breaking the circle completely.

K'aia turned around unsteadily to take in the strange new environment. She batted at a tendril of mist that was tickling her face. "What *is* this place?"

Bethany Anne left Michael and the twins to explain. She took a few steps away and paused to search the mists for any sign of the scout ship. *ADAM!*

Her heart rate spiked when there was no reply.

Bethany Anne, you need to take it down a few levels.

Bethany Anne didn't hear TOM.

Michael saw Bethany Anne walk away, and her posture made it clear she was on the hunt.

He had expected to find the dumpster and ADAM's ship immediately on entering the Etheric. Since neither were in sight, and he sensed other minds in the near distance, he could only deduce that there had been an attack and ADAM had acted to save lives.

Michael understood his wife's distress. However, emotion was not his driving factor, and there was more at stake.

He turned to the children. "There are people here. You three will find them and return to this point in the speediest manner possible. Stay together, and be ready for anything."

K'aia's bewilderment was no less than it had been when they arrived. "What *kind* of anything?"

"Nothing to worry about," Gabriel teased. "Just don't wander off."

"It is perfectly safe for you to look around," Alexis told the nervous Yollin. She threw a glare Gabriel's way. "We're all fitted with trackers, and you have limited access to Phyrro to guide you if you get lost."

"Remember that you have an objective," Michael chided. "There are people relying on the three of you. Look for the dumpster, since they will most likely be too afraid to go too far from it."

Alexis tilted her head. "What about you and Mom?"

Michael indicated Bethany Anne, who was now some distance away. "We're going to search for ADAM's ship. Gabriel, you are team leader."

Alexis made a face. "Why Gabriel?"

Michael's lips pressed together. "Because the team will be relying on you to locate the people you are searching for." He nodded in the opposite direction from the one Bethany Anne had taken. "Good luck, and if you get into any trouble, we are only a few moments away."

Alexis, Gabriel, and K'aia looked at each other after Michael headed out.

K'aia was first to speak. "So where do we find these people?"

Gabriel looked at Alexis. "I can sense them, but only generally."

Alexis pointed and set off in the direction Michael had indicated. "This way." She chatted as they walked, passing on what she knew about the realm to K'aia. "Things can get weird here. Like, if you see a storm, go the opposite way."

Gabriel nodded. "Oh, yeah. But it's calm enough right now."

K'aia looked at the swirling mists skeptically. "It doesn't look very calm. Let's just get these people to safety. I don't like it here."

Alexis paused at the revelation. "Really? I love it in the Etheric. It's so peaceful just to be here and feel the energy currents wash around."

K'aia waved her hands. "Yeah but you're all, like, powered by this place."

"If you're sticking around, Mom will probably have you go in for more enhancement," Gabriel pointed out. "Then you'll be 'powered' by the Etheric, too."

They got back to walking while K'aia chewed that over.

She was distracted from trying to decide how she felt about being given that responsibility when a dark shape materialized out of the rolling mists. "Is that the dumpster?"

They edged a little closer.

Alexis eyed the dimensions. "It looks to be the same size as the space in the alley."

Gabriel wrinkled his nose. "Ugh, it smells. I'm going to take a guess and say we found it."

K'aia tilted her head. "I hear voices. Are they singing?"

"It's a pretty big group, and yes, they are singing," Alexis confirmed. "Weird. We should get closer so I can work out how many there are."

"Wait." Gabriel held an arm out to stop Alexis from rushing over. "Call first. We might scare them."

Alexis nodded, seeing the sense in her brother's reasoning. They approached carefully, keeping their senses peeled. "Hello?" she called. "Is there anyone here who needs help?"

The chorus in the dumpster cut out immediately.

"It's okay," Alexis continued. "We came to get you out of here."

A tremulous voice called from inside. "We're dead... aren't we? Have you come to take us on to the next place?"

A child began to cry, and there was an angry murmur among the others before the singing started up again.

K'aia's mandibles clicked quietly. "There are infants in there."

Gabriel nodded somberly. "I can feel their confusion and fear."

"That can be dangerous," K'aia told them. "People make bad decisions when they're scared. I saw it in the mines, although sometimes I was able to help."

Alexis raised an eyebrow. "How do we help these people? If Mom was here, they'd see her and feel safe."

Gabriel nodded. "K'aia, what did you do to help people in the mine?"

She shrugged. "Mostly just talked to them when the

guards weren't watching. Let them know they weren't alone."

Gabriel scrunched his nose. "It seems too simple, but it's worth a try." He walked over and tapped on the side of the dumpster. "Hello? You're not dead, you were brought into another dimension to save your lives by our AI friend. We came to rescue you all."

"Do you think you could come out of there?" Alexis added hopefully.

There was a shuffle, and the lid rose a fraction. A hammy-looking man looked out at the three of them. His eyes widened in surprise when he saw Alexis and Gabriel. "You're just kids. How did you get here?"

Gabriel gave the man a friendly smile. "We came with our parents. What say we get you all out of there so we can go back to the outpost?"

A child screamed inside the dumpster. "No! There's monsters!"

Gabriel held out his hands, his voice projecting complete calm and assurance. "Our parents took care of the Ooken who attacked the outpost. It's safe, I promise."

The dumpster lid rolled back, pushed open by five of the occupants.

A woman straightened up to get a look at them. She narrowed her eyes at Alexis. "You look familiar... But we can't leave. We have children and elderly. What if we end up walking around in circles in that mist until we die?"

Gabriel reached up and touched the woman's hand. "I promise that won't happen. Our parents are a short walk away from here, and they will take you back."

The people in the dumpster murmured among themselves for a few minutes, then the man who had spoken first nodded. "Okay." He looked to figure out a way to get his leg over. "We believe you." He muttered before throwing a leg up, just missing another person. "My nose might be dead now."

Gabriel's smile was pure sunshine. "Great. Let's get you all out of there so we can get going."

K'aia held out her arms. "Here, pass me anyone who needs help."

It took a short while to get everyone out, but they were finally all assembled in front of the dumpster and ready to leave. They went slowly to accommodate the elderly woman, who bitched merrily the entire way about not having had rejuvenation therapy before she left the *Meredith Reynolds* to survey the rings.

Alexis glanced at her brother as she moved to help a young girl who had wandered out in front of them. *When did you work out how to do that on purpose?*

How to do what? Gabriel asked.

Persuade people to do what you want, Alexis clarified. *You didn't do it on purpose?*

No, Gabriel replied. *I just really wanted them to not be scared anymore so we could get them to Mom and Dad.*

Alexis continued walking, turning Gabriel's words over.

Michael walked beside Bethany Anne, blind to the mental scent she had been tracking since they'd parted with the children. His focus was on monitoring Alexis, Gabriel, and

K'aia. *Have you still got a lock on ADAM?*

She looked at him with frustration creasing her perfect features. *Yes, but it feels wrong—like there's too much of him.*

TOM interjected, **What you are feeling is the main portion of ADAM's brain.**

The yucky bit that we agreed not to talk about ever?

Well, yes.

Then how—

Bethany Anne interrupted Michael as she was hit by a massive spike in her pain level. She clapped a hand to the base of her skull, stumbling a step before she recovered her balance.

Michael had a steadying arm around her waist in an instant. *What happened?*

Bethany Anne brushed his concern off with a wave. *A headache,* she told him. *TOM is supposed to be keeping it under control.*

TOM's concern came through clearly to both of them. **Sorry, I let go to block the Kurtherian brain so you can focus on the chip in his scout ship.**

Michael frowned. *This is what is causing your headache?*

Mmhmm. Bethany Anne rubbed the back of her neck as the pain ebbed. *Can we get your shit together, TOM? How am I supposed to find anything when my brain feels like it's being constricted by barbed wire?*

Working on it. There was a pause. **And?**

A grin lit Bethany Anne's face as she turned slightly to her right. *It's gone, and now I know where ADAM's ship is.*

Michael held out a hand. *Lead the way, my love.*

Bethany Anne took his hand, and they ran through the mists until the scout ship came into sight. She was at the scorched scout ship almost before Michael noticed she'd dropped his hand.

ADAM!

>>Bethany Anne?<<

Bethany Anne felt a rush of relief when she heard ADAM speak. *You're okay. What the fuck were you thinking?*

TOM interjected on ADAM's behalf. **How is your head, Bethany Anne?**

She frowned. *Still good. Why?*

>>You were in pain?<< ADAM sounded regretful. >>That was probably my fault. I've had a bitch of a time since I got here trying to get hold of you, but something blocked me at every turn.<<

Michael turned to Bethany Anne with an icy look she knew was *all* for TOM.

She shrugged. *It's done now. ADAM is back inside my head where he belongs. No more mysterious headaches. I will think of a suitable way to thank TOM when we get back to the* Izanami.

ADAM's laughter echoed over his backdoor link to TOM. >>Trust you to land yourself in the firing line trying to get *me* out of it.<<

TOM, for his part, was mysteriously quiet.

Bethany Anne waved at the ship, and it rose a short way off the ground. *I think Jean might actually attempt murder if I leave this one behind.*

Michael turned to her, his eyes slightly unfocused. *The children were successful. They have around twenty people with them who are in need of a ride home.*

Bethany Anne laughed aloud as she set off, determination in her stride. *Queen Bitch's inter-realm taxi service coming right up.*

Federation Deep Space Research Outpost, QBS *Izanami*

The *ArchAngel II* Gated in within a few minutes of Bethany Anne requesting pickup for the rescued people.

Admiral Thomas came aboard the *Izanami* to supervise the transfer of the traumatized researchers and their families personally.

Bethany Anne took him to one side once they were aboard the transfer Pod. "You need to make sure that they all receive Pod-doc treatment." *ADAM, your job is to make sure not a one of them remembers seeing me, Michael, or the children—and* especially *not even a hint of the Etheric.*

>>**Got it.**<<

And don't disappear this time.

>>**Will I have to say it a million times? I'm sorry.**<<

Bethany Anne relented at the sincerity in his voice, but not much. *Just don't make me have to come and search for your ass. I swear I'll find a way to beat it if you ever scare me like that again.*

Admiral Thomas shuffled beside her, eager to get the rescued people on their way to the *Helena*, from which they could be transferred back to Yoll. He looked at her. "You still plan to follow the trail of the Leath ship?"

Bethany Anne nodded. "Yes. Izanami has been tracking Loralei since she left to follow them. She came out near our seventh location. I want the superdreadnoughts ready to Gate in at short notice." She made a face at his fidgeting and waved him off, shaking her head. "Go. I can see you're itching to leave. We're heading for location seven as soon as you've gotten through your Gate."

"Then I won't keep you a moment longer." Admiral Thomas walked off, turning back to raise his hands in a wide shrug. "What can I say? The shit has hit the fan."

Bethany Anne snorted. "You can relax. The shit might be adjacent to the fan, but it hasn't hit *just* yet."

17

Ooken location, Municipal Center

Akio fended off multiple tentacles as well as the blades the Ooken he was fighting wielded in its hands. He noted that John was in some trouble, but not enough for him to intercede just yet.

All teams, you can relax. Bethany Anne has recovered ADAM, along with a number of survivors.

John did not relax when the Admiral's update came over the comm.

Relaxing would, in fact, have been the worst thing he could have done, since an Ooken guard had a tentacle around his neck and it was getting tighter by the second. "You," he grunted, "are a monumental *ass.*"

The announcement had nevertheless had the positive effect of cutting through the last vestiges of the grip his opponent was attempting to put on John's mind, freeing him to concentrate on the physical aspects of the fight.

Anything that prevented him from becoming some Ooken's midnight munchie was good in John's book.

It took only a second to assess just how far up Shit Creek he'd found himself. His arms were pinned to his sides by the same tentacle, prohibiting him from ripping the fucking thing off and using it to give the sneaky bastard a taste of its own medicine.

The wishful thought, however, led to an idea. It wasn't an idea he was proud of by any stretch, but Akio had his hands full with his own guard.

"I'm John-fucking-Grimes, you fetid beaked sack of dried foreskin!"

John leaned forward, then smashed the back of his helmet into the Ooken's beak, stunning it before it had a chance to change tactics. "Mind-fucking still needs permission, asshole!"

As he felt the impact, he instructed the faceplate of his armor to open. He didn't think about what he had to do next, just sank his teeth into the tentacle and tore a huge chunk of the meat away.

Akio finished with his guard and happened to glance over at the exact moment John spat out the chunk of tentacle along with a globby spray of Ooken blood. *Really? You could have just called.*

The Ooken screeched in rage and pain, then redoubled its effort to drag John into its waiting jaws.

"Hey! No smooches!"

John jerked his head back when one of the Ooken's suckers caught his face. "I'll eat *you* before you ever get a taste of me!" he roared as the burning line over his left eye healed.

He broke through the tentacle with another bite and flexed his chest to make room to free his arms. *"Definitely does* not *taste like chicken!"* he bitched, spitting out a stray scrap of meat as he took a couple of steps to give himself room to work.

I would have thought it would have a distinct sushi flavor, Akio retorted with a glib smile. He jogged up the stairs toward the entrance. Ika, *perhaps.*

John chuckled as he pivoted and drove a fist into the Ooken's open beak. *Fuckers haven't got a single redeeming quality. They don't even have the decency to taste nice when they're forcing you to bite them.*

His punch broke through the Ooken's delicate soft palate and went straight into its brain.

He tried not to gag when the Ooken collapsed and its brain fluids ran down his forearm. *Not that cannibalism should be a thing, but we're fucking delicious. At least if a human gets eaten, they don't give the fucker who ate them indigestion.*

Akio thanked the stars he hadn't eaten yet that day. His lip curled at the mess. *How did it even get hold of you?*

John pulled his fist free of the dead Ooken, grimacing at the brain matter coating his armored glove. *Damn thing suckered me while I was taking care of the first one. Maybe Scott's tinfoil hat joke wasn't such a stupid idea.* He wiped it off and headed up the last few steps with Akio close behind.

He flung a last bit of mucus-y gunk at the wall where it made a *splunk* sound and grabbed his two corpses. "Okay, that's just nasty. Let's get these hidden and get inside before the Ooken get here."

Akio nodded, dragging the remains of his guard into cover. "I can hear them, they are aware of the deaths of these three."

John grunted, pulling the door open. "It's not news."

There was no one inside the administration build-ing,which was closed for the night, exactly how they'd planned it. They crossed the high-ceilinged atrium and hopped the counter to access the back of the building.

The first floor had nothing but meeting rooms. They headed up to the second floor and found more of the same. The door at the top of the next stairwell opened into a corridor going left to right.

Akio regarded the corridor with a look of utter disdain. *How wonderful...yet another identical corridor.*

John indicated the left-hand side to Akio. *Quick search. It has to be on this floor. When you find anything that looks like the records room, call. I'll do the same.*

Akio made his way to the nearest door, the ghost of a smile touching his lips. *How much would you like to bet that he did it?*

John considered it while he stopped to try one door that looked out of place. *Scott's tinfoil hat? Sure, I'll take that bet. Don't forget who he's partnered with. Eve would tear him to shreds and share the photos with everyone—including Cheryl Lynn.*

The nondescript door was locked. He would have dismissed it as another supply closet if not for the box at chest height on the wall beside it.

He looked over his shoulder at Akio. *Check this out. It looks like I just found our target. This door has a biometric lock.*

He looked at it, his eyebrows narrowing... "Ahhhh Shit." He turned towards Akio. *"Are any of those furry meatbags out there still intact enough that we can use them to open it?*

Akio was by his side a moment later. He bent to inspect the blank display. *I believe they may be beyond the ability to open it in any case. If the lock is biometric, where is the scanner?*

John's grin dropped away. *Well, damn. It's going to work by telepathy or some shit, isn't it? Can you trick it into recognizing you?*

Akio frowned in concentration for a few moments. *No, and we don't have long. Our clock started counting down with the first Ooken you killed.*

John grunted and shrugged. *Yeah, well, it's not as if we left a trail for them to follow. It's just the three out front. We should have a little while at least before they work out where we are.* He took a step back and examined the door when something tripped his subconscious.

Can you feel that around the door?

Akio tilted his head and surveyed the door. He felt the disturbance in the electrical field John had picked up. *It's alarmed,* he confirmed, and his eyes traveled around the door. *It goes in an unbroken line around the entry, so how do we get in without alerting the Ooken to our precise location?*

John stared at the door for a moment, then grinned and took another two steps back, then a couple to the right. *What do you think?* He nodded at a panel on the wall in front of him.

Akio made a face. *I think another half-step to be sure, and don't hold back.*

John raised an eyebrow. *Why would I do that?* He inclined his head and shuffled back more, now almost touching the wall behind him. *Good?*

Akio nodded, folding his arms. *I will be judging you for style.*

John chuckled. *Challenge accepted.*

He took two steps forward and spun precisely on one foot, twisting his hips as he brought up the other foot and stomped his armored boot into the panel. The composite the panel was made from buckled under the force of John's kick, sending a shudder through the wall.

Akio made a noncommittal noise.

John held up a finger. *Wait for it...* A moment later the panel fell forward, spilling a heap of crumbled insulation out onto the corridor floor. He swept a hand toward the hole he'd made. *One alternative entrance.*

Akio see-sawed his hand. *Almost. There's still the panel on the other side to get through. I'll give you a nine and a half, since it was excellent work in a confined space.*

John frowned. *Only nine and a half?*

Akio shrugged. *Your hip flexion was a half a degree less than it could have been during the wind-up. You lost power because of it.*

There was a moment's pause from John, who shook his head. *Damn, that's exacting. Did you learn how to critique from BA? Want some push-ups out of me?* John filed the tip away for later and looked through the hole he'd made. He turned back to Akio. *I'm kidding. I can always improve. Still, I'd like to see you make that kick—*

Akio turned a perfect rotation on the spot, his foot meeting the exact center of the remaining obstacle to their entry. The composite came away from the wall in one piece and flew into the room beyond, bouncing off of something. Sickly artificial light shone through from the other side.

John nodded in appreciation as the panel came to a

spinning stop. He gestured for Akio to go through first. *It's not cocky if you can do it.*

Akio ducked through the hole and went a few steps in before turning back to John. *It's all in the hips.* He chuckled. *You just have to be flexible.*

John grinned. *Ask my wife. She'll tell you I'm plenty flexible.* He raised an eyebrow and gyrated his pelvis a couple of times to accentuate his point.

Akio snorted, turning to get a look around the room they were in. *Of course, I'll get right on that, just as soon as I put my affairs in order and make my final wishes known.* He walked over to a door and looked inside. *Servers.*

John lifted a shoulder. *I'd say that was a wise decision on your part.*

He was only half-listening to Akio, his attention drawn to the computer on the solitary desk in the empty room.

He sat down at the desk and waved his hands over the computer in the extremely slim hope it would boot up, but nothing happened. *I'm going out on a limb here*, he sent Akio as he wiped his hand on the desk. *But this looks like more tech you need to be psychic and an Ooken to use. Can you imagine being the Ooken who had to sit in here every day to maintain all this?*

Akio came over to the desk and looked over John's shoulder. *This is definitely what Bethany Anne wanted us to find. Want to call in tech support and get started?*

John nodded and opened the comm link. *Admiral?*

Admiral Thomas' familiar voice answered. *Good to hear from you.*

You too, Admiral, Akio replied congenially.

John grunted. *Same here. If that completes the greeting*

portion of the conversation, we made it to our target with minimal disturbance. Are you ready to receive the data?

Is this the score we'd hoped for? the Admiral asked, choosing not to mention that John's start to a conversation was just as abrupt as Bethany Anne's these days.

John grinned, although Admiral Thomas couldn't see it. *How does a room full of servers ripe for the copying sound?*

Sounds damn good, John, Admiral Thomas replied, instantly forgetting his grumpiness. *I won't lie. Any clue about what you have there?*

None whatsoever, Akio told him, passing John an open case containing a toolkit and a number of small black disks, each no bigger than half a fingernail.

John ignored the toolkit and pried apart the computer casing with his bare hands. He treated the tiny disk with much more care, inserting it carefully into the computer's inner workings before he spoke again. *ADAM's device is inside the computer. Are you ready to receive?*

Admiral Thomas sounded like a kid on Christmas morning. *Hit me.*

Former Ooken Territory, SD *Atalanta,* Admiral's Office

Admiral Thomas stood in front of the war board, his eyes skipping from feed to feed. There was action across the board, enough that he was hard-pressed to keep up with everything that was happening on the Ooken worlds.

They owned everything between QT2 and location three, but the word had gotten out and the Ooken were beginning to fight back.

Of course, it was too little, too late. The Ooken had

signed their death warrants the very first time they committed a heinous act in the name of their advancement.

It had just taken this long for someone strong enough to come along and enforce it, and Bethany Anne wasn't one to fuck around.

Both minor locations had been taken care of. John and Akio had hit the jackpot at their second target. Now they were headed over to give Gabrielle and Eric support, and the superdreadnoughts had Gated in and begun the bombardment of the colony as they were leaving.

Early progress was looking good, despite the setback Bethany Anne and Michael had with the Leath. He was glad about the progress since the unfolding intelligence was revealing the bigger picture to be more complex with every new report he received.

The information pouring in from the teams was at once revealing and horrifying. It wasn't just technology the Ooken had stolen. The third location and the surrounding area of space had originally belonged to another species, the Moen.

This species were so damned submissive the Ooken had, in essence, showed up on their doorstep one day demanding to be served, and the Moen had rolled over to show their bellies and thanked their new overlords for the privilege.

Definitely not a typical human response.

Scott and Eve had sent this in from the first place they'd hit at location three. The issues the scout ship EIs had come up against were no obstacle to Eve. They had uploaded from two locations so far.

Admiral Thomas was waiting to hear that they'd reached the other information repository the largest colony possessed.

He didn't need to speak to Bethany Anne to know how she was going to react to what they'd learned once she checked in.

He sighed aloud. "You are dead bastards. You just need to get with the program."

Location Seven, QBS *Izanami*

Bethany Anne waited on the bridge while Izanami brought the ship in relatively close to Loralei's locator beacon and messaged the EI. She had her couch in the upright position and her eyes on the screen with a live feed to the ship bay Loralei was headed toward.

The scout ship slid silently through the translucent barrier. "Give me audio to the bay, Izanami." She paused a beat for Izanami to comply. "Good job, Loralei. Where have they taken our kidnapped Leath?"

Loralei's ship came to a soft stop. "I've already sent my logs to Izanami, my Queen. She reminded me there are, and I quote, 'children on board who don't need to hear my dirty mouth.'"

Bethany Anne smirked. "My children are not here right now, Loralei. Go ahead, but keep it short and sweet."

"Okay, then." The EI laid it out in the simplest terms. "Izanami told me to go after the Leath ship, so I followed them through the Gate. The Ooken didn't catch me, so I kept on after them. They took the Leath ship to the coordinates I gave Izanami. That's all I know, because there are three of those huge fucking ships guarding the colony, so I hid my ass and waited for you to send someone for me."

Bethany Anne wasn't worried. Izanami could get in and out without being detected. The question was, could she and Michael do the same? She was definitely making the children remain aboard this time.

Her fingers began tapping as she considered her options. "Well, fuck. This is a complication I hadn't counted on."

Michael stepped out of the elevator just as she spoke. "What complication?"

Bethany Anne turned in her seat. "Three Ooken dreadnoughts between the Leath we came here to liberate and us. Not a problem."

"Of course not." Michael smiled warmly as he took his couch. "Our dreadnoughts are *much* bigger than their dreadnoughts."

"This is not a size comparison," Izanami retorted. "You can have a heavy hitter in a small ship."

Michael snorted. "Check your databanks. It is *ALWAYS* about size."

18

Devon, QBBS *Guardian*, Station Commander's Office

"Tim, are you listening?"

Tim snapped out of his daydream and focused on the holoscreen. "Sorry, babe, you just got me thinking for a moment then." Sabine gave him the Look—the one that made him squirm in his seat. "Babe, can you not look so mad? It's not helping."

Sabine sighed, and her cute frown vanished. "As if I could be mad at you for long. Did you hear what I said?"

Tim flashed a grin. "I *was* listening..." He racked his brain to see if he could shake loose what Sabine had been telling him while he'd been imagining the various ways they could have fun with a few sets of zip ties and a large pot of Yollin honey and almost got lost in the daydream all over again.

"Tim!" Sabine waved her hands to bring him back. "You have no idea, do you?"

He hung his head and held up his hands. "You're right, I

wasn't listening," he admitted. "But in my defense, you totally distracted me."

Sabine chuckled, her blue eyes sparkling. "I was just wishing you luck for your meeting with Peter. I will see you tomorrow, no?"

Her eyebrow quirked a bit and Tim's concentration almost went again. "With bells on."

Sabine giggled. "Now, *that* I would love to see."

The screen went dark, and Tim sat there for a few minutes to shake off the dazed feeling Sabine always left him with. That woman was a witch; he was sure of it.

CEREBRO pinged the speaker on Tim's desk, dragging him reluctantly back to reality. "What's up?"

One of CEREBRO's more businesslike voices came from the speaker. "The *Achronyx* is due to arrive at dock zero-zero-one within the next half-hour. Commander Silvers has just filed the flight plan with us."

Tim pushed his chair back, getting to his feet. "Shit!" He grabbed his jacket from the hook by the door and slid his arms into the sleeves. "He's getting here early?"

"He asked us to inform you that he will be taking a walk around the station before your meeting."

"Thanks, CEREBRO." Tim headed out the door, opening a link to Rickie and Joel. *Guys, Peter got here early, and it looks like he's here for more than discussing this month's rotation. Please tell me we're ready for the surprise inspection he's calling a "walk."*

Oh, sure, Rickie deadpanned. *I'll just run around and close up all the drug dens and brothels we got running all over the station before Peter notices them. Shit, Tim. Chill.*

Joel cut in, *Shut it, Rickie. We're good, boss. That's the old*

Tim talking. You've got everything under control. I'm even looking forward to giving my report on the teams.

Tim waited for CEREBRO to open the elevator door and stepped in. *I know. Hell, I'm impressed at how effectively the system is working.*

Joel's enthusiasm was contagious.

Rickie didn't *need* any extra pep. *It just makes too much sense to steer the adventure seekers toward the fight they're looking for.*

The inspection isn't a problem, Joel continued, *Peter is fair. It could be much worse; we could be getting a visit from the Admiral's wife.*

Tim shuddered, remembering Mrs. Foxton-Thomas' last visit to the station. *We should count ourselves lucky. She's almost as demanding as the Queen.*

Rickie's reply was laced with admiration. *Yeah, but she's shit-hot at recruiting all the unruly assholes who turn up here into the Navy.*

The elevator opened, and Tim spotted a pair of those same assholes getting into it in a seating area by the vending machines.

He ground his teeth when he saw the damage they'd caused with their petty drama and strode over. "What's going on here?" he demanded, grabbing the two young men by their hair to pull them apart.

They struggled until they saw who had hold of them. Then they went pale, recognizing Tim's face from the orientation video.

Tim released the pair of them once he was satisfied they'd calmed down.

They glared at each other, and each of the Weres began accusing the other at the same time.

Tim folded his arms across his chest. *"Enough!"* he roared at the young Weres. "This is a battle station, not the Wild fucking West. Whatever the hell you two are fighting over, I don't care. It's done."

He pointed around at the vending machine guts strewn about. "Both of you will clean up this fucking disrespect you showed my station and then report to maintenance. You can spend the rest of the day there as an apology for the mess you caused here."

He pointed vaguely at the ceiling, seeing the stubborn looks they were trying to hide. "CEREBRO will inform me if you fail to arrive, and I'll have you shipped straight back to the Federation. Now, get started before I change my mind about giving you a chance to readjust your damned mindset."

He shook his head in disappointment and turned his back as the two young men scrambled for the spilled contents of the broken vending machine, cursing each other for the dirty work they'd been given.

Tim shook his head. "Fuckin' clownshoes. What, am I a bouncer in an officer's uniform?" He continued to the dock, bitching under his breath that the pain in his ass testosterone-fueled shenanigans like that caused was supposed to be a thing of the past.

As intimidating as he found the Admiral's wife, the prospect of her visit always became somewhat more attractive when the order he worked to maintain was upset by an overabundance of assholes aboard the station.

Peter had just disembarked when Tim arrived at the

VIP dock. He met Tim with a back-slapping bearhug. "Long time, dude. Long time."

Tim nodded as he returned the hug. "I know, right? It's good to see you. I was sorry to miss you when you picked Sabine up on your way down to the city."

Peter waved him off. "Nah, we were only here a few minutes. It had been a big day for Todd already."

"Sabine has told me enough that I feel like I've met the kid already." Tim's voice softened. "It's great that you honored Todd that way. I know how much his death hurt you."

Peter nodded. "It hurt us all. But I didn't name our son, Tabitha did."

Tim let out a low whistle. "Wow, that must have meant a lot to you. You guys were always the tightest."

Peter grinned. "Which is why it's the perfect name for our son." He swept a hand to ask Tim to show him the way. "Let's get this tour done and dusted so we can catch up for a spell."

Devon, First City, The Hexagon, Penthouse Apartment

Peter crept through the door so as not to wake Tabitha or Todd.

The after-meeting catch-up with Tim, Rickie, and Joel had run for a few hours longer than expected. It was good to be working with the guys again, and he was satisfied that they had their end of the Interdiction handled.

What he *really* appreciated was that they were competent enough that he would be able to spend most of his time at the apartment with Tabitha and Todd.

Peter dropped the breakfast he'd picked up on his way home on the kitchen counter and tiptoed into the bedroom. He took a second to appreciate how cute Tabitha looked when she was asleep with the sheets scrunched around her curled-up body before peering in at his sleeping son in the Pod-crib.

He slipped into bed beside Tabitha and nuzzled her neck. "Good morning, beautiful."

"Morning," Tabitha murmured, "or is it still night? I hope to God it's still night." She turned over and pulled the sheets tighter around herself. "Fair warning, Todd slept for a grand total of, like, an hour since you left for the station, so anything that pokes me in the back is likely to get snapped off."

Peter made a pained face and skooched backward. "You get some sleep. I'll take care of Todd's breakfast, then we'll go down to the kids' apartment. Sabine's always happy to get some time with our tiny terror."

Tabitha half-rolled over and pried an eye open to look at Peter. "You're my angel." She blew him a kiss and flopped back over.

Peter took the Pod-crib into the kitchen and hummed to himself as he put Todd's food in the microwave, or whatever the hell they called it. He supposed he should take the time to find out what the correct name was, but it was kind of funny to get everyone to call the magic heat-the-food-up gizmo a microwave instead of the real name.

He snorted softly to himself and got on with preparing the baby's breakfast.

Todd woke as the smell of his breakfast permeated the

kitchen. The side of his Pod-crib became translucent as he pulled himself to a sitting position and cooed at Peter.

Peter walked over to pick him up, glad he'd thought to get in Tabitha's good books by ordering in a bulk consignment of the diapers that worked similarly to the waste disposal system in the old atmosuits. "Hi, buddy! Mommy told me you kept her awake all night." He pressed a soft kiss to Todd's head and deposited him in his high chair. "Something tells me you'll be eating and going back to sleep."

Todd banged the high chair's tray while he babbled an indignant reply.

Peter grinned, making up Todd's side of the conversation as he often did. "Really? You look pretty tired to me." He placed Todd's bowl on the table and took a seat beside the high chair with his own breakfast.

Todd's excitement grew when he smelled the contents of his bowl.

Peter chuckled softly and held out a spoonful of the sausage and tomato baby food. "We won't tell your mom I made this instead of your oats, okay?"

Tabitha strolled down the stairs and blinked sleepily at Peter, rubbing her eyes. "Mommy already knows."

Peter hung his head and grinned ruefully. "Busted. What are you doing up? You should be sleeping."

Tabitha ruffled her bedhead. "Nah, I'm awake. Besides, we have appointments today."

Peter groaned. "What's the point? You haven't liked a single one of the properties we've viewed so far." He made a spaceship out of the next spoonful.

Tabitha bent to kiss Todd on her way to the fridge. "I

feel good about today." She took out the juice and poured herself a glass, leaving the carton on the counter as she sipped.

Peter kept his tone cheerful as he obliged Todd with another spoonful. "That's what you said about the last billion places we looked at." He paused for a moment, looking up as if in thought. "Sorry, I sit corrected. Billion and one."

"Ass." Tabitha placed her glass on the counter next to the open carton and strutted over to the table to drape her arms around Peter's shoulders. "And I'll keep saying it until we find the perfect place. I don't see this war being over and done with anywhere near as quickly as Bethany Anne wants. There are some things even she has no control over, and I kind of like it here. Don't you?"

"I like wherever you are, Tabbie. You know that." Peter turned his head to look at her and Todd knocked the spoon out of his hand. He grabbed a towel to wipe up the mess. "Fast little...fff..iretruck." He dodged the swipe coming in from Tabitha. "But it's not the worst place, if you overlook the crime rate."

Tabitha kissed Peter and released him. "Actually, the crime rate is one of the attractive parts. Think of all the fun we could have reducing it!"

Peter shook his head in disbelief. "Really?"

Tabitha nodded, smiling sweetly over the rim of the glass she'd just retrieved. "Didn't you know? Vigilantism is all the rage these days."

Peter nodded. "Sure, but you hate to follow the crowd. Besides, the teams are doing good work down here. Joel tells me they're part of the scenery now, and some of the outreach services they've set up are starting to get some uptake."

Tabitha narrowed her eyes. "So you're not even going to play along? I'm pleased that the teams are doing well, but wouldn't I look super-cute in a cape?"

Peter shook his head. "Nope." He made a face when he realized what he'd said. "Well, yeah. But if you want some action, why don't you take a few fights downstairs?"

Tabitha's lip curled. "It's not exactly action when you're the walking manifestation of Lady Death and the competition is a bunch of untrained streetfighters. The regulars are a bit more disciplined, but not much."

"Okay..." Peter complied with Todd's demands for another spoonful of his breakfast while he prodded his tired brain for an answer to Tabitha's restlessness. "What if you... I don't know, train some of them? The ones who can take a beating and get up again."

Tabitha grinned and squeezed Peter. "That might not be the worst thing you ever came up with. I could be a modern-day Miyagi, passing on my wisdom to the worthy."

Peter chuckled at the dreamy quality of her voice. "You and your decidedly ungirly obsession with eighties movies."

Tabitha leaned into his ear and whispered, "Can you tell me that you *don't* want to snuggle up and watch *Karate Kid* once Todd goes down for the night?"

Peter groaned, knowing when he was beaten. "No." He opened his mouth to return her teasing, but all that came out was a yawn.

Tabitha took in the luggage he was carrying under his

eyes, the stubble coating his jaw, and his generally wrung-out appearance. "Yeah, I'm going to cancel our appointments for today. Get some sleep. We'll go visit with the kids."

Peter couldn't hide the yawn in his reply. "If you insist, I'm not going to argue."

Tabitha took Todd's bowl from him and bumped him with her hip to get him out of the chair. "Nurse Tabitha says you need sleep. You can tell me about your meeting when you wake up."

Peter stretched and let out another huge yawn. "If I'm a good patient, will I get a house call from Nurse Tabitha?"

Tabitha grinned and shooed him out with Todd's spoon. "Go to bed, and maybe you'll find out later."

Location Seven, QBS *Izanami*, Bridge

Michael lifted a hand to touch Bethany Anne's arm as she paced the space between the couches yet again. *That will not make our window for sneaking through the blockade come around any faster.*

Bethany Anne resisted the brief urge to see if she really *could* shoot lasers from her eyes. *It isn't a secret how I feel about waiting.*

Michael dipped his head in acknowledgment. *It is known, my love. However, we know that the captured Leath are being treated reasonably well for now.*

Bethany Anne snorted. **They're in the middle of a strange planet, exposed to the elements in a fucking pit. How is that being treated well? The Leath are by no means my favorites, but I wouldn't keep them like that.**

Michael raised an eyebrow. *Sweetheart, you're not the taking-prisoners kind. If you had been the one who captured them, they wouldn't be alive to be rescued. Besides, I've seen worse.* He shrugged at the pointed look she gave him. *I didn't say they were comfortable, but they will be fine for a few hours longer until we can get there.*

She sighed and sat down on the edge of his couch. **Okay. It's just that we're so close. Are you sure about leaving the children alone on the ship?**

We will need Addix, or they may refuse to be rescued, Michael qualified. *Many Leath still fear you too much.*

Bethany Anne scowled. **Why do you think I'm still here, fucking waiting? If I didn't think there was a high chance they'd lose their shit at the sight of me, I would have just gone through the Etheric and gotten them already.**

Michael's mouth twitched. *That could very well occur whether Addix and I are present or not.*

Bethany Anne got to her feet. **In that case, there's no reason for me to work myself up about it. In fact, getting in some pre-mission mother-daughter relaxation is a much better use of my time.**

Michael raised an eyebrow. *You're taking Alexis to the spa scenario.*

Bethany Anne looked back as the elevator door opened. **You bet your peachy ass I am. Mama wants a mud pack and a sugar scrub.**

Michael smiled and waved his fingers at her. *That sounds like an excellent idea. I'm sure Gabriel and I will find something to entertain ourselves.*

19

Training and Recreation Scenario: Earth, Mongolia, 1176AD

Gabriel lifted his snowshoe and shook off the drift that had accumulated there. *This is grim, Dad. Did you really stay in a place like this?*

Michael nodded, forging ahead to cut their path into a stand of thin trees through the shin-deep snow. *I traveled most of Earth long before I met your mother. Eve constructed this scenario directly from my memories.*

Gabriel ducked to avoid a shower of snow from an overhead branch as he hurried to keep up with his father. *What's the objective in this scenario?* he inquired.

Not so much an objective, Michael told him, *as an experience to be gained.*

Gabriel looked plaintively at his father. *Is that all you're going to tell me?*

Michael chuckled dryly. *Yes. I want you to reach your own conclusions, not adopt mine without deciding if you agree.*

Gabriel pondered that while they trekked through the

stark frozen environment. A group of winged white creatures burst skyward, startling him into speaking aloud. "What are those?"

Ptarmigan, Michael supplied. *Birds.* A smile touched the corner of his mouth at a memory. *They tasted good wrapped in herbs and leaves and baked underground.*

Of course, he continued, *food always tastes better when you've caught it with your own two hands and the brain in your head. And spiced by hunger.*

Is that why you were so obsessed with the dinosaur that time? Gabriel teased.

Michael fixed his son with a look. *One day you'll understand, son. This experience might just be the first step toward that day.* He lifted a hand to point out a long shadow in the distance. *There, in the shade of the rise. That is our destination.*

The shadow resolved into multiple shadows, then bulky tents on the backs of wagons. Gabriel drank it in. *I've never seen anything like it!* he exclaimed when the light of many small fires appeared as they neared the camp Michael had led them to. *What are those beasts?*

Michael chuckled. *They are steppe ponies. A word of caution: don't breathe too deeply at first. The particular aroma of the nomad clans takes a little bit of time to acclimatize to, thanks to those creatures.*

A gruff voice challenged them from the shadows at the edge of the camp. "Who are you to come to our home?"

Michael called back, "We do not come empty-handed." He reached into thin air and pulled out a pair of jewel-encrusted gold vambraces.

A vast bearded fur-covered man emerged from the shadows belly-first. His dark eyes shone at the sight of the gold and his hostile grimace melted into a wide smile. "Welcome, weary travelers."

Gabriel glanced at the vambraces scornfully as Michael handed them to the hair mountain. *What's the point of those? The first person who wears them into battle is going to lose both their hands.*

It is a cultural thing. Michael shook his head, smiling wryly. *When this scenario occurred for real, I was ignorant of this clan's customs. I made the error of offering my sword as a guest-gift in return for their hospitality.*

Gabriel frowned, missing the point. *Why would that be a mistake? A blade is a more acceptable gift than...*those.

If you insist, go ahead, Michael conceded. *This is* your *experience, after all.*

He reached out again and handed Gabriel the well-made and serviceable but plain sword he manifested. *But I hope your proficiency with that weapon is adequate, since by offering it you are claiming you can best any warrior here.*

Gabriel's normally passive expression shifted when he handed the sword over and the man eyed him skeptically. *It should be interesting. How old were you when you experienced this?*

Michael lifted a shoulder as they walked side by side behind the man through the wagon circle. *Around twenty-seven. I had a good grasp of my powers, such as they were at that stage, but I had little of your training.*

Gabriel grinned at his father. *So I'm probably going to die horribly, but I'll look spectacular doing it.*

Michael lifted his hands, feeling a surge of pride at Gabriel's lack of hesitation. *Who knows? I survived it. The clan fights honorably—mostly. If you do die, I suppose it won't be the worst death you ever have.*

Location Seven, QBS *Izanami*, Vid-doc Room

Addix and K'aia stood facing each other over the Vid-doc made for the four-legged.

"Look. I'm not getting back inside that thing until you tell me why you want me to do it."

The Ixtali was the picture of calm in the face of the young Yollin's mistrust. "I like that you are suspicious, K'aia. It will serve you well in your future role."

K'aia glared at Addix. "What do you know? You're just a nanny."

"At first glance, it may appear so." Addix's mandibles twitched in amusement. "I *have* been taking care of Alexis and Gabriel since they were born, after all. However, I have lived many lives, young one. I may have the honor of protecting my Queen's children, but I have also been her spymistress for more years than I truly recall. Before *that*, I was a highly-placed official in the Ixtali government. Do not be taken in by first appearances."

K'aia dropped her defensive posture. "So you're not just being crazy, then." She settled back and unfolded her arms. "I'm sorry for being such an ass, but would you tell me why you want me to get in there? I only just got out of the damn thing."

Addix nodded. "Good. I was beginning to wonder what it was Michael saw in you. As you so kindly pointed out, Alexis and Gabriel are almost too old to need me around, so it's time to train my replacement. Before we begin,

Bethany Anne has left instructions that you go into the Vid-doc for further enhancement."

K'aia looked at Addix and the Vid-doc. "I don't know. What kind of enhancement?"

Addix smiled. "You've heard of the Bitches, right?"

"Yes. What have they got to do with..." K'aia tilted her head as comprehension dawned. "Oh. *Oh*. Then I guess I'll do it. But I don't want to get out of the Vid-doc and suddenly know what everyone is thinking, okay?"

She climbed in and glanced at the humanoid-shaped Vid-docs as the lid closed over her. "I hope this does not go horribly wrong."

Addix started to assure K'aia that she was perfectly safe, but the Yollin was already under from the sedation. Her mandibles twitched merrily as she input the slide with the single drop of blood Bethany Anne had given her and handed control of the Vid-doc over to Izanami.

The AI appeared by Bethany Anne's Vid-doc. "The process is underway."

"Excellent," Addix replied, walking over to join the AI. She glanced at the wallscreens, one of which had a simple privacy notice.

The other showed an icy white land and a circle of men, with Gabriel locked in a fight for his life in the center.

Addix chuckled at the ferocity with which Michael screamed encouragement to his son from the sidelines while ending anyone dishonorable enough to intercede with his son's battle.

Izanami spoke, pulling Addix from her enthrallment. "Bethany Anne and Alexis are in the rejuvenation cycle."

Addix nodded and went back to watching Gabriel fight.

This was something of a sad time for her, in a way even worse than when her own children had grown up and left her.

Bethany Anne and Michael's children had burrowed their way into her heart from the first time she had laid eyes on them as wriggly pink infants. They had been so helpless then.

Onscreen, Gabriel pulled a maneuver that had him roll over his opponent's back, giving him space to swing the sword and part the man from his head.

They weren't so vulnerable now.

Addix could only hope that this Yollin would be more than the protector the children's parents had decided they needed. Not just a guard, but a friend they could relate to. Someone they could trust and rely on once they were of an age to be on their own.

They were going to need as many of those as they could get, and youth was in short supply in their circle.

Bethany Anne exited her Vid-doc, unnoticed by the pensive Ixtali. She felt the sadness coming from Addix, something she'd noticed more than once in recent days. "Penny for your thoughts?"

Addix turned gracefully to face Bethany Anne. "I think the translation on that needs some work. You want to pay me for thinking?"

Bethany Anne snorted softly. "It means I'm listening. What's on your mind, old friend?"

"Oh." Addix placed a hand on K'aia's Vid-doc. "Gabriel and Alexis. I was ruminating on what path life will take once K'aia is trained and I become surplus to their requirements."

Bethany Anne scrutinized Addix. "Are you thinking of leaving?"

Addix shook her head emphatically. "Not at all. But I think it will take some time to come to terms with this shift in the twins' needs." Her mandibles worked through her mixed emotions as she spoke. "I am proud of them, but human children mature quickly, Bethany Anne. I blinked, and they are almost adults."

Bethany Anne placed a comforting hand on Addix's arm. "You are their aunt, Addix, blood or not. They will always need you in their lives in one way or another."

Addix shrugged with a fatalistic air. "Children grow up. It will be as it is meant to be."

Alexis' Vid-doc completed its unlocking cycle and she climbed out, stretching lazily once her feet were on solid ground. "Mom, we *have* to do that for real when we get back home."

Bethany Anne grinned. "I've been waiting for you to say that. There's this little place on one of my stations we can go that has the *best* masseuse."

She glanced at the wallscreen and did a double-take at the surreal scene of Michael and Gabriel sitting around a campfire with a bunch of... "Are those *Huns* they're eating with?"

Bethany Anne's eyes widened when she saw one of the men pass her battered and bloodied son what looked to be a skin filled with liquid. "Izanami, get them out of there *right now*."

She stood at the end of Michael's Vid-doc with her arms crossed over her chest, her foot tapping an angry staccato while she waited for it to open.

Michael emerged with a look of concern. "Why have you pulled us out? Has something happened with the Leath?"

Bethany Anne pursed her lips. "Please tell me you didn't allow our fourteen-year-old child to drink alcohol?"

Michael furrowed his eyebrows in confusion. "Well, yes —and no. The celebration called for the fermented milk to be consumed, but there was no way for Gabriel to have become intoxicated."

Gabriel fairly erupted from his Vid-doc when it opened. "Mom, Aunt Addix, did you see me? They just kept coming, and I was like," he jumped around reenacting the fight, "and *then* two huge guys that looked like bears tried cutting in and Dad just took them down."

Michael beamed at Gabriel's joy in his victory. "Our son did exceptionally well," he bragged to Bethany Anne. "He defeated seventeen fully-grown warriors one after the other in single combat."

Bethany Anne kissed Gabriel on the forehead. "Well done, honey."

Gabriel scrubbed the kiss away with the back of his hand. "Mom! You've gotta stop doing that. I'm a man now, and men don't get kisses from their moms."

Bethany Anne shared a glance with Michael. "Is that so?"

Gabriel nodded. "It's true. There was a ceremony, and the clansmen told stories of when they became men and sang songs and gave me a gold arm ring."

Alexis pouted. "Sorry, Mom, but I kind of wish I'd done Dad's thing, too. Why can't I be in two places at once?"

Gabriel chuckled. "That's weird, because I would love to be in a hot tub right now."

Bethany Anne smiled and flourished her hands. "There we go; problem solved. Next time we go fight with the Huns together, then we all spa afterward."

Devon, Interdiction

CEREBRO's early warning system registered a series of blips a good way past the outer boundary of the Interdiction.

They enacted the contact protocols immediately, and the alert spread back to the QBBS *Guardian* within just a few seconds.

CEREBRO activated all weapons systems along the projected path of the unidentified objects and waited for their scanners to identify the class of the approaching objects.

The next set of data identified the blips as a tight group of fast-moving bodies.

Enough of the EI group agreed that the bodies were moving too fast to be natural phenomena that they did not preemptively fire upon them.

Space trash could be blown to dust, no problem. Trade convoys, not so much.

There was a return contact from the *Guardian*. "What have we got, CEREBRO?"

"We are uncertain as of yet, Commander Kinley," they replied. "Next set of scans in three, two... Ships, Commander. We have ships. What are your orders?"

Commander Kinley's reply came instantly. "Activate the Interdiction and alert the fleet. I'm on my way."

Tim dropped the connection to CEREBRO and scooted to the edge of the bed. He winced when he woke Sabine getting out of bed despite his efforts to slide out without disturbing her.

"Where are you going, Beefy?" she murmured, her voice husky from sleep. "'Cause if you were planning some kind of eat, fuck, and leave move, then you got it the wrong way around. You're supposed to take me to my place."

Tim pounced back onto the bed and kissed her. "There's something going on at the Interdiction. I would be more than happy if you were still here, exactly like this, when I get back."

Sabine rolled onto her side the second Tim got up. "There's a good chance I will be. It's the middle of the damn night." She fluttered dark lashes at him. "Will you bring breakfast when you get back?"

"Of course, babe." Tim rescued his pants from the bedroom floor and did the dance of getting them on. He headed for the door, shimmying his hips as he went. "I'll even *be* breakfast, if you like."

Sabine giggled and threw a pillow at his retreating back. "You're an ass, Tim."

Tim slapped his rear end as he left the room. "I've got a nice ass? Thanks for noticing." His teasing smile fell away as he heard movement from Sabine before the bedroom door clicked closed behind him.

He opened a mental connection to CEREBRO as he left his quarters. *What's the status out there?*

CEREBRO fed the reports to Tim's internal HUD. *The fleet is still headed toward Devon.*

Tim's jaw dropped when he read through the updates. So much for breakfast. *Shiiit, that's a hell of a lot of ships. Do you know whose they are?*

We count fifty-three, Commander, CEREBRO informed him, *and no, we have not yet been able to identify the fleet's origin, since there are so many different energy signatures. We will know more once the head of the fleet comes into communication range.*

Tim paused walking to re-read the data. *That doesn't match what we know about Ooken ships.*

The probability of the approaching fleet belonging to the Ooken is low, CEREBRO confirmed. *However, we also calculate that the probability of the Ooken being involved is high enough to mention.*

Tim noted something in the report that gave him a better idea of what was going on than the EI group had. *CEREBRO, that's a refugee fleet. Get confirmation before standing the Interdiction down, but this looks like a humanitarian situation to me.*

He dropped the link to CEREBRO and hit Joel and Rickie up.

Rickie was first to answer. *Dude...*

Tim cut across his bitching. *Wake up, jackass. We've got a situation out at the Interdiction.*

Joel sounded half-asleep as well. *What's the situation, big guy?*

Tim messaged Sabine as he got into the elevator,

wishing he had Bethany Anne's ability to just vanish and appear wherever she wanted to be.

I want you both at the docks ten minutes ago. We have an unidentified fleet approaching.

Dammit! Joel cursed softly. *Hostile or friendlies?*

Tim sighed. *Again, we don't know yet, but to me, it looks like a bunch of people fleeing for their lives. Rickie, you're gonna stay here and coordinate the relief effort. Joel, inform the crisis teams that they're needed out there, and scramble the ground teams in the cities to keep things calm.*

Devon, First City, The Hexagon, Commentary Box

Ricole switched on the announcer's mic and leaned in to speak clearly after Captain Holt's all-teams bulletin had finished playing for the second time. "Training's over for the day, people. Instructors, report to the armory, there's a team call."

She stood and glanced out of the box to the arena below, where a rehearsal for the month's acting event was breaking up at her announcement.

Jacqueline pinged her on the team link. *What's going on? I saw the notification while I was on the floor teaching.*

Give me a minute, I'll be right down, Ricole replied. Jacqueline was waiting at the base of the box's stairs when Ricole got there. "Captain Holt has ordered all the ground teams to peacekeeping duty. Except ours. We're to get our asses out to the Interdiction. His instructions are to come loaded for *everything.*"

They headed over to the private elevator and waited for Winstanley to bring the car.

It arrived a whole minute later and contained one battle-ready former Ranger fully armed with a stupidly large plasma rifle and a shit-eating grin. Tabitha waved them in with the rifle. "C'mon. Joel called like, twenty minutes ago. Get your asses suited up and meet me at the *Achronyx*, I've got a couple of babysitters to round up."

20

Devon, First City, The Hexagon, Private Dock

Tabitha brought the Pod-crib to a stop by Hirotoshi and Ryu and bearhugged them both. "Thanks for babysitting your nephew."

"Our pleasure," Hirotoshi wheezed as she squeezed his ribs tightly.

Peter stood at the bottom of the ramp, looking skeptically at Hirotoshi and Ryu. "Are you guys sure you know how to take care of a baby?"

Ryu drew a breath to recover from the hug. "We took care of Tabitha for years and look how well she turned out."

Tabitha rolled her eyes. "Ryu, you're such a dick sometimes. Hirotoshi is now my favorite forever." She laughed at Ryu's indignant protest and headed aboard the ship.

Hirotoshi dipped his head in Peter's direction. "I cannot speak for Ryu, but I had a family once. Todd is safe in our care."

Ryu shrugged. "It can't be so hard, can it?"

Peter looked in on his sleeping son's Pod-crib. "Sorry, it's just hard to leave him with anyone. I appreciate that you volunteered so Tabbie and I could both go help out."

"Pete, come on!" Tabitha yelled from inside the ship.

Ryu grinned and bumped an elbow into Hirotoshi's side. "I do not miss *that*."

Hirotoshi bent to program the Pod-crib to follow him. "I cannot completely agree. It has been my greatest honor to guide and protect our Lady Kemosabe, although it is pleasant to take a more relaxed pace for a while."

"You mean it's nice to eat in places that serve human food while we're traveling," Ryu countered. "My nanocytes thank me for ceasing to test them with toxic alien 'delicacies.'"

Hirotoshi shrugged and turned to leave. "I suppose if you look at it from that perspective…"

Peter waved them off and headed up the ramp.

Tabitha was on the bridge with her feet up on the console and a bag of popcorn in her lap. "Hey, babe."

Peter snagged a handful of the popcorn as he passed her. "You came prepared."

Tabitha snickered and lifted the arm of her captain's chair to reveal a cavity stuffed full of her favorite snacks. "I just dipped into my emergency stash."

He shook his head, chuckling, and took the XO's chair next to hers. "Are we good to go?"

Tabitha looked up. "Achronyx, are we waiting for anyone?"

"Sabine was last to arrive," Achronyx informed her. "Demon got nervous about leaving, so Sabine had to come down to the Hexagon for her."

Tabitha wrinkled her nose. "Poor kitty. They're aboard now though, right?"

"Everyone is aboard," the AI replied. "Sabine and Demon are in the cargo bay you assigned to the cat. Jacqueline, Mark, and Ricole are in the galley making a mess."

Tabitha rolled her eyes. "Kids. They'd better clean up when they're done." She grinned at Peter and clapped her hands. "But if we're all here, take us up to the *Guardian*, Achronyx."

"*As you wish*, Tabitha." There was no mistaking the teasing edge to the AI's voice.

Tabitha raised a hand and gave the finger to the bridge in general. "Screw you, Achronyx."

Peter repressed a snicker as she smiled sweetly and grabbed a handful of popcorn.

Devon, QBBS *Guardian*

Tim maintained a brisk pace, knowing he was cutting it fine to catch his ride. He reached the VIP hangar just as the ground crew was finishing up. He held the door while they pushed their trolleys past into the corridor, then headed over to the *Achronyx*.

Peter was waiting at the top of the ramp for Tim. He raised a hand to hurry Tim, then dropped it again, his attention captured by one of the ground crew. "*Mother-fucker*! Grim'Zee, is that you?"

The two-legged Yollin named Grim'Zee turned and almost dropped the stacked catering trays he was carrying when he saw it was Peter calling. "Peter?" He steadied the trays a little. "Good to see you, my friend!"

Peter waved Tim aboard and jogged down the ramp and over to the Yollin. "What are you doing here? I mean, I get that you decided to be a cook, but I thought you stayed on Yoll?"

Grim glanced down at his chef's whites. "I got bored being in one place, so I decided to work my way around for a while. I just need to finish up here, and we'll catch up a minute."

Tim boarded the ship and made a beeline for Sabine, having no wish to run into Tabitha in case he'd pissed her off being late. He followed the sweet scent of Sabine to a small, clean, cargo bay where he found her getting Demon comfortable.

He tapped on the door as he entered, more out of good manners than for any other reason. "Hey, babe."

Sabine looked over from the crate she was kneeling next to and smiled warmly. "Hey, you made it. I thought Tabitha might leave without you." She finished unpacking Demon's bedding and got to her feet.

"She probably would have, but Peter bumped into someone he knew and bought me a few minutes to get aboard." He walked across the cargo bay and offered his hand for Demon to face-bump or ignore as she wished. "How's my favorite feline today?"

Demon chose to greet Tim this time. *I am excited about the hunt.*

Tim made a face, taking a seat on one of the crates Sabine had arranged to create a cubby for Demon. "You know, I don't think we'll be doing too much fighting today,

Demon. We'll be ready for it, but I'm convinced that these ships are filled with people needing our help."

Sabine lifted her chin, her eyes cold. "We will help them, and then we will find out who made them run and repay them with the same hurt."

Tim shifted on the crate, getting a splinter in his ass for his trouble. He stood and reached around to pull it out from where it had lodged in his pants leg. "Unless a threat comes knocking, we're not going to see any action. I'm just not getting an aggressive vibe from these ships. They're too bunched up to implement any kind of attack."

Demon yawned affectedly, her long tongue overlapping her lower jaw. *You may come to whatever conclusion your inferior senses tell you. There is a fight coming.*

Her tail made one precise swish, and then another. *I can taste it.*

Devon, Interdiction

CEREBRO did not stand the Interdiction down completely. The satellites lay dormant for now, but they were ready to burst into action should CEREBRO command it.

The incoming fleet was within weapons interception distance but was not replying to the message CEREBRO had playing on all known frequencies.

More disturbing was the miscalculation CEREBRO had made when counting the number of ships headed their way. They did not make errors, yet there were only forty-nine ships on the approach.

Commander Kinley spoke. "Status, CEREBRO. We're entering the Interdiction zone. What are we heading into?"

"The fleet is still some distance away," CEREBRO reported. "They have not responded to my hails."

A large gate spiraled into existence in the distance, and the SD *Adrastea* slid out, a shadow of death against the star-pricked backdrop. The *Achronyx* Gated in next, followed by ten more battleships. CEREBRO checked the status reports of each ship as they spread out to form a defensive line.

When they got to the *Achronyx*, they asked nicely.

The fleet as a whole slowed rapidly at the appearance of Devon's defenders, apart from a small group of ships that veered off from the main mass, apparently unwilling to find out what kind of welcome awaited them.

Over on the *Achronyx*, Tabitha waved her arms and yelled at the viewscreen. "Where are they going? There's nothing that way for millions of kilometers except asteroids."

Sabine shrugged. "Maybe they're not the visiting type." Her poor attempt at humor did little to mask the concern she felt. Demon's prediction had stuck with her, and she could not shift the unease that smothered her like an itchy too-big sweater.

Tabitha turned back to the screen showing the mismatched collection of ships. "What are they waiting for?"

Seconds later, one of the splinter group exploded.

Peter jumped to his feet. "What the fuck?"

Tabitha became even more animated. "Tim, get someone over there."

"Already on it." Tim lifted his hands. "What's going on

here? The other ships are still just sitting there. CEREBRO says they're still not answering, either."

Tabitha dropped her popcorn back into the secret compartment in her chair, then pulled her sleeves and touched the soft bands around her wrists to activate them. "Well, if they don't want to answer, I guess I'll have to break in. You know, to check that they're okay."

She relaxed her arms in her lap and her fingers began to move, going through the motions of typing on her crossed leg. "Just... And the translation..." She looked around with a slightly too-bright grin. "We're good. They're trying to get to High Tortuga, they don't know why they're here."

Tim's head jerked up. "Are you in their systems?"

Tabitha grinned. "Nah, I hacked the speaker system on the lead ship. They're arguing about where they are and what to do. Wait, I have their cameras, too. Achronyx, feed it to the viewscreen and get me up on theirs. Let's see if we can get them chatting while you keep digging."

A number of frightened and angry voices came from the screen, then a grainy image appeared that stabilized into a view of the bridge on the lead ship.

Tabitha sat up and raised her hands in front of her. The crew was made up of a few different species, none of which they'd seen before. "Well, hello. Welcome to Devon."

The startled crew of the other ship clammed up when she spoke, but that was fine. Tabitha had never been one to let stunned silence get in the way of starting a conversation. "I'm glad to see there's someone there, although why you were ignoring us is a mystery. Who are you, and what brings you this way in such a hurry?"

The silence dragged on. Tabitha pouted. "Achronyx, why aren't they talking to me?"

One of the alien crew spoke finally. "The gods of war have pursued us across half the galaxy. We are in desperate need of a safe place to hide, but we dare not pause for long."

Tim stood to get a better view of the screen. "We can offer you all sanctuary," he told the alien.

"Hold up a minute," Tabitha told them. *Achronyx, does their story check out?*

It appears to, Achronyx replied. *I'll keep searching.*

Another voice cut over the first. "We cannot in good conscience risk any more lives. It is wrong to ask for anyone to defend us against the insurmountable. Anyone who helps us will be destroyed."

Tabitha tilted her head. "Let me get this straight. You're being chased by some big-bad and you don't think you can win, but you don't want to ask for help because you don't want to put others in danger?"

The alien made a hand gesture that the translation software interpreted as a variant of a nod. "Thank you for your generous offer, but we will be on our way."

Tabitha raised her eyebrow. "Um, no. Like Tim said, we're granting you sanctuary. You will be safe here. We will handle whoever was chasing you if they show up."

The aliens looked as though they would refuse again, but Tabitha held up a finger. "No arguments. Sometimes the universe lends good people a helping hand, and today's your day to receive it."

She waved her hand to cut the connection and turned her head to make a comment to Hirotoshi about how effective the Mom Voice was, then sighed when she remembered that he wasn't there.

Peter reached over and covered her hand with his for a second. "You're missing your Tontos?"

Tabitha blinked away the shine that threatened to escape her eyes. "A little." She sighed at Peter's questioning look. "It's the damn hormones, okay?"

"I didn't say a thing," Peter promised.

Tim looked up from the console he was using to communicate his orders to the defensive line. "I've sent them a safe route through."

The ragtag fleet began to move again. Slowly, the ships began to make their way through the gap in the defensive line on Tim's command.

Achronyx spoke up in Tabitha's mind when the procession was about halfway through. *We may have a problem.*

What problem? she asked.

Most of these ships have no prior affiliation with each other. Looking at the flight path of each ship, I was able to ascertain that the fleet grew in size as it traveled. There's only one explanation for that.

Tabitha was focused on a speck of light that had just blinked into existence some way behind the refugee fleet. *Are you going to tell me what it is?*

The twinkling point bloomed into the familiar pale light of a Gate. An Ooken ship emerged, making Achronyx's reply redundant.

They've been driven toward us.

21

Location Seven, QBS *Izanami*

Bethany Anne and Michael met Addix in the bay with the drop doors.

Alexis, Gabriel, and K'aia hung around near the back of the bay, talking among themselves while the adults prepared to get the rescue underway.

Alexis leaned up against the wall with her arms folded, her bottom lip set to a certain petulant angle. "I still think we can be more useful than Mom and Dad are allowing."

Gabriel shrugged. "Pouting about it isn't going to make them change their minds. Besides, we're responsible for helping Izanami prepare the triage area for the rescued crew."

Izanami floated over. "I had the bots deliver the supplies we need for the task to the bay next door."

"Like *that's* going to take long," Alexis grumped. She got off the wall and raised her voice enough to be heard. "Mom, can't Izanami use the bots instead, and we come with you?"

Michael fixed Alexis with a stern look. "Didn't we have that talk about duty not so long ago?"

Alexis nodded, still pouting. "This isn't going to take long, and then we'll just be sitting around."

Bethany Anne looked up from checking that the knives in her boots were secure. "If that's the case, the three of you can grab some game time until we get back."

Gabriel whooped, pumping the air with his fist. "See, I *told* you we wouldn't be bored. We can play some of those ancient games Aunt Tabitha recreated for us."

K'aia's reaction was somewhat more subdued. "Oh joy, more games."

Alexis narrowed her eyes at her mother, looking for the catch.

Bethany Anne raised an eyebrow. "You will be running the APA scenario under Izanami's guidance. Team training is essential for bonding, after all. Go!" She waved her hands at them. "Get started. We'll be back soon enough."

Michael watched the children leave, then turned to Bethany Anne. "Are you sure about taking us through the Etheric? What about the armor issue?"

Bethany Anne held out a hand for Addix to take. "That's why I had us switch out for the lighter armor. It's a risk if we get caught in any big fights, but we're not planning on that." She smiled pointedly at her husband. "Are we?"

Michael shrugged. "I wasn't planning on it. However, if anyone *does* start one, I will have no choice but to end it. We are not at home now."

Bethany Anne rolled her eyes. "Men." She took them into the Etheric and brought them out in a shadowed area behind the outpost wall. ***The pit they have the prisoners in is*** *near here. Let's get this over and done with, so we can get on with the actual war.* She led them out and into the outpost, using the crawl spaces under the buildings as cover.

Addix peeked over the ledge and looked around, her mandibles showing more bemusement with every turn of her head. *What kind of layout is this? It's chaos.*

Michael looked at the Ooken construction, which was more of what he and Bethany Anne had seen previously. *It is how they build. I quite like the style. It's efficient for the way they move.*

I think you must be mad, Addix replied. *I've never seen anything so convoluted, and I've visited Triome. You know how weird that place is on the senses if you move your head too quickly?*

Bethany Anne snickered. *We went there in a delegation one time, and Darryl threw up so often I ended up sending him back to the ship.* She ventured out of the shadows, sensing that the area was clear. *It's not going to matter when there's no Ooken architecture left to debate.*

They made good progress. Since the Ooken didn't use the ground at all they didn't think to check there, making it relatively simple for the three to work their way along without being spotted.

It's always a bonus if I get to use the enemy's cultural ignorance against them, Bethany Anne remarked as she and Michael waited for an Ooken to pass overhead so Addix could make her way across to them.

Of course, it isn't a new tactic for you, Addix chuckled.

Her humor melted away when another Ooken joined the first and they paused on the walkway overhead. *Oh, screw this. I can use the environment to my advantage, too.* She leapt and grabbed hold of the underside of the walkway, then worked her way over to Bethany Anne and Michael that way. *I have to mention how much easier this is without pounds of useless fabric hanging from my body.*

She dropped onto her feet. *I also prefer this light armor to the regular heavy armor. Here's to traveling through the Etheric all the time.*

Bethany Anne snickered. ***Nice try, but no.***

I thought it was worth it, Addix told her good-naturedly and pointed. *Is that the pit they're keeping the Leath in?*

Bethany Anne and Michael looked in the direction Addix was indicating.

Michael's lip curled when he touched the minds within and felt their fear. *It is.*

How many? Bethany Anne asked.

Twenty-one, he replied. *Too many for one trip?*

Hmmm. She conferred quickly with ADAM and TOM, then sent a message to Izanami with the details of how many to prepare for. ***No, we'll be fine. Addix, you're on. We've got you covered.***

Addix stayed low and darted across to the six-foot cage over the top of the pit. She ducked so as not to be seen and whispered to the Leath below. "Hello, my name is Addix, and we're here to get you out of there."

The Leath looked up. "No. You can't do anything."

Addix risked standing enough to peer down into the pit. Twenty-one angry Leath stared up at her. "You don't look very subjugated," she commented, testing the cage and finding it could be easily broken. "Why can't we do anything? Come to think of it, why did you allow them to take you in the first place? I watched it happen, and you backed down a bit quickly for Leath warriors."

"Do we look like warriors?" one of the Leath hissed. "We're merchants. We took a consignment for a Federation general to pay for fuel to take our family home to Leath, and those abominations took our young."

Bethany Anne heard all this from her place in the shadows. She sighed angrily, rubbing her eyes with a thumb and forefinger. *Why do they* **always** *take the kids? Doesn't matter where we go or who "they" even fucking* **are.** *They always take the kids, and I fucking* **hate** *it.*

Addix and I will take care of getting the Leath free, Michael assured her. *You work on getting their young to safety.*

Bethany Anne walked through the Etheric—right into the pit with the Leath.

Who all but shat themselves.

She held up a hand. "I know, I'm not supposed to be here. Big surprise, the human lied. Now, if we're all done with the truth part, let's get you all the fuck out of this pit so I can do what I do best and reduce this fucking planet to rubble."

The Leath remained frozen to the spot until Bethany Anne clapped her hands. "Come on. I haven't got all day. Your children need to be rescued."

Devon, Interdiction, QBS *Achronyx*, Pod Bay

The six fighter Pods spread out as they exited the *Achronyx*.

They formed up loosely behind Peter and went straight

in to attack, pushing back against the smaller Ooken ships that were nipping at the tail end of the refugee fleet.

The Guardian teams joined the line, pushing the drones into the path of CEREBRO's tender care—and the railguns mounted on the satellites.

Tim took a position where he could see the whole operation to direct it and accepted the request for communications from the lead refugee ship.

"Commander," the captain's trembling voice began. "We are sorry for this attack. We did not want this."

Tim dismissed the apology. "This was their plan all along, and there's no blame to any of you. You were only ever bait as far as the Ooken were concerned. It's us they want. Just keep everyone calm and orderly and moving. The sooner you're all safe behind the line, the sooner we can deal with them."

Tim requested a private channel with Peter. "I'm pretty fucking nervous, Pete. What if it all goes to shit out there?"

"Then it goes to shit and you deal with *that*," Peter replied. "You've got this, Tim. It's your show. I'm just here to remove the unwelcome houseguests from my front door."

"You know, paternity leave only counts if you actually *leave*," Tim pointed out. "You didn't have to come out here today."

Peter's humor faded at the reminder of why he was here. "This is every bit as much of a part of my duty as a father as changing Todd's diapers. My son will have a place to live in safety, and the people who fled this way in terror will sleep soundly tonight in the knowledge we are watching over them."

Tim struggled to speak for a moment. "Dude, I think I want to hug you right now. Go fight for your kid. I've got this."

Peter turned his fighter in a tight arc above the beleaguered convoy, opening fire on a group of small drones that had managed to get past the other defenses.

There was time for a single deep breath before Tim opened the channel to the Devon fleet. "Hey, Peter, how much you looking forward to showing these kids how to kick Ooken ass in style?"

Peter's easy grin returned. "Oh, man, like you wouldn't believe." He tuned the rest of the fleet out, keeping it to just the five of them, with Achronyx listening in and relaying comments for Tabitha.

"More like we're gonna show *you* up," Ricole retorted.

"Yeah," Mark cut in. "You're talking to a man who has an unbelievable amount of experience in the flight simulator."

"You tell the old men how it is, baby." Jacqueline snickered. "Even if the amount of experience you're claiming really *is* unbelievable."

"Hey!" Mark exclaimed.

Peter joined in the protest. "Who are you calling an old man?"

Mark snorted. "Didn't you used to know Jacqueline's dad back in the day?"

Jacqueline cracked up. "He's got you there."

"You're a traitor to male solidarity, Mark." Peter grinned as he spun his Pod to avoid being hit. "Besides, if *I'm* old, what the hell does that make *you*?"

"A rare vintage," Jacqueline replied airily. "Finely matured and aged to perfection."

"Yeah, right." Ricole snickered as she shot back at a seeker. "As if that's going to beat out our generation's oneness with tech."

Jacqueline took out two drones with one puck. "Did you see that?" She turned her fighter on the spot and released another into the seeker the Pod's EI alerted her to. "Okay, you want to play it that way? We'll see whether experience or youth wins in the end. One point for a drone, two for a seeker. Most points wins."

Achronyx spoke in Peter's mind, cracking him up. He cut in over the others. "Tabitha wants to know how many points she gets for taking out a destroyer."

Tim dropped into their chat for a moment. "Tell Tabitha no fair," he complained. "She's got a freaking battleship!"

Peter laughed again. "I did, but she says she's counting that destroyer either way."

"She's welcome to it," Sabine told him. "What's the prize?"

"Not money," Ricole added as a condition. "That's actually getting to the point where it's boring, we have so much of it."

"Speak for yourself," Mark countered. "I wouldn't say no to a few zeroes being added to my account balance."

Another Gate opened nearby. Ricole and Mark pivoted their fighters and sent a barrage of Etheric charges into the shimmering light.

"I wouldn't mind your account getting those zeroes, either," Jacqueline murmured, joining them to fire a spread of her own before the Gate destabilized and collapsed in on itself. "I saw these shoes the other day..."

"What is it with women and shoes?" Peter demanded.

Jacqueline chuckled. "You'll have to ask Bethany Anne, since I was thinking of them as a gift for her. They were beyond my price range in any case."

"Just how expensive *were* they?" Sabine inquired. "I do your accounts, so I know you're not hurting for funds."

Jacqueline casually dropped a number and the only sound over the team comm for the next few seconds was silence. "Exactly. I suggest we all put a thousand credits in, and then whoever tallies the highest score chooses the prize."

"You would, if you're planning to drop *that* much on a pair of shoes," Sabine teased.

"I'd like to know why you're not doing *my* accounts," Mark bitched.

"Because *you* don't pay me for doing them," Sabine shot back. A flash of light distracted her from any further snarky reply. "Shit, what's happening now?"

Two more Gates spiraled open, one on each side of the Interdiction line. The Gates solidified, casting an eerie light over the battle for the lives of the refugee fleet.

Tim let the EI take the strain of running the Pod while he cycled through the masses of incoming reports. He thanked fuck yet again for Bethany Anne's gift of enhancement to his cognitive function and jumped back in on the fleet-wide channel. "The *Astraea* will be inbound shortly," he informed the teams. "We also have more destroyers incoming from the other side."

He wanted the numbers to even up. *CEREBRO, it's play-time. Get your ass in the game and give those ships some cover.*

We thought you would never ask, Commander, the many voices of the EI group replied. The sides of the satellites fell open and CEREBRO activated their drones, each group remotely piloted by an EI with a grudge to settle and a scoreboard to top.

Achronyx contacted CEREBRO when the satellites released the first wave. *Can I borrow a couple hundred of those?*

CEREBRO redirected the requested number of drones to the *Achronyx* and sent the rest to back up the teams in the fighter Pods.

The drones moved to blanket the space around the convoy, making it impossible for the Ooken drones to get near. It became a stalemate, drones on each side, the Guardians in their Pods outmatching the unmanned Ooken seekers, the larger battleships and destroyers facing off uneasily.

The QBS ships stood fast, backed up by the might of two of Bethany Anne's superdreadnoughts. The *Adrastea* and the *Astraea* were more than intimidating enough to keep the Ooken destroyers at bay.

On the *Achronyx*, Tabitha jumped up and down at her console. "You know, it's looking like we have the upper hand," she squealed, punching the air. "Is it wrong that this is the most excited I've been in what feels like years? I kind of get why Bethany Anne went all stabby-killy-kill when we ran into those grubs."

"I like that we pulled their own dirty move on them and stole their technology," Achronyx proclaimed.

Tabitha grinned. "I know, right? But of course, we improved on it. The Ooken version is dependent on time to build up the payload. Since we're using the Etheric instead of messy old plasma, it's more efficient on all counts."

"How do you know all of that?" Achronyx received the last of the drones from CEREBRO and got to work reprogramming them.

Tabitha made a face. "Very funny, Achronyx. Michael and I saw some of the reverse-engineering process while we were visiting William about something else."

"Oh, yes?"

She waved a hand distractedly. "Michael wanted to arrange another hunt, but then this war happened, so I suppose it's on the backburner for now." She cursed softly when twin Gates appeared on the Ooken side, followed by two more, then four more.

Everywhere Tabitha looked, more Gates winked into existence, each spitting out another Ooken ship.

"Damn," Achronyx piped up.

"'Damn' doesn't even begin to cover it," she forced out between gritted teeth. "Pete's out there with the kids. They're screwed."

"Not while I'm around," Achronyx' tone was resolute. "I'll have to say 'watch this,' since I don't have a beer to ask you to hold..."

Devon, First City, The Hexagon

Winstanley observed the odd group approaching the main entrance. She contacted the penthouse apartment's hub and was answered by Hirotoshi. "Hirotoshi, there is a group of Bakas behaving suspiciously outside."

"In what way are they acting suspiciously?" he asked.

Winstanley checked the observations that her system had flagged. "They are dressed strangely, and they have approached the door twice and backed off."

"I'll go speak with them," Hirotoshi told Winstanley.

She followed Hirotoshi on the cameras while maintaining surveillance on the four Bakas. He slipped out of the main entrance and approached the Bakas in a friendly manner. The logic of that did not compute for Winstanley since Bakas were unfriendly toward humans as a rule.

Still, they did not initiate violence, as she had anticipated. Instead, Hirotoshi spoke with the Bakas for a few minutes, then left with them.

22

Outside the Interdiction, QBS *Achronyx*

Having his bonded human grieve when there was something he could have done to prevent it was *not* an outcome Achronyx considered. All the AIs knew how it had been for ADAM when Michael had died and there was nothing he could do for Bethany Anne except be present for her during the worst of it.

That was *not* happening to his Tabitha.

He checked on the progress of his drones as he took the ship off the line. The others took this as permission, word from Tim or not, and the battle was joined for real.

The Interdiction zone was instantly filled with projectiles of all kinds from both sides, plasma fire and Etheric charges adding to the mood lighting provided by the open Gates.

Tabitha covered her eyes as Achronyx veered the ship into a corkscrew. Peter spoke in Tabitha's mind. *Tim's not too happy you jumped the gun, Tabbie.*

Tabitha peered out from between her fingers, hardly

daring to look but unable to take her eyes off the viewscreen. *Don't look at me! My crazy AI decided to come rescue your ass.* Drones and seekers exploded all around the *Achronyx* as Achronyx pounded the crap out of them with pucks. "Achronyx, are we going to make it?"

"It's going to be close," Achronyx admitted. "But as long as they keep sending things that blow up so nicely, I'll have enough material lying around to keep making new pucks to clear a path with."

Be ready, she told Peter. *The second it's clear, we're gonna get out there and cause some real damage.*

You weren't kidding about the destroyers, huh?

Tabitha heard the laughter and love in his voice. *Oh, sweetie, did you think I was?*

Peter snorted softly. *Not for one minute, babe. Just watch yourself, okay?*

You know I will. Achronyx won't let anything happen. She grinned at the screen, where Achronyx was taking out an Ooken ship every few seconds, then scooping up the remains to use to destroy the next. *We've got this. He's killing it out here, literally.*

She tilted her head when Peter dropped the link. "We do have what we need to take a few of those out, right?"

"Oh, yes." Achronyx sounded smug. "I've saved all the best stuff for last."

Tabitha's lip curled. "Good." She looked back at the screen. "The refugees are almost through. It will be our turn in a minute."

"I count five ships remaining," Achronyx confirmed.

The fighters shielded the final ship to cross the line,

opening up the field for the Devon fleet to do more than defend.

Tim's voice came over the speakers. "All ships of the fleet. We are clear to engage. The Interdiction will be live in two minutes, and I don't want to see any fucknuts getting fried by those satellites unless they've got tentacles hanging from their faces."

His voice grew passionate as the Gates continued to spit out Ooken ships just out of weapons range. "You might be looking at all of those ships right now and be wondering how we're going to win against so many. Have faith in yourselves, and trust your teammates. We might be outnumbered, but we are *never* outgunned. The Ooken have destroyed worlds just to test our defenses. *Now get out there and show those fuckers what we do to homewreckers!*"

Tabitha grinned. She remembered when Tim was just another punk Were with a chip the size of Texas on his shoulder. "You heard the Commander, Achronyx. Both barrels hot, and don't fucking stop until there's not a single one of them left."

Achronyx had the ship at peak efficiency. He zipped around firing pucks in every direction. "I'll do my best, but maybe it would be nice to save some for everyone else?"

Tabitha sneered. "If they want any, they'll have to fight for them. My baby is down there! You have no idea how fucking *pissed* I am that they came to our home."

"Oh, I have. It's a 'perk' of being both onboard and sentient. I get feedback from *all* your emotions these days."

Tabitha snickered. "Must suck to be you at least one week in four."

"Yet if *I* made that joke, you'd find new and even more inventive ways to threaten me." Achronyx huffed.

Tabitha shrugged. "Should have chosen to be female."

They broke through another line of Ooken ships, edging ever closer to the destroyers.

"The fecaloid freaks know how to play the numbers game," she admitted, her eyes glancing at the screens giving her feedback. "There are so many of them."

"We should do something about that," Achronyx remarked in a tone that suggested he had something in the works.

"What have you got?" Tabitha asked, walking over to her console to look through their inventory. "Where did those drones in the cargo bays come from?"

"I borrowed them from CEREBRO," he told her. "Just don't disturb them in any way, okay?"

"O-kaaay." Tabitha's hand, which had been hovering over the activation sequences, pulled back. "Why?"

The earlier lightness returned to his tone. "Let me just get us out of friendly-fire range and closer to one of those destroyers and I'll show you." There was a brief pause. "Oh, wait. I'm low on ammo."

Achronyx flipped the ship and dropped them into a sickening perpendicular dive, preceded by the hail of pucks he sent ahead to clear the way.

"FUCKING HELLLLLLL!" It didn't matter that Tabitha felt none of it, the rapid rollercoaster motion on the screen made her feel like she needed to throw her hands in the air and scream her lungs out.

Achronyx reached the trough and tipped the nose of the

ship back up to gather the debris from the destruction he'd caused on the way down. "Almost done…"

He didn't bother to compact the shards of metal into pucks this time, just loaded all six sets of Jean Dukes rail-guns over and over and sprayed them like superheated buckshot at the enemy ships.

Despite this, the drones kept being gracious enough to provide the means for their own termination all the way to the nearest Ooken destroyer.

"Watch the marker," Achronyx instructed as a yellow triangle appeared on the screen.

"Ummm…" Tabitha chewed on her lip. "It's not on the ship," Tabitha pointed out.

"Just watch." Achronyx released five of his repro-grammed drones. Four vanished into the Etheric, and the fifth shot toward the destroyer. "Dammit."

Tabitha gaped. "What did you do?"

"I read the plans for the ELF and adapted the drones to fulfill a similar function. *That* one is about to fail spectacu-larly." The one headed for the destroyer suddenly picked up speed.

Tabitha snickered, her eyes on the drone. "Was that what William called it? What's the acronym for, and how on a cold day in hell did he get that name past Bethany Anne?"

"I have no idea, and I have *no* idea." Achronyx shifted the ship, and the view tilted again while the external cameras adjusted for the new trajectory. "One moment while I get us out of range of that rogue drone."

Tabitha frowned at the screen. "Um, we're not near the drone."

"We're *too* near," Achronyx muttered distractedly.

Tabitha watched the drone warily as it grew smaller on the screen. "Is it…glowing? Just what did you do to those drones, Achronyx?"

"I told you." Achronyx huffed. "It should still be very effective."

The drone exploded, throwing Etheric energy outward in a bright corona that burned everything around it for hundreds of kilometers to ash.

Beyond that, there were four more detonations. The flash was eyeball-searing, and Tabitha threw up an arm to protect herself.

When she dropped it, the destroyer was gone.

Tabitha raised an eyebrow at the ash cloud drifting away on the solar currents, all that remained of the Ooken ship. Her voice was soft this time.

"Yeah, Jean's going to want a couple of those to play with."

Location Seven, Ooken Outpost

Bethany Anne seriously considered the logistics of just knocking the adult Leath out and floating them to the Izanami through the Etheric if they didn't stop arguing with her before they drew the attention of the Ooken.

Luckily for them—and her—at least a few had been sensible enough to see that her time would be better spent finding their children and persuaded the others to allow her to lead them out of the pit to where Michael and Addix waited.

Bethany Anne opened a link to Izanami as she left

Michael and Addix to lead the Leath out of the outpost. *How are the children doing?*

They completed the task well, Izanami reported. *The Pod-docs are all set up and waiting.*

Good. I want Alexis and Gabriel safely in the Vid-docs before a single Leath sets foot aboard the ship. Also, we have a few more coming aboard than we planned for, and Michael and Addix will need pickup with the twenty-one we were expecting.

I understand, Izanami told her. *I have dispatched two Pods to Michael's projected destination. I wouldn't worry about the extra. I can take care of that.*

That's exactly what I was hoping to hear. Etheric jumping would just have to be saved for the children. They were being kept somewhere not too far from there. The adults had told her they'd heard crying while she was getting them out of the pit. *Now, can you take a guess at where I would find a bunch of children in this place?*

I can do better than that, Izanami told her, pride in her voice. *I'm able to pinpoint life signs that belong to the Leath you are searching for. I've sent directions to ADAM.*

>>Yeah, and when we get back, I want my ship's scanners upgraded to match Izanami's.<<

Bethany Anne snorted. *Um, yeah,* no. *I'm a hundred percent certain we've already discussed that you're not getting back into that ship anytime soon.*

>>Whatever.<< He sulked, going quiet again.

Bethany Anne followed the route overlaid on her internal HUD until she came to a point where she couldn't avoid being seen and then slipped into the Etheric.

The route map vanished. Bethany Anne rolled her eyes and headed in the general direction she'd been traveling in.

"Well, that's just fucking great." She looked left and then right, but walked straight ahead. "Guesswork is *always* my favorite way to conduct a rescue mission." She kept bitching as a way to deal with the Etheric strain. "I mean, having your onboard AI, your alien stowaway, or even a single fucking clue where you're going aren't at *all* fucking necessary when there are lives hanging in the balance, are they?"

ADAM and TOM exchanged the mental equivalent of a knowing glance without Bethany Anne noticing. Neither of them were going to offer themselves as a target for her simmering murderous feelings.

Bethany Anne ran a hand over the left thigh of her armor and accepted the sword hilt that pressed itself into her palm. She activated the Etheric blade and poked her head out to check her position, then pulled it straight back in again when she came face-to-face with a nest of tentacles.

She reached out with her free hand and dragged the surprised Ooken into the Etheric with her, then tossed it roughly to the ground and pressed the tip of her sword into the fleshy part under its tentacles.

The Ooken squirmed until the edge of Bethany Anne's blade nicked a tentacle.

"What to do with you? Will the others know I killed you if you die in here?" Her lips pressed together in consideration for a second, then she shrugged. "I guess I'll find out." She flicked the sword hilt with a practiced twist of her wrist, and the Ooken's head dropped onto the pile of its severed tentacles.

Bethany Anne wrinkled her nose as she turned away. "I

think I might avoid spaghetti and meatballs for a while." She gacked, and a moment later she peered out of the Etheric again, remembering to sense ahead this time to check that it was clear.

The route map reappeared in the top corner of her vision, and she saw that the building ahead and a level up was her target.

Ooken minds might be beyond Bethany Anne's ability to read like Michael could, but she could easily sense when they were in the vicinity.

Like now.

However, Bethany Anne had her target in sight. Another short hop through the Etheric took her inside the building where the Ooken held the Leath children hostage against their parents' good behavior.

Bethany Anne repressed her reaction to the conditions the children were being kept in. The single room had no bathroom, and the children had no food or water that she could see. She wanted more than anything to destroy the whole vile place.

Soon.

The children were asleep, huddled together in a rough bed that looked to Bethany Anne like it was made from whatever they'd been able to scavenge.

One of the larger children opened an eye, sensing that something had changed. He saw Bethany Anne standing in the shadows and jumped up in terror. He managed a single horrified word. "Empress!"

The other children woke up and had similar reactions. One of the smallest let out a shrill squeak and the air suddenly carried the tang of fresh urine.

Bethany Anne took a knee and held her hands out in a non-threatening way. It didn't take a mind reader or a genius to work out that she was the proverbial monster in the closet to generations of Leath. "Hey, it's okay. I'm here to help."

The children scuttled back against the wall as though she'd just told them they'd make good ingredients in a soup.

It wasn't unexpected. Not every species she'd made contact with considered her a savior, and in the case of the Leath, it had taken a century of persuasion for her to convince them that their affiliation with the Seven would bring about their ultimate end.

She should be grateful she wasn't here as Baba Yaga.

Of course, she *was* the end she had warned them about, and although the Leath had disavowed their false gods, it came as no surprise to find herself the object of the cautionary tales they passed down to future generations.

It didn't solve Bethany Anne's current dilemma, though.

Unfortunately, she'd had enough experience of situations like this. Well, too much, and she didn't deny it. She knew there was nothing she could do for these children except wipe herself from their memories.

Doubly unfortunate was that the mind wipe rendered the children unconscious.

Bethany Anne didn't feel as bad about the side-effect as she thought she should. After all, *she* wasn't the one who had scared these children with stories of a woman who would in actuality defend them with her last breath if it came to it.

If she could save the children the extra layer of trauma

that seeing their boogey-empress had caused, then a short nap wasn't a huge factor in the decision.

Bethany Anne shrugged and waved a hand over the children. Their peacefully sleeping bodies rose into the air on the cushions of Etheric energy she had formed beneath them, and they bobbed behind her into the Etheric.

The fact that she was finding it much easier to get them aboard the *Izanami* now they weren't likely to bolt had nothing to do with her lack of guilt.

Nothing whatsoever.

23

___

Devon, Interdiction

CEREBRO registered the massive pulse of Etheric energy near the *Achronyx's* position. They requested a report from Achronyx, adding the response to the mass of inputs they were processing from all over the Interdiction.

Data trickled back from the drones to the core group faster than human thought, giving CEREBRO the means to choreograph the mechanical side of the efforts and keep the organics alive.

Over by the satellites, the battle raged thick.

Tim whooped as his Pod completed its barrel roll by releasing two guided Etheric charges after the seeker. "Missed me, you mangy sphincter twinge!"

Sabine snickered, jerking her Pod up at the last moment and leaving her pursuer to get fried like a bug on a zapper in the active laser net. "*Ma petit boulette*, such passion, and all for a machine with no Ooken inside."

Tim accepted her gentle teasing. "Just wait and see how 'passionate' I get if I get the chance to meet any of the squirmy-faced little fuck-knuckles in person." There was a tiny pause. "What's the team's status?"

Sabine flipped her Pod around, spraying the drones around her location with tiny explosive pucks. "We're doing great. A couple of minor scrapes, but otherwise the biggest challenge is keeping the area around us clear enough to work. They're swamping us the second we defend elsewhere."

Tim frowned at the expected news. "I'm getting that from across the fleet. But the Ooken can't have infinite resources. The tide will turn, babe."

"Be sure to let me know when that happens," she told him softly before dropping the connection.

Tim wanted nothing more than to tell her it already had. Bethany Anne had warned him about the Ooken numbers game, but it had to be experienced to be understood. However, the majority of the Gates had been taken out, and Tabitha was pulling some crazy shit right in the middle of it all.

Tim didn't think the Ooken as a species were too bright. Their swarm tactics might have worked wherever they went before, but they hadn't backed off at the realization that they'd kicked whatever their version of a hornet's nest was. That made them dumber than a football in Tim's opinion.

In fact, he thought they were even stupider than that, since *this* nest was filled with super-enhanced humans who were more than happy to scrub the chance of that stupidity spreading from the galactic stage completely.

Altogether, it was looking good.

He opened a mental link to Rickie back on the *Guardian*.

Rickie was his usual ebullient self. *Heeeey, how's it hanging? Having fun without me?*

Tim rolled his eyes. *The time of my fucking life, dude. It's the quietest it's been for weeks. Are all the refugees safely aboard the station?*

We're just processing the last few groups through triage, Rickie told him. *How's it really going?*

Tim returned to the fleet reports as he spoke. *We're going to win, I have no doubt about that.*

Buuuut? Rickie pressed.

But nothing, Tim repeated, his voice taking on that edge that meant there would be no argument. *We're going to win.*

Aw, shit.

Tim made a face. *What?*

It's just that I've got some private ships requesting permission to Gate out to the Interdiction, Rickie informed him. *I kinda want to let them lend a hand.*

What do you mean by "private ships?" Tim frowned, thinking that a few civilian ships were only going to distract the military fighters, who would feel duty-bound to protect them. *Who are the owners?*

Rickie was quiet for a moment. *I just sent you the list.*

Tim received Rickie's list and scrolled through it in his internal HUD. *This looks like...everyone planetside with a ship.*

Pretty much, Rickie confirmed. *What are your orders?*

Tim considered it for a long moment before lifting his hands. *Devon has spoken, so what else can I do? Let them through.*

. . .

The Etheric

Bethany Anne strode through the mists with the sleeping Leath children floating behind her at waist height. The strain of carrying the children increased with every step. *You WILL get them home. You WILL deal with the strain or you WILL let John stand on your back...in high heels.* Her lips, pressed together due to the strain, cracked a bit at that last thought.

She'd get them to the ship, and that was all there was to it.

Her feet weighed whole universes, but still she put one in front of the other, pushing forward and honing in on the beacon that was her own children. Alexis and Gabriel's physical location was a warmth to her senses, guiding her back to the *Izanami*.

Eventually, after what felt like her entire life lived over again, Bethany Anne opened the way out of the Etheric. She staggered slightly as she guided the sleeping children into the repurposed cargo bay where Alexis and Gabriel were waiting on standby for her return.

They turned as one when she stepped into the bay with the Leath children still Etherically tethered to her. "Mom!"

Bethany Anne grinned tiredly at them. "Hey, kids. I'm home."

The twins leapt into action immediately, adding their support to the energy Bethany Anne was using to hold the Leath children aloft.

Michael appeared in the bay's transfer area a bare second later and took the load from her completely. Between the three of them, they got the children loaded into the empty Pod-docs.

Bethany Anne sank gratefully down on the closest flat surface, which happened to be the floor where she was standing. *Where are the adults?* she sent to Michael.

Michael looked at his wife, his brow furrowing when he saw her sitting cross-legged with her head resting on her folded hands. *Mindwiped, sedated, and safely aboard their ship.*

Bethany Anne lifted her head fractionally to raise an eyebrow. *You got their ship? Color me impressed.*

Michael winked. *That was what Izanami said when she showed up with the Pods. Leave this to us. We have it all in hand.*

Bethany Anne knew all too well what that twinkle in his eye meant. However, Michael would be Michael, and she was fucking *exhausted* from the constant drain-pull of getting them to the ship in the first place.

Thank you. She got to her reluctant feet and set them to walking once more. *Now, if you don't mind, I've got a date with my pillow, and it's going to run for at least two hours.*

ADAM spoke up again finally. >>Yeah, I don't think you're going to get that nap. I didn't want to distract you while you were busy with the Leath kids, but there's a situation at Devon.<<

Bethany Anne's fatigue fell away in an instant. "What situation at Devon?" she asked aloud for Michael's benefit.

ADAM transferred his voice to the speaker. "The Ooken have attacked at the Interdiction. Achronyx is feeding me a play-by-play. It's getting pretty big."

"How big?" Gabriel asked, looking at the speaker. "Is the planet okay?"

"The planet is fine," ADAM assured him.

Michael walked over to Bethany Anne and took her

hand. "You still need to rest and recover from the effort of saving those children. I will wake you when we arrive."

Bethany Anne squeezed his hand and let go. "You and I both know that's not happening. I'll be in my chambers if this," she waved a finger over the Pod-docs, "doesn't go as you expect and you need me." She blew a kiss to Alexis and Gabriel. "Love you both. Be good for your father."

Alexis put a hand to her chest, feigning offense. "Who, us?"

Bethany Anne chuckled softly as she left the bay. She didn't technically need to make any of her calls using conventional methods, but she was getting back into the habit of making a physical call every now and then—when it mattered to her the most. That could wait until she got to her chambers.

Speaking to Admiral Thomas was her first priority, and she didn't need to see his face to get this portion of her mental checklist completed. *Admiral, report in. How is the operation progressing?*

Almost complete, he replied. *Hello to you, too, Bethany Anne.*

The thought occurred that maybe he did have a point about her abruptness. *One of these days we'll meet when we're not in a dire situation and I'll remember.*

Admiral Thomas laughed aloud. *Not today, though?*

Bethany Anne chuckled coldly. *No. Devon is under attack.*

By the Ooken?

Your astuteness is comforting, as usual. I'm going straight there, and I want the others to meet me there when they're done. Can you coordinate the rest of the operation from there without us?

Um...

Bethany Anne pressed her lips together. *There's a problem?* She accessed the operations logs, her eyes flicking from side to side as she read through while she walked. *What is it? All I see is debris where there used to be planets, which is exactly what I asked for. Oh, location three is still active.*

Admiral Thomas sighed in exasperation. *It's more of a complication. Remember I told you about the Moen? The servile species?*

Mmhmm. She reached her chambers and stepped through the wall to get inside. *What about them?*

Well, we're having some trouble freeing them. They're suffering from some kind of alien version of Stockholm syndrome or something.

Bethany Anne touched her hand to her forehead and did something she hadn't done for a very long time. She prayed for the patience to see this through without losing her shit at the absurdity of it all. *Of course, they are.*

If I apologize, will it help?

Bethany Anne snorted softly. *Not really? But we need to do something about ensuring the Ooken don't use the Moen as leverage. Okay, get the other locations wrapped up, then put a blockade on location three. Nothing and no one out, nothing in except for supplies approved by us. Make sure the Ooken know we're watching them.*

How long do you expect to need this blockade? Admiral Thomas asked.

However long it is until I get back from Devon, of course.

Goodbye, Admiral. Bethany Anne cut the connection and waved a hand over her desk to activate the holoscreen.

Her call to the *Achronyx* went unanswered, and she tried again, with the same result. Bethany Anne was aware that the battle was still going on. She pinged Tabitha over their mental link.

She tapped a foot while she waited for an answer from Tabitha. Which didn't come, because Tabitha had Achronyx screening for her.

Bethany Anne's patience had already worn thin. "ADAM, put me through to the bridge."

The bridge of the *Achronyx* was empty. She tapped her fingers on the desk. "Clearly it's not a life or death situation, so where *is* she?"

>>**You should have called ahead,**<< ADAM joked.

Bethany Anne frowned, then shrugged. "It's not too late for that. Give me the ship's speakers."

Devon, Interdiction

Tabitha tipped her captain's chair back and squinted at the overwhelming light flooding the entire screen. "That's a big-ass Gate."

"It is indeed," Achronyx replied. "Shall we break it? I still have a few drones remaining."

Tabitha grinned. "We *could* do that...but I have another idea. Can you get me CEREBRO?"

Achronyx provided the necessary link between Tabitha's mind and the core of the EI group.

Hey, CEREBRO. Do you have anything on the other side of the Gates?

Regretfully, we do not, the EI group replied. *Everything we've sent through was destroyed before any data could be returned.*

Tabitha smirked, lacing her hands behind her head as she arranged her feet on the console to get perfectly comfortable. *I want to know where they're coming from and what resources they have. That could be the homeworld sitting just on the other side. How about we work together and see if we can't get an idea of what this group has to keep throwing at us so we can double it and be done here?*

We like the odds of that, CEREBRO replied.

Oh, you all like to bet? Tabitha grinned. *What am I talking about? You live for that shit.* She sat forward and laced her hands under her chin. "Here's what we're going to do…"

At the other end of the battlefield, Tim's Pod reached the open Gate as the first ships of the people's fleet came through.

He heard his own voice issuing the first set of recorded instructions he'd given to CEREBRO to play into every personal ship that crossed the Gate.

The shimmering light was pierced by the smaller groups first—the angry citizens, the transport workers, and the everyday people who had access to a ship.

Tim saw ships of every kind, from tiny individual transports that bristled with weaponry designed to ward off chancers in the mean skies of Devon to gigantic freighters with massive company logos emblazoned across their flanks so that pirates knew who to call for the ransom. They all moved off to their assigned areas with more or less a minimum of drama.

Next came the mercenary companies, and Tim's

message switched to direct the skilled crews over to the main effort.

First out of the Gate were five battered junker-looking ships that Tim knew nevertheless would probably outlast cockroaches. Tim was well enough acquainted with the Shrillexian company commander to drink with her and a few others on occasion, and Lai-pen and her crew were just as durable as their ships.

They exited the event horizon and dropped out of sight before he could see a single bleeding skull badge painted on the sides of the ships.

The rest of the merc companies were close behind, mixing with each other in their hurry to be next to cross. Tim chuckled, wondering how Lai-pen had gotten the Skull-Fuckers ahead of the pack.

He fired off a message to the *Victory in Death* inviting them over to the *Guardian* to celebrate after the battle and got back to monitoring the overview.

Scanning through, Tim decided that CEREBRO needed a freaking medal or whatever upgrade they wanted after this battle was done. Every report he read had a mention of the EI group in there, assisting the efforts and saving the lives of his people.

CEREBRO, you're all doing a great job out there.

Commander? the EIs inquired.

I don't know if EIs need to hear that kind of thing, but you're invaluable. Our asses would be so far in the air right now without you all. His eyes flickered as he scanned through the report for the *Lucky Run* and moved on to the next—which was unavailable. *Shit...where has the* Achronyx *gotten to?*

Over by the largest Ooken Gate with a number of us,

CEREBRO replied. They sounded somewhat thinner than usual. *We are attempting to get readings from the other side of the Ooken Gate.*

CEREBRO, are you good? Tim inquired. *You sound like you're missing some of yourselves.*

We are optimal, thank you, Commander. We are just spread far and wide at the present time.

Tim shrugged. The EIs knew better than he did. *What's this with Tabitha and Achronyx?*

Tabitha cut in. *It's time-sensitive, and you're hogging CEREBRO's bandwidth. Can you chat later, when we've gotten at least one freaking drone through this Gate intact?*

Sure, Tim replied, but they were already gone.

In the lee of the Gate, Tabitha stamped a foot as the drone configuration failed to fail—*again.* "Fuck it five ways to Friday! Why can't we replicate one simple error?"

Achronyx sounded equally frustrated. "Because we can't replicate it without knowing the exact reason the drone went rogue in the first place. If just one sensor had remained functional, I would know what caused the drone to malfunction and we could create that malfunction in the rest of them."

Tabitha kicked the drone. "Instead of digging around in the guts of this thing."

"Oh."

Tabitha looked up at the surprised tone in Achronyx' voice. "What is it?"

"Could you kick the drone again, same place, same strength."

Tabitha shrugged. "Sure." This time her boot left a small dent in the drone's shell.

"Interesting…"

Tabitha growled in frustration. "C'mon, just tell me, already!"

"Well," Achronyx dragged it out just to annoy her, "it looks like an impact on launch may have been responsible for the malfunction."

"You mean I've been sweating all this for nothing?"

Achronyx made a noise of uncertainty. "If you could just wait while I have another drone brought up…"

Tabitha was about to tell Achronyx exactly where he could stick his drone when Bethany Anne's voice reverberated through the ship. "Tabithaaaa. Where are youuuuu?"

"Oh, dear," Achronyx muttered.

Tabitha narrowed her eyes. "What now, Achronyx?"

"Um, Bethany Anne might have tried to contact you a couple of times while we were working."

Tabitha's heart sank. "How many times? Like one or two?"

"Sure, one or two…"

Tabitha made a sympathetic face. "You do know I can tell when you're lying, right? Bethany Anne might not kill me, but I'd start making final arrangements if I were you."

She got to her feet and headed for the bridge at a brisk jog, taking a moment to kick Achronyx' drone as the anti-grav pallet carrying it passed her. "Here, finish your testing. If you have something good to tell Bethany Anne when I throw you under the bus, she might not pull your plug."

24

Devon, QBBS *Guardian*

Michael nodded and patted Hk'lhrr's arm briefly. "I appreciate this. Just get them within hailing distance of the Leath homeworld."

The Leath Marine nodded. "Of course, sir. Do you want me to be there when they wake?"

Michael shook his head. "I want you to be long gone by then. There is to be nothing that leads them back to this part of space." He raised a finger. "And I'll need you to confirm your success."

Hk'lhrr nodded again. "I'll send my report as soon as the assignment is complete, sir."

Michael gestured for Alexis, Gabriel, and K'aia to follow him and they left the hangar.

Gabriel had retreated into his usual observant mode. "What are we doing here, Dad?"

Michael paused at an intersection to check the location designation stenciled on the wall, then took a decisive left.

"Your mother and I agree that the best place for the three of you until the battle is over is the Hexagon."

Gabriel regarded the faint line in his father's forehead. "Wouldn't you rather be out there fighting?"

"No." Michael lifted a shoulder. "Your mother and Aunt Tabitha have everything in hand."

Alexis gave Gabriel a nudge. "He means that they went out for a girls' night and he got stuck looking after us."

"I meant," Michael corrected sternly, "exactly what I said. It is not necessary for me to be by your mother's side every minute, and neither is it conducive to her focus to be worried about your safety. Besides, a fight is what you make of it, and there are two overly chatty children in need of some instruction right here who require my attention."

Michael turned and narrowed his eyes at K'aia when the young Yollin snickered. "My apologies. Three."

Rickie scrolled down the checklist on his datapad. "Damn, that's a lot of people. Where the fuck am I supposed to *put* them all?"

"There are always the orientation lounges," CEREBRO suggested.

Rickie almost missed his turn. "CEREBRO, you're a freaking grade-A genius." He grimaced. "Even so, is that enough space for them all?"

"The lounges can hold sixty thousand comfortably," CEREBRO reminded Rickie. "They were originally intended as temporary accommodations for colonists."

Rickie nodded and looked down at his datapad again.

"Okay, then. Next...clothing and food for the people who aren't being taken straight to medical."

He located the site for kitchen orders, but it was unavailable because the staff was out at the Interdiction.

"Oh, shit. C'mon, Rickie, *think*..."

Inspiration hit. He'd noticed people regularly using one catering company around the station. Maybe they could help? A quick call confirmed that they would be able to provide a team for each orientation lounge.

Rickie grinned to himself as he headed over to Requisitions to see what they had in the way of warm blankets and other basic necessities. "Rickie, you might not suck at management after all."

Devon, Interdiction, QBS *Achronyx*

Tabitha grabbed the doorframe to steady herself as she made the turn onto the bridge at breakneck speed. "I'm here!"

Bethany Anne looked at her from the viewscreen, her face stern and unmoving. "You're not dead, then."

Tabitha grinned and dropped into the captain's chair. "No, but I can offer up Achronyx as a sacrifice to appease your anger if you'd like?" She put her feet up, ignoring the look she received. "Since it was him who blocked you."

"I did nothing of the sort!" Achronyx protested over the speakers. "I blocked *all* external inputs so you could process working with so much of CEREBRO."

"Here, watch this." She forwarded the video of Achronyx's modified drones.

Bethany Anne's eyes moved rapidly, a smile creeping

onto her face as explosions tore the Ooken destroyers to shreds.

Bethany Anne raised an eyebrow once it was done. "Nice!"

Tabitha stood up and shimmied victoriously "I know, right? CEREBRO provided the drones, and Achronyx and I—"

"Um…"

Tabitha rolled her eyes. "Fine, *Achronyx* figured out what to do with the Etheric charges."

Bethany Anne chuckled. "Well, in that case, I'm not as annoyed with you, Achronyx."

"Which I appreciate immensely, my Queen," Achronyx replied gravely.

Tabitha dropped back into her chair. "I knew you'd understand. What was so important you had ADAM hack my ship?"

Bethany Anne waved a hand. "Oh, just that we're almost home. We'll be docking at the *Guardian* in two jumps."

Tabitha's head snapped up. "Really?" A grin appeared on her face at the same time an idea popped into her mind. "You're planning on coming out here?"

Bethany Anne looked at her skeptically. "Yes. Why do you have that crazy look on your face, Tabitha?"

Tabitha couldn't see her own face, but judging by the tightness in her jaw and the angle of Bethany Anne's eyebrow, she thought she could probably give the Cheshire Cat a run for its money at that moment. "Oh, you need to get here *soonest*. We've come up with a way to get a look at what we think is the homeworld, and you don't want to miss it."

A satisfied smile touched Bethany Anne's lips. "That's my girl."

Devon, Interdiction, QBS *Izanami*, Bridge

Bethany Anne leaned forward, hands on the console, as the *Izanami* Gated into the midst of the battle. "Where's the *Achronyx*?"

There was a massive explosion of Etheric energy off in the distance.

Bethany Anne reached out with her mind to discern the source. "Never mind, I've found them. Take us over there, Izanami."

Izanami's eyes blazed like rubies in the snow. "Of course, my Queen." The AI's aura glitched shades of red that pooled around her feet, flowing behind her in pixelated bloody-looking contrails as she glided around the bridge.

Bethany Anne read the fleet reports as Izanami guided the ship across the battlefield. She fired off a message to Tim to tell him she would discuss his decision to allow the general citizenry of Devon to participate.

Izanami appeared beside Bethany Anne. "We are at the *Achronyx*'s location, my Queen."

Bethany Anne stepped through the Etheric to the *Achronyx*, exiting in the bay where she sensed Tabitha's presence. She gazed down from the walkway above the bay as Tabitha laid a boot into one of the drones she had lined up in rows.

Bethany Anne watched, confused, as Tabitha paused a moment before moving to the next drone and kicking that one, too. She walked over to the railing and inspected the damage to the drone directly beneath her. "What did they do to you?"

Tabitha looked up from the drone when Bethany Anne called to her. "Cool, you're here!" She made her way over. "I'm damaging them for a reason."

Bethany Anne's leaned over the railing, her curiosity getting the better of her. "I'll bite. What's the deal?"

Tabitha hopped onto the nose of the drone Bethany Anne had been looking at, then jumped to grab the railing and swung herself over with ease. "Did you notice the Gate in the video I sent?"

Bethany Anne nodded. "I did. Was there something special about it other than the size?"

Tabitha shrugged and leaned against the railing. "That's the thing—we don't know. All our efforts so far to get a look at the other side have failed. Whatever we sent through got destroyed the second it crossed, and now the Ooken are bunched up around the Gate like hemorrhoids so we can't get near it. "

Bethany Anne pursed her lips, making the decision. "I can get us there. The Ooken can't detect the *Izanami*." She waved a hand at the floor below. "Pack up. We're going to pay them a return visit."

Tabitha wiggled her eyebrows. "I was really hoping you would say that." She vaulted the rail, already conferring with Achronyx on the logistics.

Bethany Anne went back to the *Izanami* to wait for Tabitha, heading straight for the armory to exchange the light armor she was currently wearing for full battle gear.

The case containing her heavy battle armor opened as

Bethany Anne entered the armory. No simple crate for this set, it was housed in an unbreakable glass cabinet with the Jean Dukes logo handpainted on the doors above Bethany Anne's Queen Bitch badge.

A small chuckle escaped her lips when she realized that even TOM and ADAM were absent for the moment. It was a rare thing to be alone long enough to contemplate.

"I guess there's nobody around to think I'm crazy if I talk to myself." She trailed her fingers over the rack of under armor suits, grabbing the one she wanted before crossing the room to get space to change into it.

Then came the fight to get out of the light armor. "Can I just get a happy medium when it comes to my armor?" she bitched, tugging at the skintight nano-infused fabric until it peeled away from her back with a snap. "Something comfortable that I can wear while I'm in the Etheric and not have to worry about healing bullet holes when I walk out?"

She extracted her legs and dropped the stiff suit on the floor, then retrieved the under armor suit and slipped a foot into the soft material.

The armor unfurled from the center outward when she was five steps away from the case. "The only thing that would make *this* beauty better was if it had heels built in."

Bethany Anne smirked at the thought and raised her arms slightly as she walked up the two steps to enter the cabinet.

She turned to face the room as she took the final step backward into the embrace of Jean's best work yet. The armor assembled itself around her body from her feet up, each section locking seamlessly into the next until she was completely protected from neck to toes.

She hummed as she stepped down, flexing her hands inside the gauntlets. They made the connection to the Etheric and a tingle raced over her bare skin. Keeping it simple, she selected her faithful katanas and her Jean Dukes specials.

If she couldn't beat the Ooken with her swords, her guns, and her brain…

Bethany Anne laughed. "I can't even continue that thought. It's too ridiculous." She left the armory and set off for the bridge.

Tabitha came aboard while Bethany Anne was finishing the review of CEREBRO's logs pertaining to the attempts. She flounced out of the elevator and over to the larger couch, where she flopped down on her stomach and rested her chin on her hands. "Are we good to go?"

Bethany Anne shrugged. "Near as I can tell. Izanami, is our way home secure?"

Izanami appeared at Bethany Anne's side in a swirl of pixels. "As secure as a Gate jump can be," the AI replied. "In short, yes."

Bethany Anne waved her finger in a circle. "Then why are we not moving? Let's go."

Izanami dipped her head and vanished. The Ooken Gate came into view on the wraparound screens a few moments later.

Bethany Anne's eyes darted around, taking note of the various groups clustered around the Gate as the *Izanami* approached.

Ooken destroyers swarmed around the threshold.

Their plasma weapons glowed brightly, warning off any ships that got too close. "They sure have enough of those destroyers. Didn't you take a shit-ton of them out?"

"They just kept bringing more through the damned Gate," Tabitha bitched. She untucked a hand from her chin and flapped it at the line the Ooken had made around the Gate. "This is how far we got with the *Achronyx* before they all swooped in like vultures."

The Izanami passed the line without challenge.

Tabitha sighed heavily, then looked at Bethany Anne and shrugged. "I knew we were good, but it was still squeaky-ass time for a second while we tested it."

Bethany Anne shook her head and turned back to regard the screen through narrowed eyes. "Izanami, take us through that Gate."

Beyond the Gate, QBS *Izanami*, Bridge

Bethany Anne got her first look at the area beyond the Gate as the ship nosed over the threshold. The *Izanami* was a mere speck in comparison to the sprawling construction they'd arrived at.

She cursed softly, noting the heavy defenses on every flat surface. Patrol ships swept back and forth between the many active Gates scattered around the asymmetric arrangement of platforms that made up the staging post. "I guess we know why none of the drones made it through," she commented as they passed unnoticed between two ships armed with turret guns.

Tabitha frowned as they surveyed the nine gigantic cubes that were linked in the Ooken manner by tunnels and scaffolding. "I'm gonna go out on a limb and say that this is not the homeworld."

"You don't say!" Bethany Anne closed her eyes for a second, wrapping her hope up tightly to save it for another day. She opened them again and turned to Tabitha. "It's not *all* bad news. I think we are in a position to deal the Ooken some real hurt. Look closely... Those Gates are going to other places than Devon. This is an important location for them."

Tabitha's face contorted when she connected Bethany Anne's words to the steady flow of inbound ships from the surrounding Gates. "Greedy fucking assholes. Is that their only motivation for all this? Stripping every world they come to for every resource it has?"

Bethany Anne nodded calmly, her outward serenity a sharp contrast to the tumultuous anger boiling within. "Yes, but not for long. Did you bring enough of those drones to make a scene?"

Tabitha gave Bethany Anne a shark-like grin, the maniacal glint back in her eyes. "Oh, *hells* yes. Where do you want to start?"

Bethany Anne glanced at the screen and pressed her lips together in thought. "Hmmm. Good question. Izanami, can you poke around in their systems without them figuring out that we're here?"

Izanami floated across to Bethany Anne, a hint of darkness rippling through her aura. "I already have, and I've identified several areas of interest."

A holomap overlaid the live feed and a colored marker appeared on one cube that was slightly offset from the center of the staging post. "This area, however, was the one that caught my attention first."

Bethany Anne looked over at the AI. "Why?"

Izanami glitched out, reappearing on the other side of the map in a burst of pixels. "It is covered by the same type of shielding we encountered over the first colony."

Bethany Anne pressed her lips together. "Okay. That's not entirely unexpected. What have they got going on here that we can see? Give me everything you've identified."

Tabitha walked around the map, selecting the different-colored markers that popped up all over the map. "They're pretty organized. So, Izanami, the blue markers away from the shielded area are the manufacturing sites?"

"They are," the AI confirmed.

Bethany Anne raised an eyebrow. "Are you thinking what I'm thinking?"

"That depends," Tabitha replied offhandedly. "Are you thinking about blowing the shit out of this place?"

Bethany Anne nodded somberly. "That's pretty much the plan."

Izanami vanished again as the ship neared the shielded area. Her voice came from the speaker in the headrest of Bethany Anne's couch as a small drawer in her console slid open. "Take this with you, my Queen. It will disable the shielding, and I left a little gift of my own in there for the Ooken."

Bethany Anne picked up the tiny translucent cube within and held it to the light to examine the ripple of the Etheric energy inside. "Pretty. How does it work?"

"Just press it to the shield generator. It will do all the heavy lifting for you," Izanami informed her.

The corners of Bethany Anne's mouth turned up as she stashed the cube in one of her armor's compartments. "Handy thing to have."

ADAM spoke up. >>**It can do much more than that with a little bit of tweaking.**<<

You have a considerable amount of training ahead of you before you get to even **think** *about touching the Etheric again,* Bethany Anne told him firmly. *Still, good to know.* She filed the information away for later use and turned to Tabitha. "Ready?"

Tabitha grinned, hooking an arm through the sling of her rifle. "You bet your ass I am."

25

Beyond The Gate, Staging Post, QBS *Izanami*

Bethany Anne and Tabitha stood at the open drop door in the cargo bay while Izanami brought the ship in to hover above an access hatch near the shielded section of the central cube.

Bethany Anne leaned out to line up the hatch, holding the overhead strap for balance. "Make sure you don't fuck the landing."

Tabitha narrowed her eyes and made the jump. "I do not 'fuck landings,'" she protested hotly as Bethany Anne landed beside her. "Sometimes they just get away from me, is all."

Bethany Anne snickered as she bent to tear the hatch free. "Oookay, sure." She checked her mental image of Izanami's map and stepped inside the hatch onto the ladder. "This goes down a ways. We leave this shaft three exits down and then work our way across to the shielded section."

Tabitha climbed into the hatch after Bethany Anne. "What do you think we're going to find?"

Bethany Anne peered into the first exit as she passed it. "I couldn't even begin to guess. Whatever it is, it was valuable enough to the Ooken to put all that shielding on it, so it must be worth blowing up."

She passed the second exit, which was as empty as the first. Tabitha was quiet—for Tabitha, at least. "You okay?"

Tabitha made a noncommittal sound, not wanting to raise the subject with her. "I'm good."

Bethany Anne sensed Tabitha's reluctance to talk. She took the rungs a little bit faster, seeing their exit. "Nice try. What's eating you? You know you can tell me if you aren't happy on Devon." She stepped into the horizontal shaft and waited for Tabitha to join her.

"Are you kidding?" Tabitha caught up a moment later and fell into step behind Bethany Anne, and the two women made their way deeper into the cube. "I *love* Devon. High Tortuga has gotten so stuffy that you can't even find a decent bar fight there anymore."

Bethany Anne frowned, checking their route again before taking the right turn at an intersection that led them into a wide corridor. "You and Peter are okay? Todd's health is good, or you would have told me about it."

"It's nothing like that." Tabitha shrugged. "There's no point anyway. You made your decision about Nickie, I know you won't budge on bringing her home."

Bethany Anne raised an eyebrow. "Damn straight. Seven years is seven years, and I'll be honest and say I'm not expecting much change when that time is up—not based on the reports I've been getting."

"You too?" Tabitha's voice wavered. "I hate that she's out there alone, Bethany Anne. You just don't know her like I do. She needs someone to believe in her, or my worst fear might just come true, and the next time I see her will be when her body is returned to us."

Bethany Anne pushed Tabitha into the shadow of a recess before they turned into another corridor. *Wait a moment—I'm sensing Ooken nearby. What do you want me to do about Nickie?* she asked. *Even if I wanted to let her come home early—which I'm not inclined to do at this point—how does* that *teach her anything?*

Tabitha pressed herself against the wall. *It doesn't. All I'm asking is that you allow me to send someone to watch her back and give her a nudge in the right direction.*

The Ooken got within smelling distance. Bethany Anne guessed they were about to turn onto the corridor she and Tabitha were in.

Bethany Anne looked hard at Tabitha. *We will discuss this when we're back on the right side of the Gate.*

Thank you. Tabitha nodded toward the two Ooken. *Which one do you want?*

Neither. I'm really sick of sneaking around, but if we kill one, they ALL come running.

Oh. Yeah. Tabitha pouted. *I've got to say, this deviation from your usual in-your-face badassery is not your best look.*

I know, right? Bethany Anne grimaced. *But what else can I do? It's a different challenge completely when the enemy is telepathic.*

Tabitha felt her best friend's turmoil. *Don't stress it. Something will come along that tips the balance completely in our favor.*

You're right. Bethany Anne grabbed Tabitha's hand and pulled her along the corridor. *But when have I ever waited for serendipity to drop the solution into my lap when I can tip the scale myself? Now,* run.

Bethany Anne and Tabitha blurred around the corner, moving too fast for the Ooken they passed to realize something had just blasted by and sprinted down the corridors at full speed.

They slowed upon reaching the shield, which covered the turn into a much wider, brightly lit corridor.

"Over here," Tabitha called, indicating the hidden access panel she'd found farther along the wall. "It will only take a minute to open."

Bethany Anne walked over and put her fist through the panel, ripping it off as she removed her hand. "Not even half a second if you do it my way." She took Izanami's cube from the compartment in her armor she'd put it in for safekeeping, made a space to push it through the ropes of wires inside the wall, and pressed it to the inner workings.

The cube glowed, then melted into the circuit board. A few seconds later, Bethany Anne had access to the Ooken mainframe.

"Did it work?" Tabitha asked.

Bethany Anne nodded slowly, then shook her head when nothing happened with the shielding. "Yeah…no." She fixed Tabitha with a sparkling smile. "I don't speak Ooken, which makes me doubly glad I brought tech support along for the trip. Oh, and TOM. "

>>Hey,<< ADAM complained. >>**What about me?**<<
You're grounded. Indefinitely.

>> **Whatever.**<< ADAM huffed and went silent again.

I don't know why, TOM piped up, **but** *somehow* **the Mom voice is worse than the Empress voice.**

Bethany Anne rolled her eyes. *Can we just focus, please? It's like trying to think with a bunch of damned squirrels arguing in my head.*

It's about to get a little bit more unpleasant, TOM told her apologetically. **I have to make you speak Ooken.**

So? She waved off his concern. *We've done that almost too many times.*

Not with a psionic language. I suggest you brace yourself. This is going to hurt.

Bethany Anne considered why she wasn't more surprised by that information. "I don't give a shit if it hurts as long as it works."

Tabitha looked at her with concern. "If what hurts?"

"Speaking Ooken," Bethany Anne told her quickly. "Okay, just get it over with. It can't be worse than the headache you caused fucking around with ADAM's chip."

Frankly, yes it can. There's no point in sugarcoating it. I have to overstimulate a part of your brain that humans don't normally use in this way.

Sudden pressure behind her eyes almost made her scream. Bethany Anne pressed a hand to her eyes, staggering from the intensity of the pain. *FUCK! It wasn't a damned* **challenge, TOM***!*

I'm sorry! Almost done.

The shield across the corridor disappeared.

Bethany Anne gritted her teeth and waited. The pressure behind her eyes vanished as suddenly as it had occurred. "Dammit, TOM."

Tabitha was by her side in the next moment. "You

okay?" she asked, her brow furrowed with concern. "It looked like you were going to faint or something."

Bethany Anne shook off the residual pain. "I'm fine. Let's go." She drew her katanas and headed for the now-unrestricted corridor.

Beyond the Gate, Staging Post, Shielded Area

The corridor led Bethany Anne and Tabitha to an imposing set of doors, which Bethany Anne opened with a generous application of her boot.

The two women strode in with their weapons raised—straight into the waiting tentacles of several Ooken guards. There wasn't even time to admire the huge tank that took up most of the room.

Tabitha ducked out from under the reaching tentacles and tossed a tiny drone into its snapping beak.

The Ooken stepped back, clutching its throat where the drone had stuck.

Tabitha winced when she realized exactly which drone she'd thrown. *Bethany Anne?*

Bethany Anne turned from the corpse of the guard she'd dispatched as the head of Tabitha's guard exploded. ***Really?***

Tabitha winced as Bethany Anne wiped a hand down her face to remove the brain splatter. *Um, duck?*

Bethany Anne narrowed her eyes.

Tabitha made herself busy to avoid the glare. *How long do we have?*

Bethany Anne flicked her hand to remove the goop. ***Ten, fifteen minutes maybe until every Ooken here comes*** *baying for our blood.*

Tabitha looked around. *Then we should start searching for whatever it is they're hiding before we have to leave everything behind.*

Bethany Anne pointed behind Tabitha at the tank, gaping in amazement. **They're not hiding anything.**

Tabitha turned her head from one side to the other, trying to understand the dimensions of the creature before her. "Are you a squid? You look a bit like a squid."

The not-a-squid threw back its tentacles, revealing a familiar-looking beak.

Bethany Anne sensed more to the beast than the animal instinct it was showing them. "I think it might be Ooken, too, without the 'ook' part."

You are correct, TOM cut in. **It seems that this is what the Ooken were before they were altered.**

By the Kurtherians.

Yes, Bethany Anne, by the Kurtherians. I believe it wishes to communicate with us.

Bethany Anne regarded the creature with a mixture of suspicion and curiosity. *But it's an Ooken. They don't communicate, just attack.*

She glanced at Tabitha. "Apparently, TOM and I are going to attempt a conversation with this creature."

Tabitha shrugged. "I've seen weirder things happen. I'll keep watch."

TOM established the mental link between him and Bethany Anne and the creature.

We are the Collective, it began. *And we wish for death.*

Bethany Anne snorted. *I figured that out from the way I*

keep killing you and you all keep turning up on my doorstep again.

The creature thrashed as though it were in pain. *They are the Chosen. We are not the Chosen. We are alone.*

TOM made a sound of sympathy. **Bethany Anne, this being is separate from the hive mind.**

We hate the Chosen. We wish them to die. We will help you.

Bethany Anne grinned at the mass of writhing tentacles inside the tank. ***Well, shit, I guess that makes us friends. What can you tell me that will help?***

Everything.

She was hit by a flood containing the sum of knowledge of the mind inside the tank. ***TOM, are you getting all this?***

TOM's voice was tight. **It wasn't exaggerating. This is a whole lot of data, much of it random. It's going to take ADAM and me some time to turn it into something you can use.**

That's fine. I can wait until we get back to Devon.

How generous of you.

Bethany Anne shrugged. ***Actually, you're right. You can get started now, and I'll hear it on the way home.*** She looked back at the solitary creature in the tank. ***Are you sure you don't want to come back with us?***

The creature was gone in a flash of tentacles. *Destroy this place. We will die happy.*

Bethany Anne went to find Tabitha.

Tabitha almost ran into Bethany Anne, returning from the corridor just as Bethany Anne left the tank room. "Yeah, um…we should probably get going. I think I just pissed them off more than they already were."

Bethany Anne didn't need to try to hear the Ooken's

minds; they were everywhere. Hundreds of Ooken spilled into the corridor, all screeching for blood.

"This way." Bethany Anne opened a link to the ship as she and Tabitha raced in the opposite direction to avoid being overrun. *Izanami, we're ready for pickup.*

The AI replied immediately. *The ship awaits, my Queen.*

Tabitha fired into the mass as Bethany Anne grabbed her and pulled them both into the Etheric. She dropped onto her ass when they emerged on the bridge of the *Izanami*, panting heavily around gales of laughter. "That was the craziest shit we've done in forever!"

Bethany Anne walked over to the screens and stared at the staging post as the ship moved toward the Gate. "I think we're far enough away, Izanami. Activate the drones."

Izanami appeared, dressed all in black. "Of course, my Queen."

Bethany Anne grasped the Etheric and poured more energy into the drones as they sped away.

"Are you giving them more power?" Tabitha asked in awe. "After seeing what they do *without* a boost?"

Bethany Anne nodded, her face set in hard lines. "I want to be sure the creature who helped us does not suffer —and that every other Ooken aboard those cubes does."

A few moments later, dozens of explosions lit the staging post as the drones detonated. The cubes were shredded by the Etheric energy hitting them from all sides.

The whole structure collapsed. Slowly at first, then all at once.

Bethany Anne saw a Gate snap shut near the one back to Devon. "Izanami, take us home."

Izanami inclined her head. "If you would give me a moment to deliver my blow to this place?"

Bethany Anne smiled. "Go for it, Izanami."

The AI bowed her head, and the tiny flaws in her avatar ceased to flicker in the air around her for a moment. "It is done."

Tabitha clutched her hands in front of her chest as a fresh wave of explosions ripped through the remains of the staging post. "I always forget how awesome fireworks are until we do something like this."

Bethany Anne grinned. "Let's go home, Tabitha."

Devon, First City, The Hexagon

"I want to see my boys!" Tabitha barged past Bethany Anne and Michael and ran over to where Peter stood waiting for her with Todd.

Bethany Anne grinned at Michael as Tabitha stormed down the ramp at high speed. "Did you ever think she would settle down like that?"

Michael shrugged. "I had those two pegged the first time I saw them together."

"MOOOOOM!"

Bethany Anne spun at the combined yells of Alexis and Gabriel. She got her arms out in time but was still almost knocked on her ass by the force of her children throwing their arms around her.

Alexis buried her face in Bethany Anne's shoulder, scolding her mother even as she clung to her. "Mom, we were so worried when you dropped off like that."

Gabriel gripped her in a vice-like hug. "If it wasn't for ADAM, we would have come after you."

Bethany Anne understood her children's concerns. "Heeeey," she soothed. "It's all good. I'm home."

Alexis and Gabriel looked up at her with identical expressions. "We know you're home," they mumbled in unison, reverting to ritual as their emotion ran over.

Bethany Anne held her children close, kissing their heads one at a time. "I know you know," she finished softly.

Michael completed the circle, wrapping his arms around the children while he touched his forehead to Bethany Anne's. "Everyone else is waiting in the conference room for the debrief, and our children have a shuttle to catch."

Bethany Anne took a second to breathe him in, groaning at the thought of dragging her tired ass to a meeting when all she wanted was a duvet and a soft pillow. "A shuttle?"

Gabriel ducked out of his parents' embrace. "To the *Guardian*. We are taking a shift helping out in the orientation lounges," he told her. "Dad said it would be character-building, but we were going to volunteer anyway, so it all works out."

Alexis squeezed her mother tighter for a second before letting go. "We should go or we'll be late."

Bethany Anne watched her children leave, then turned to Michael. "Let's get this done so we can go home."

"Home?" he asked as they set off for the meeting room.

Bethany Anne closed her eyes as the temptation to move the debrief to the morning flickered through her mind. "Mmhmm, which right now means wherever there is a bed I can get into and not emerge from for at least eight hours."

Michael slipped an arm around her. "You can rest tonight, my love."

Bethany Anne tucked her head into the hollow of Michael's shoulder as they walked. "I fully intend to. But, debriefing first."

"Tomorrow we get up and fight all over again."

FINIS

Have you started the new weekly Zoo series from Michael Todd (Anderle)? New Soldiers of Fame and Fortune books are coming every Wednesday. Book one is Nobody's Fool. Get started today!

Available at Amazon

THANK YOU for not only reading this story but these *Author Notes* as well.

(I think I've been good with always opening with "thank you." If not, I need to edit the other *Author Notes*!)

RANDOM (*sometimes*) THOUGHTS?

I often refuse to talk politics, because some readers (like me) are not wild about reading them in my stories, and certainly not in my *Author Notes*.

However, they get into the stories, since politics are often part of the story (can't help it, politicians are often assholes.)

The reason I bring this up is due to an explanation to a fellow author about how what we write, at times, can come across as the opposite of what we believe.

Case in point. A few months ago, I received a Facebook Messenger message from a *very* displeased reader who was castigating me about a negative attitude toward the President in the story and assumed I was allowing the present President of the United States to be the point of my irritation.

I was not.

I tried to explain, in as short an amount of time possible, since arguing is usually pointless, that I am a WORLD-CLASS cynic about politicians and politics.

I hate them all equally and assume the worst of them all unless overwhelming evidence contradicts me.

True story—I was writing a Kurtherian Gambit book (somewhere in the first twelve books) when the FINAL Presidential election was being held. I had the new President's gender as female in the book but had to wait until the election was over before releasing.

A guy won, so I changed the book to fit the new gender. (Hey, I was just going by what the polls were proclaiming. While I did vote, I didn't vote for either of them.)

I was a dick to *whichever* President won because I didn't base my character on the real person. It just so happens the gender changed, and it became a man instead of a woman.

Yet, some assume I actually care who is in the office. While I might personally, I don't do that in my stories.

So, if you think I hate the present President (even if you are reading this in 2026) the answer is I might not hate the person, but I am very cynical about what they are doing for my country.

HOW TO MARKET FOR BOOKS YOU LOVE

We are able to support our efforts with you reading our books, and we appreciate you doing this!

If you enjoyed this or ANY book by any author, especially Indie-published, we always appreciate if you make the time to review a book, since it lets other readers who might be on the fence to take a chance on it as well.

AROUND THE WORLD IN 80 DAYS

One of the interesting (at least to me) aspects of my life is the ability to work from anywhere and at any time. In the future, I hope to re-read my own *Author Notes* and remember my life as a diary entry.

Christmas Eve 2018 Baby!

I'm in California eating frozen candy corns left over from Halloween (actually, I think maybe Thanksgiving… I don't remember.)

Either way, frozen candy corns are freaking delicious. They aren't so hard just out of the freezer that it hurts if you rush and chomp on them (not great, but they aren't a hard candy) and they melt to room temperature pretty fast.

They also, I found out, coat my fingers with sugar, and it messes up my laptop's keyboard.

Crap.

Also, the Trans-Siberian Orchestra's Christmas music is stellar!

FAN PRICING

If you would like to find out what LMBPN is doing and the books we will be publishing, just sign up at http://lmbpn.com/email/. When you sign up, we notify you of books coming out for the week, any new posts of interest in the books and pop culture arena, and the fan pricing on Saturday.

Ad Aeternitatem,

Michael Anderle

www.ingramcontent.com/pod-product-compliance
Lightning Source LLC
Chambersburg PA
CBHW031613100726
47898CB00006B/1768